The Purchased Bride

THE
PURCHASED
BRIDE

Peter Constantine

DEEP VELLUM PUBLISHING

DALLAS, TEXAS

Deep Vellum Publishing
3000 Commerce St., Dallas, Texas 75226
deepvellum.org · @deepvellum

Deep Vellum is a 501c3 nonprofit literary arts organization
founded in 2013 with the mission to bring
the world into conversation through literature.

First Edition, 2022

LIBRARY OF CONGRESS CATALOGING-IN-PUBLICATION DATA
Names: Constantine, Peter, 1963- author.
Title: The purchased bride / Peter Constantine.
Description: First edition. | Dallas, Texas : Deep Vellum Publishing, 2022.
Identifiers: LCCN 2022047457 | ISBN 9781646052271 (trade paperback) |
ISBN 9781646052530 (ebook)
Subjects: LCSH: Constantine, Peter, 1963—Family—Fiction. | Constantine
family—Fiction. | LCGFT: Biographical fiction. | Novels.
Classification: LCC PS3603.O5585 P87 2022 | DDC 813/.6--dc23/
eng/20221017
LC record available at https://lccn.loc.gov/2022047457

ISBN (TPB) 978-1-64605-227-1
ISBN (Ebook) 978-1-64605-253-0

Cover design by Kyle G. Hunter

Cover images: Antique photo of girl: © ilbusca / iStock
Lace pattern: © ajuga / iStock

Interior layout and typesetting by KGT

PRINTED IN CANADA

1

The Viewing, Summer 1909, Constantinople

MY GRANDFATHER WALKS DOWN THE long corridor to the room where Maria and the other two girls he has purchased are waiting to be viewed. Maria has not seen the other girls before; they are both fifteen, like she is. They have been brought from across the border in Batum, and like her they have each been sequestered in a separate room for a week before this final viewing that will decide their fates.

Despite the warm afternoon, my grandfather is in formal attire, a monocle that glints in the light, and white gloves fine enough for his rings to fit over the fingers. He is both a modern Ottoman and a conservative Muslim, so he considers the choosing of girls for his household a solemn occasion. It is now to be seen whether the girls will please him enough to stay on as concubines, please him only mildly and stay on as servants, or please him not at all and be sent away to be sold to other households. By the time my grandmother Maria entered his home, my grandfather had been purchasing girls for over thirty years, and during this time a fixed protocol had evolved. He and his first wife, Grandmother Zekiyé, whom he married when he was twenty and she was sixteen, review the girls together, each with their own set of priorities. Grandfather looks for beauty, grace, European features, a lean-but-busty line, a natural demureness, and what he calls a *many-pronged wit*—once a girl is accepted into his household as a concubine, she is there to stay, and within a decade her wit might be her only recourse against the fading of her charms. Grandmother Zekiyé views the purchased girls through a narrower prism: her eye probes torsos and thighs in search of imperfections a man might not immediately notice. If a girl is to be resold, it will have to be before Grandfather takes her virginity, so Zekiyé looks for any flaws that might dampen his interest after his initial excitement pales. She also has a knack for evaluating the durability of a teenage breast, chin, or hip. Slim at thirteen does not mean slim at eighteen; one chin can turn into three. A girl might be prone to pimples, which is acceptable, even charming, but only if the pimples are not the kind that leave blemishes.

An equally important purpose of Zekiyé's inspection is to determine if a girl will fit into the inflexible hierarchy of the household. Is the newcomer a quick learner, clever enough to acquire elegant Turkish? Will she be good at taking direction? Will she manage to keep a pleasing individuality but still bow to the senior women of the harem? In the three decades that Grandmother Zekiyé has been running grandfather's household, no wives, concubines, or maidservants have entered the harem without her approval. But her choices have always been right, and Grandfather has always been pleased with them. Many of Grandfather's peers have found life at home a strain, their peace soured by ill-tempered wives and warring concubines. There is a growing trend in Constantinople and the larger towns of the Ottoman Empire for even the wealthiest men to turn their backs on the Islamic dispensation that allows them four wives and as many concubines as they can afford to keep, and instead to limit themselves to one wife and perhaps one or two women outside the house, women they keep in private villas and visit secretly. Zekiyé prefers the old ways that allow her to keep an eye on things. A well-run house can make its master's life pleasant, and Grandfather has found himself able to avoid the drabness of marital monotony through the occasional introduction of fresh faces into his home.

The drawing-room door opens and Grandfather enters. Zekiyé puts down the book she has been reading and hurries over to him. She, too, is dressed formally, in a floor-length evening gown. She holds her ostrich fan to her cheek, whispers something to Grandfather in French, and then points at the three girls, who are standing by the large window that opens out onto one of the harem gardens. Grandfather smiles and whispers something in reply, at which she pouts playfully and taps him on the shoulder with her fan. She hangs her arm in his, and they walk across the drawing room toward the frightened girls.

The girls, though unveiled, are dressed in long silk jackets that reach to the floor. Their first appearance before Grandfather is to be in the guise of modest Turkish maidens, the kind with which an Ottoman gentleman might wish to fill his household.

"They are an attractive assortment," Grandmother Zekiyé says in French.

"That they are," Grandfather replies.

"I am particularly pleased with the green-eyed one," Zekiyé continues, pointing her fan at my grandmother Maria. "Shall we view her first?"

They walk up to Maria, who looks directly into Grandfather's eyes and then slowly lowers her gaze, as Zekiyé told her to do when she prepared the girls for the viewing. Your future master will want to see your eyes, Zekiyé said, but only for an instant; a girl must not stare into a man's eyes for too long, even if he is to be her master.

"She speaks a pretty Turkish," Zekiyé says. "It's strange, and *un peu tartare*, but it is pretty."

"Greetings. I am Mehmet," Grandfather says to Maria.

"Greetings. I am Maria," Maria answers, looking up again, though she is not sure whether she is supposed to. His monocle catches her eye, and she is amazed that the round piece of glass can remain in place. He is older than she expected. There is silver in his hair. She had thought her future husband would perhaps be her brothers' age, but now realizes how foolish that thought was: a great man, a grandee, would be one who has done many things in his life, not a boy. Still, Mr. Mehmet is too distinguished to be a bridegroom, she thinks, surmising that he must be her master's father, the head of the household, who has come to view the girls who are to be the brides of his sons. This morning Zekiyé did not introduce herself to the girls—she just assembled them in a small chamber and with gestures and simple Turkish phrases told them what to do. So Maria believes Zekiyé might be her master's mother. What if they don't like me and send me away, she suddenly wonders in fear.

"Greetings, Maria," Grandfather says, pronouncing her name in a strange and foreign way.

"Greetings. I am Maria," she says, and then smiles, realizing she has just repeated herself. Grandfather smiles too.

"She has a pleasant voice," he says to Zekiyé. "She does not mind looking me in the eye. *Très vivace.*"

With her fan, Zekiyé motions Maria to lower her eyes. Maria lowers them. There is gold everywhere in the room. Large vases stand in all the corners and on the tables; they are old, perhaps even ancient, but they look so clean and polished they might be new. Maria wants to raise her head and look around but knows that she must not. She rests her eyes on the lowest shelf of books lining the wall before her. She has never seen so many books. In her Greek village back in the Caucasus, the priest had a Bible and two thin volumes of Byzantine chants, and Black Melpo the Medicine Mixer had the piles of yellowed penny novels written in Pontic Greek. But Maria has never seen beautifully bound volumes like these, their spines covered with strange gold letters.

"She is thin, but in a good way," Zekiyé says in Turkish. "Her thinness has not affected her breasts. And her hips will widen when the time is right." She taps Maria's hip. "She might well bear you some boys."

Maria looks up. She has understood Zekiyé's words about bearing boys, and realizes that Mr. Mehmet is not her master's father, but her master. She is so startled by this that she cannot tell if she is pleased or dismayed. Zekiyé does not notice that Maria has raised her eyes again. Grandfather steps back a few paces to view her from a distance. He smiles. She breathes in carefully so he will not think she is flustered. She looks at his face, then lowers her eyes again. So this is the face of the man who is to be her husband. He is clearly a good man, a kind man, she thinks, even if his eyes are difficult to read. He has smiled at her, which probably means that he is pleased; he has saved her family and all the others by sending them so many gold coins before even having met her. She doesn't dare raise her head again but thinks she can feel his cool eyes on her. His eyes are a bright hazel and were the first thing she noticed about him when he entered the room. They are unusual eyes, she thinks.

Outside, in the harem garden, two little girls in frilly white dresses are chasing a boy of about ten who is wearing a sailor suit and hat. Maria watches them out of the corner of her eye. The boy shouts shrilly as the taller of the two girls catches him and pushes him to the ground. Zekiyé opens the French doors that lead onto a terrace and waves her fan at the children. "You naughty things!" she calls out. "You are disturbing your Papa! Papa cannot hear himself think!"

The children run down the path past a pond and disappear among the trees beyond it.

Zekiyé closes the French doors and smiles apologetically at Grandfather, even though the children are not hers, but his third wife's. She goes over to a large oil painting of a young shepherdess in a white and pink dress, stares up at it, and then glances at Grandfather, who is looking at Maria with thoughtful eyes. Maria looks at the painting, knowing she is expected to avoid his gaze. She notices that the shepherdess is holding a stringed instrument, its precious lacquered wood gleaming; there is a diadem of blossoms in her hair—a princess perhaps, dressed up as a shepherdess, Maria thinks, but then sees that the subject of the painting is undoubtedly Madame Zekiyé as she must have looked many years ago. Madame Zekiyé quickly walks toward Maria. "Pretty eyes, pretty complexion, good breasts, *mon cher*," she says to Grandfather, reaching out and touching Maria's chest with her forefinger. Maria steps back in alarm, holding her hand over her breasts. Zekiyé smiles and wags a finger at her, and Maria smiles back at her nervously.

2

Four Months Earlier, Spring 1909,
in a Greek Settlement in the Caucasus

AS THEY FLEE, THE TEA plantation below the village is burn-ing. The great lady of the house, a Russian noblewoman, has been slaughtered along with her daughters and servants and all the guards. The village elder, who tried to hide in her stables, is mur-dered as well. The priest runs barefoot and sobbing through the muddy field, his cassock hitched above his knees, thorns and stones cutting his feet, but the men catch him at the line of trees at the end of the field, the tall ash trees blocking his escape. Their machetes hack at his hands and feet, and he tumbles into the mud, his blood pouring onto his murderers as he tries to crawl away. Platoons of marauders are dragging the wounded and dying out onto the burn-ing field where the dead priest lies, tearing off their victims' smocks and trousers and defiling them in unspeakable ways, guffawing and firing their rifles. They torch the grand house and its granaries and barns, throwing into the flames boxes of flaring cartridges, walls of fire stretching down into the valley beyond the plantation. The massacring horde comes swarming up toward the village, and with the church bells ringing the villagers flee, dragging the old and the sick with them toward the forests. Maria's father opens the sheds and the sheep pen under the house to let the animals escape; he slits grain sacks and tears open cupboards, cursing and shouting profanities. His fields and goods, Maria's dowry, everything is lost, and his wife Heraclea runs at him, shrieking, beating his back with her fists, "We must go, we must go! They will cut our throats!" As she throws woolen smocks, shirts, and pantaloons into a bundle, he tries to set fire to the house so the marauders will find nothing, and Heraclea pulls him away, ripping his shirt in her frenzy. She grabs Maria by the hand and drags her out of the house, ready to abandon her husband to his fate, but he follows them, crying like a boy, holding his rifle and the bundle of clothes that Heraclea has thrown into an empty flour sack. "I will shoot anyone who comes here, I will shoot them all," he weeps. There is a shelf above the door with a row of large round loaves of bread, and Maria, too short to reach it, throws her bundle at it, the loaves toppling onto the floor. "Run! Run!" her mother screams, her flailing hand hitting Maria across the cheek, but Maria snatches up two loaves, one falling and rolling into the ditch as she runs out of the house.

•

A swarm of refugees is descending from the raided Greek mountain villages of the Caucasus, trudging through the forests and over narrow mountain paths toward the borderlands of the Ottoman Empire. Fifteen-year-old Maria is among a group of villagers who have gathered from various burned-down settlements. More and more people join Maria and her parents as they make their way toward the border river. Some have been marching for two weeks, some for three, sleeping in the open, their campfires keeping forest dogs and wolves away. They are all hard people, having lived like their ancestors through generations of disaster, upheaval, and plague. The land once belonged to Colchis, to which Medea had brought shame and destruction; it has not been Greek for a thousand years, and although they continue to live there, their numbers are dwindling as the raids grow fiercer, the plagues more frequent.

The refugees cross over the fast-flowing river and into Ottoman territory in leaky boats and climb up a winding mud trail in the rain, toward a place where, they have been told, there are some abandoned barracks. Maria's father, Kostis, is leading the way, climbing over brambles and fallen branches. His rifle is slung over his shoulder, and on his back he is carrying the large flour sack filled with clothes and blankets, now wet and heavy in the rain. He beats at weeds and bushes with a stick to clear the way for the others. Camels graze among the trees by the side of the path, gaunt and skeletal animals that have barely survived the winter and are not worth shooting for a few strips of meat. A scent of eucalyptus and putrefaction hangs in the air. Since railway lines now cross Anatolia, the great caravans have been disbanded and the camels released to die in the wilderness. Kostis sees a deer and tries to take a shot at it, but the primer in his rifle is wet from the rain. They could have strung up the deer on a tree, out of the reach of the jackals and wolves, he says, and then come back for it once they had found the barracks. "No point wasting bullets now," Heraclea tells him in a low voice, so that the others won't hear her talking down to her husband.

Kostis turns and looks back at Maria, then looks away again. Her mother is walking some distance behind him, her feet slipping in the mud, a bundle in her arms as large as his but heavier, for as they fled she scooped up a tin bowl that had been part of her dowry many years before, as well as three boxes of cartridges. Kostis in his confusion and rage was about to take the rifle with a single cartridge in it; had Heraclea's mind not been as nimble as it was, he'd now be carrying a whole rifle for nothing, with just a single shot. The barracks to which they are heading, she knows, are in the middle of nowhere; the nearest settlement, the people at the river said, lies a day's ride north. Heraclea has ten rubles hidden in the hem of her skirt, but none of that must go for cartridges. She stares at the path in front of her feet, her lips moving as she counts every stone larger than her shoe; if someone were to give her a kopeck coin for every ten stones, she might have a whole ruble by the time they reach the barracks, maybe more, and she imagines all the things she could buy. Maria knows it is best not to disturb her mother during these counting games in which she gathers imaginary coins for things she sees, people who cross her path, or the number of birdcalls she hears. Heraclea would get angry if she lost count. Maria walks sullenly behind her mother in the rain, careful where she steps because she is wearing the shoes she has previously worn only on Sundays and at church feasts, the pair in which she was to have been married and buried. Village girls like her spend their lives barefoot in summer and wearing straw sandals wrapped in fur in winter, but Maria had the foresight to snatch up these shoes as they fled their burning village. She wears them now, knowing that even a small cut on a sharp stone can fester into a gangrenous wound in these dangerous valleys.

"I see trouble ahead, lots of trouble," Heraclea mutters.

Maria looks at her.

"What are we going to eat?" Heraclea says, wiping her wet sleeve across her face, her voice low enough that only Maria can hear. "Those dried-up camels that look more dead than alive?

Nothing but mud and brambles since we crossed the river. We'll starve before the week's out."

Maria looks at the junipers and oaks and alders just beyond the mud trail, the trees gathering into a dense forest deeper in the valley. There is much more than mud and brambles here, she thinks.

"We'll starve before the week's out," Heraclea says again. "I'm hungry already."

Maria says nothing. She knows her mother is not interested in a reply or an opinion. Her mother can't be hungry: her father bought lamb shanks from a tribesman by the river yesterday; they ate some of the meat last night, half raw and bloody, and the rest this morning. The tribesman had demanded fifteen kopecks. "If you want it, you buy it. If you don't want it, you don't buy it," he had said. Kostis had managed to buy the meat for nine kopecks, pressing the battered coins into the man's hand, but Heraclea saw the expensive transaction as a symbol of calamities to come. "It's a harsh land," Heraclea says. "Who'd think crossing a river you'd be in another world, just like that? You'd think both sides of a river would be the same. I wouldn't have come here for fifty rubles if I'd had a choice, nor sixty neither."

Kostis glances back, thinking Heraclea is speaking to him, but looks ahead again.

3

THE BARRACKS ARE DILAPIDATED; THEY have stood empty for more than twenty-five years. The walls are made of roughly packed logs and cracked wood blocks, scorpions and beetles nesting in the chinks and hollows. Some of the window frames have been covered with thin, almost transparent oil paper, something that must have been done recently or the paper would have torn in the wind, but most of the windows are only gaping holes. There will be little shelter from the cold if the weather turns. It is still early in the spring, and though the rain showers are warm, even summery, snowstorms can still blow down from the mountains. She watches her father and a small group of men surveying the three rickety buildings.

"Women and children in this one!" Kostis calls out. He is standing in front of the sturdiest of the barracks, tapping the logs of the wall with his stick. "What do you think?" he says to the other men.

They nod.

"We'll be in that one," he says, pointing to the barrack next to it. "Or maybe that one over there. Whichever's better inside."

The men nod again.

"These barracks look sturdy enough, they'll do. Anyway, they'll keep us dry," he calls out to the refugees standing in the rain. "It'll be raining at least through tomorrow."

The wet ground is covered with shards of clay pots and broken pitchers; it seems that the barracks have been used as storehouses and raided by a pillaging army in one of the many border skirmishes over the past hundred years in which the Sultan's troops and the Russian army have fought each other for control of these remote outposts of their empires. There are empty cartridges and broken musket latches and rifle pins strewn about the meadows, lying with the pale bones of the dead among the grasses and weeds. And yet the barracks are surprisingly clean inside. The rough floorboards have been swept, scrubbed, and sanded, and blankets and straw sacks for bedding are piled against the back walls. It looks, Maria thinks, as if a troop of washerwomen with rags and pails had come up the river to this godforsaken place, vigorously scrubbed the floors, and quickly, strangely, left downriver again. There is a trunk with "Bread" painted in large Greek letters on the top, and in the trunk are stacks of dried flatbread to stave off hunger pangs until a field kitchen can be set up. Maria's legs are bruised from the rough river crossing. The boat was little more than a flat-bottomed tub, pushed this way and that by the rushing torrent, water seeping between its uncaulked planks, its prow banging against rocks and sandbanks. "We're going to drown now," she thought, "we're going to drown, we're going to drown." All the refugees had come from mountain villages—no one had ever been in a boat before; no one could swim. In the last few days death has snatched at them many times. Maria feels a hard knot in her stomach, but thinks that the trunk filled with flatbreads and the unexpected cleanliness and fresh straw sacks in the barracks are a good sign.

"So this is it," Kostis says to Heraclea, pulling two sacks away from the wall and putting their bundles on top of them. "This is it. If you need anything, shout for me through the window."

He picks up his rifle, and Heraclea smiles and bows her head like a meek wife, a mere show before the other women. Kostis glances at one of them sitting by the far wall; she is without a kerchief or cap, her head and hair completely bare. She has one thick braid hanging down her back, the other over her breast, in the way of virgins at village feasts. But she is not a virgin; Kostis can tell. He also senses that she is alone here, without a husband. The braid over her breast is long, its end lying in a coil between her legs. She is wearing three necklaces, each with a gold cross—not out of Christian zeal, Kostis thinks, but because of their value and because they catch the eye and draw it to the white skin above her breasts. He had not noticed her before, and wonders how that can be. Her eyes meet his and she tugs at her scarf and covers her head, looking away.

"So you'll be in the barrack over there?" Heraclea says, pointing to the window.

"Yes, that's where I'll be," Kostis says. "We've set up shifts to stand guard, you never know what's in those forests. I'm doing the next shift with two other men." He points at his rifle and Heraclea nods.

Leaving them to sort out their belongings, Kostis goes outside. Maria sees the woman with the long braids glance at him. Kostis doesn't know any of the other men—most have fled from the north during the slaughter, some are from villages hundreds of miles away. The whole Caucasus, with all its tribes and peoples, is up in arms: Tatars and Armenians fighting one another, Muslims and Christians and Mountain Jews pitched against each other by the Russians. And we Greeks, Kostis thinks, who have lived in the Caucasus since the days of Noah, are caught in the middle, shot at and plundered by all sides. So many decades of unrest, but now the whole land back home behind the border is aflame. The Russian governor general Prince Golitsyn and his wife had been attacked on the highroad outside Tiflis, the prince shot in the head, his wife stabbing the sharpened tip of her parasol into the gunman's eye. This is how it had all begun. Prince Golitsyn's headwound had not been fatal, but his wife's forward lunge, using her parasol as a sword, first blinded and ultimately killed one of the freedom fighters. Reprisals followed reprisals, and a wave of assassinations began. First the Russian Governors of Elizavetapol and Surmalu were shot dead, and the Russian governor of Baku was killed by a bomb thrown into his carriage. Their Russian councilors were assassinated one by one, and the officials who had been sent out to seize the malefactors' lands were ambushed and shot dead as they rode out of the capital in a phalanx. Then the peasants of Guria torched Russian government houses and seized the estates of the Georgian nobility. A Gurian Peasant Republic was proclaimed, a violent and lawless land that spiraled into arson and terror once the Russians managed to reoccupy it.

Kostis sees a group of men huddling outside the barrack under some planks protruding from the roof. Their clothes are wet, even though they are standing out of the rain. One man is talking intently as the others shake their heads. He is wearing long silver chains around his neck and expensive cartridge belts and bandoliers across his chest, as if dressed for a feast. The man raises his hand in greeting to Kostis and then continues talking to the others.

During the Khan Day celebrations, he tells the men, the Russians arrested his brother, who was impersonating the czar in the village pantomime. The entire Caucasus makes fun of the czar on Khan Day, he says, just one day of fun, only one day, and this year all the thousand czar pantomimes throughout the land had been raided, and the Russians had shot at some of the drunken czars who were raising their cassocks, gaudy imitations of imperial robes, showing their bare knees to the laughing crowd. The men shake their heads and say that all the marauding and murder is the Russians' fault. It has only been a hundred years that the Russians have ruled the land, but it has been a hundred years of famine, plague, and war.

Kostis walks away toward the empty barrack. He feels uneasy among so many strangers, all the more as they sometimes speak an almost incomprehensible Greek. Who are these people? Are all of them even Greek? He has heard that some Armenians and Mountain Jews can speak Greek as if it were their mother tongue, and then there are Greeks who over the centuries have forgotten much of their language, mixing stuttered Greek words with Svan and Georgian and other strange mountain speech. He is worried that his wife and daughter will be sleeping in a separate barrack, but with so many people here and more arriving every day, the women have to sleep apart from the men. He thinks of the woman with the thick braids; he has a way with women and knows she will go for a short walk with him into the forest. There will not be much food to be had here in the barracks, and he will be catching game with traps; there is much she might do for a strip of meat.

But men and women living in such close quarters will cause trouble. The women will have to bathe by themselves, upriver in the shallows. He will speak to Heraclea, he decides, and have her gather the women into shifts for bathing. Back in the village, his daughter had been hidden away in his house, weaving and stitching her dowry until they could find her a bridegroom. Now she will sit among men, eat among men, be spoken to by men and boys. A thousand years of tradition have been torn away in a single day of terror. What adds to his worry is Maria's beauty. It came quite suddenly; nobody had expected it. Until three summers ago she had been plain and skinny, her face sunburned and boyish, her nimble fingers brown and stained from picking tea leaves on the plantation covering the foothills below their village. But seeds do not reveal the flowers within them; a remarkable transformation came over her. Her face was fuller; her hair was a deep chestnut brown like his, long and rich, unlike her mother's hair, which hung in thin graying strands that she always hid in a kerchief, even in the house. He now finds it hard to look at Maria, angry at himself for the thoughts that flare up, just for an instant, as if to spite him. She has become a beauty, and it was from him, not from Heraclea, that she inherited her looks. Heraclea was plain when he married her and is even plainer now that she is almost forty. Kostis is a year younger than her, which was unusual in the Greek villages, but she had had a large dowry, so much larger than he could have expected, and she had made a useful wife for him. Heraclea's father had not agreed to such a disadvantageous marriage, but fate decreed against him. When Kostis married Heraclea he was a destitute young man still in his teens, an orphan, bringing to the marriage only a strong pair of hands and his good looks, which counted for nothing in a wedding contract. His grandfather had gambled away the family's house and fields and then died in the great Batum plague without a kopeck to his name, the plague also carrying away his sons, one of them Kostis's father. Kostis and his brothers grew up destitute, and then in the spring of the year he was to marry Heraclea, his four brothers died of the cholera that came up from Persia, and

Kostis's mother hanged herself in the village granary. Kostis, then eighteen, was the only one of the family to survive. He had swallowed strips of yellowing paper, inscribed with words copied out of the Bible in bitter ink and blessed in the village church, and prayed to Saint Kassandra of Trebizond. As his brothers died, their souls seeping out of their mouths, he had dragged their corpses one by one out into the field, their bodies wrapped in foul, reeking sacks. He had then stripped off his tainted clothes and burned them, returning home naked and barefoot, the shadows of carrion birds crossing his path. His brothers too had swallowed strips of paper with words from the Bible, but the illness had nevertheless seized them and struck them down. As they died one after the other and his mother went mad, Kostis was certain he would be next. He waited for the flashes and stabs in his innards, but they never came. Aphrodite the Witch, the medicine mixer of the village, had told him to keep washing his whole body again and again, and to drink only the water from the springs higher up on the mountain, a half hour's climb from the pest houses; villagers were washing cholera rags and death sheets in the streams, poisoning them with pestilence. "Better one mouthful of pure water than an entire tainted sea," Aphrodite the Witch had said. "Burn everything your brothers touched, and burn all their clothes. Keep nothing of theirs."

With so many deaths it was not right for a wedding to take place, but the cholera had struck down Heraclea's people too, along with hundreds of other villagers throughout the valley. Heraclea had been left alone and unprotected. It was a marriage born of desperation, for she could not live in the village without a father, a brother, or a husband to protect her. The only village spinster was Aphrodite the Witch, who was twice her age and whose poisons kept her safe. During the plague year something had died within

Kostis too, though he was not sure what it was. At eighteen he was without family or land, while Heraclea at nineteen was without family, but with a field and two olive groves that were only a half hour's walk from the village, as well as the blankets, pots, and spoons that every bride's parents would send to the house of the groom. As Heraclea's parents and sisters were dead, her dowry had tripled, and was enough to set up an entire household. It was a good marriage, though it had sprung from a plague.

Over the years Kostis met many other women and girls in the town on the coast, where he sold the cheese and butter from his herds. He met them in bawdy houses and drinking halls, and paid for their company. Most of the girls were not much older than Maria is now, and some, despite their trade, would not take his money, hoping he would come again, would perhaps remain with them and take rooms in the port, perhaps even marry them. A handsome man has two gods, people said, a beautiful girl has none. Handsomeness in a man has its uses, but beauty in a village girl like Maria is a curse. Men will be drawn to her with lust, trapped by her looks, and she will be ruined, unwanted as a bride. Such beauty in a girl is an unbearable burden for a family. No hardworking villager wants a beautiful wife in his house, men knocking at the door while he is off herding his sheep up the mountainside, men waiting for his wife at the well, or lurking among his vines and olive groves. The sweetest grape puddings, old village women say, draw flies from as far away as Isfahan. The perfect bride is not one with a sweetness that beguiles men, but one with thick thighs and wide hips, like his wife Heraclea, signs that she can carry heavy loads on her back and will give birth to son after son. That, he thinks with bitterness, will not be his daughter's lot. Fate offers sweet melons to some, sour melons to others, and as far as he can see, there are only sour melons in Maria's future.

4

DESPITE THE CLEANLINESS OF THE floors in the barrack, Maria thinks she can smell an odor of decay, as if something has died and lies mummified beneath the planks of the floor. Some of the wood looks bleached by the sun, clearly salvaged from the river, and she thinks how strange it is that someone would have gone to the trouble of laying a plank floor in a barrack such as this. The planks would allow the snake spirit of goodness to live beneath the floor, but what spirit would want to live in a place like this? A hard mud floor would have been better. She takes a crumbled wheat cake from the pocket of her smock, a last remnant of the food she managed to bring from the village; it had been baked in the clay oven in their yard. She wonders if their house is still standing. She presses the cake to her nose; it smells of honey and mold. As they fled the burning village, running with their bundles up the path toward the forest, their feet slipping in the mud, Maria saw Old Mother Sotitsa sitting on a big stone, arm in arm with Granny Simela. "They need help!" Maria had thought. "They've been abandoned!" They were sitting with their arms linked as if they were beloved sisters whom fate had separated but who had found one another again. Granny

Simela had long ago forgotten who she was and spent her days sitting in the back of her son's smithy. Old Mother Sotitsa's mind was as sharp as that of a young woman, but she had fallen and broken her hip that winter and could barely walk. Their sons Petro the Blacksmith and Pericles the Coat Sewer must have tried to take them along as they fled, but then left them behind. Perhaps the marauders would take pity on them—the marauders had mothers and grandmothers themselves. Maria saw that Granny Simela was wearing only one shoe and was trying to hide her bare, muddy foot under the folds of her smock as they passed. Maria tripped, her foot catching on a stone, and almost dropped her bundle. Granny Simela reached out toward her as if to help her, or perhaps to beg her for help, and Maria stopped; but her mother grabbed her wrist, dragging her on toward the forest. Maria wanted to shout back to the old women, "Go to the trees, the first trees, the killers might not see you there!" Instead she ran on, panting, behind her mother.

As the terrible scenes flood back into her mind, Maria feels a chill. The village songs tell how the poisons brewed by the old medicine mixers spread like cold fear through one's veins, red blood turning black, a slow chill; this is how that must feel. And yet it is as if everything she saw as they fled the village were someone else's memories. She looks at the large lantern hanging from the barrack ceiling. Its red and turquoise glass panels throw colored shadows onto the planks of the ceiling. She wonders how in all the years the barrack has stood empty nobody has stolen it. Probably nobody ever came here. The nearest inhabited village is a day's ride downriver, she has heard. She listens for sounds from outside that might hint at danger, but hears only distant shrieks and night noises from the restless forest. Granny Simela and Old Mother Sotitsa are surely dead by now, she thinks. Even if the murderers spared them, how would they have survived? She imagines the two old women limping arm in arm through the ruins of the village. She wonders if she would have abandoned her mother in order to save herself. But both Petro the Blacksmith and Pericles the Coat Sewer had children to think of—Petro's little boy was just five, and his daughters three and two; Pericles had a son and a daughter who were about ten years old. Fleeing up the mountain path, the two men clearly had to decide between their mothers and their children. Perhaps, before reaching the safety of the borderland river, they would also have had to decide between their sons and daughters. Neither Petro nor Pericles is among the refugees here at the barracks, but many families from the raided villages of the foothills have fled north to the safety of the higher mountains in the hope of crossing into the new Peasant Republic that has just been occupied by the Russians again. It will be a temporary safety, Maria thinks, for the Peasant Republic is now an ungoverned land with brigands on every path and Russian soldiers shooting in all directions. The only real safety lies across the borders and in the faraway lands of Greece.

There is a strange sound outside in the nearby forest, like geese barking, but Maria realizes it must be vixens yelping at each other in their springtime fights. It has stopped raining and the forest seems louder than usual, with the screeching of owls and the clicking and barking of polecats. She is shivering and crosses her arms over the top of her shift, her fingers caressing her neck. Though her clothes are wet, the air is warm, and she knows she doesn't have a fever. She wonders if her mother would have left her behind if she had sprained her foot and wasn't able to keep up. Her mother is a practical woman, Maria thinks; she would have stood by her if it made sense and abandoned her if that was the thing to do. And yet, as Maria knows, young girls would never be left behind alive sitting by the side of a path as Old Mother Sotitsa and Granny Simela had been. During the uprisings and slaughter many years before, the village priest Father Kyriakos, a young man at the time, saved his sons, strong boys who could run as fast as he could, even faster. But his daughters had been plump girls who spent their days embroidering, weaving, and eating honeyed cakes; they had never run up mountainsides or jumped over brooks. As the murderers closed in on the fleeing priest and his family, he suddenly, and with the cold eyes of a desperate man, the villagers later said, turned to his panting, stumbling daughters and pushed them over the mountain ledge, and they fell shrieking into the deep ravine, their bodies remaining Christian, safe from the pillaging horde. Now the old village priest lies dead in the fields by the tea plantation, abandoned by the sons he saved.

Sounds of hammering come from the men's barrack; Maria is surprised that they have found tools, until she realizes that they must be using river stones. She looks at her mother, who despite the noise is lying on her back in a deep sleep, her mouth hanging open and her legs stretched out immodestly. She wonders if her mother would have killed her to save her from the marauders. If Maria had sprained her foot as they fled up the path toward the forest, she decides, her mother would have shouted "Christ and Holy Virgin! Can you still run, can you run?" If Maria had shaken her head, her mother would have pried loose a large stone from the path, raised it high in the air, and shouting "God embrace and welcome you!" would have brought it down on her head, again and again. She imagines herself lying on the path, her heart no longer beating, her smock covered in blood, her mother and father running alone toward the trees, the two old abandoned women sitting arm in arm waiting for the first murderers to appear by the ruined wall of Blind Nektario's sheep pen.

Maria takes a deep breath and looks up at the lantern and its colored glass. "But I didn't fall and I didn't sprain my foot," she says to herself. "And perhaps my mother would have stayed with me, and my father too." She knows that you can never tell what people will do in a moment of great danger, when one action might mean life, another death.

As they were reaching the first trees of the forest, her mother leading the way, Maria thought she saw—just for an instant—Widow Manthena, down at the edge of the village, covered in mud and crawling with her daughter along the path coiling up toward the houses. They seemed to have lost something and were foolishly looking for it among the stones and weeds of the wet, mud-filled ditch. Then Maria caught a glimpse of small figures running through the fields just below the village, and realized that they were the marauders. How could Widow Manthena stop to search for something when the murdering men were so close, Maria thought as she ran, panting for breath. And to flee the village in dresses caked with mud—where could they wash them in the forests? She looked back one last time at the two women and realized that what from so far away looked like mud was blood. She could now only see Widow Manthena, two men hugging her as she lay in the ditch, rolling with her in the mud as if they were fighting over her. The widow broke free, clawing her way out of the ditch, but they caught up with her, and a third man jumped into the ditch, and a fourth. Maria wanted to drop the sack of clothes she was carrying so she could run faster, but the smocks and dresses might soon be the difference between living and dying. If it snowed in the night, she could wear two or three smocks, one over the other; she could wrap herself in her shawls and live.

Neither Maria, Heraclea, nor Kostis will ever mention the village again, or Old Mother Sotitsa, or Widow Manthena and her daughter Agoritsa. Nor will they mention Kostis's madness, when he put all their lives at risk and Heraclea raised her hand to him and took charge. For Maria that had been a terrible thing—seeing her father, who had always ruled his household, lose control of himself at such a moment. All the refugees who have gathered at the barracks are now looking to him to tell them what they should do, where they should sleep, where their next meal will come from, how they should protect themselves, but Maria knows that when faced by true danger, he cannot be relied on. This makes these new surroundings much more frightening. If marauders come here too, she will have to rely on her mother—or on herself. She will run to the riverbank, men with knives close after her. She will crouch behind the smoke trees along the water's edge, their mass of pinkish gray leaves hiding her like a curtain of fire. But if she slips and falls into the river she will surely drown, as the water just downstream from the barracks is treacherous and will drag her under.

She looks at her mother, lying next to her on her back, her head propped up on her bundle. Heraclea has taken off her wet kerchief, which lies folded neatly next to her. Her sparse hair is tangled, and barely reaches her shoulders. She keeps cutting it in the hope that it will grow back richer and fuller so she can wear it in long thick braids. Her mouth hangs open, and though she is asleep her eyes are only half shut, the pupils pointing upward. Heraclea has a round face and a broad double-chin, which now in sleep is resting on her chest, and her expression reminds Maria of Granny Simela, who had forgotten who she was, her eyes seeing yet unseeing, her mouth hanging loose.

Alarmed, Maria leans over to her mother, touches her eyes to make her close them completely, and pushes her chin upward, the way, she suddenly realizes, a grieving daughter closes the gaping mouth of her dead mother. Heraclea, deep in sleep, turns her head angrily to one side, then to the other, as if to shake Maria off, and Maria quickly pulls her hand back, horrified that her gesture might have been a terrible sacrilege. She suddenly notices that Elpida, a sharp-faced midwife with thin snakelike braids, is staring at her. She is a woman who would not smile at warm bread, Maria thinks. She comes from a Greek village in the northern Caucasus where they speak a harsher, somehow alarming Greek. As a child, Elpida had been struck down by the plague but survived and became an outcast in the village, a plague girl. Her brothers had died but she had not, something for which her mother never forgave her. Elpida looks at Maria coldly and Maria turns away. She hears Elpida mutter something about foolish women and their useless handsome men, and knows it is meant as an insult to her mother and father. As far back as she can remember people have always made comments about her parents, usually in roundabout ways; such a very handsome man, such a very plain woman. She and her matchmakers must have whispered spells and poured potions. But Elpida the midwife does not whisper behind people's backs; she is a blunt and brutal woman, prepared to speak an insult to one's face. Maria imagines her as a child of eight or nine walking through a dark, plague-ridden village, perhaps hand in hand with another plague child, their faces marked by the plague that did not kill them, the villagers retreating like shadows into their houses, the clicking of locks and bolts.

The other women are huddling in the corners of the barrack, claiming straw sacks of their own and trying to settle the children. A young woman sitting alone on a sack next to Maria coughs, holding a dirty rag to her mouth. She is clearly a lady from a town, perhaps Batum, but her long skirts are muddy and wet, as are her wide sash and jacket. There is a tangle of silver chains and talismans around her neck that would be snatched and ripped away by the toll guards and sentries along the path to the Black Sea, Maria thinks. She is not wearing a kerchief, but a beaded round cap tied in place with ribbons, like a rich woman at a wedding.

"What do you think of this place?" she asks Maria, almost in a whisper so she will not wake Heraclea.

"It's better than I hoped," Maria whispers back. "We've been sleeping in the open the last few nights."

"Us too," the young woman says. "That's how I caught my cold."

She coughs again; the hollow and rattling cough of consumption, Maria thinks. The young woman eyes her. "I caught the cough from sleeping outside," she quickly whispers. "The night was too cold. I began coughing yesterday." She looks at Maria to see if she believes her.

"Is your husband with the other men?" Maria asks—a foolish question, she knows; where else would he be?

The young woman nods. "He's on guard shift, he's got his own rifle, a pistol too. And look, it's started raining again. My poor Epifanios will get wet. But we're not staying."

"You're not?"

The young woman leans toward her. "I'm going to need some medicine before my cold gets any worse."

"But we were told at the river to come here to the barracks and wait," Maria says. "Where are you going to go without travel papers? They said there'll be soldiers all along the road."

"My husband wants us to go," the woman says. She gets up and walks to the door, where she stands and looks out into the rain.

It is clear she comes from a town, not a village. Maria thinks it is good she will be leaving in the morning, as the other refugees will not allow her to stay once they realize that she has more than a cold, that she might have a fatal illness that will spread; better to leave now than to be chased away. The rain has gotten heavier, and streams of water are falling from the roof onto the sagging wooden planks that have been hammered into rain spouts, leading the water into the ditches of the makeshift latrines. Maria glances in Elpida's direction, but the midwife is arranging and rearranging her bundles, her eyes darting about as if one of the women might steal her things the moment she looks away. There must be coins hidden in there, Maria thinks. To her relief, Elpida and her daughter are settling down far enough away. For some reason the young woman has gone out into the rain, and now comes back, her clothes and hair wet. "There's a draft here," she says to Maria with a drawn smile. "I think I'll sleep over there." She points to the wall on the opposite side of the barrack and Maria nods, regretting that she mentioned the soldiers and the travel papers that everyone is so worried about.

5

MARIA IS SITTING ON HER straw sack with nothing to do for the first time since they fled their village. She is thirsty and wonders if there is a well nearby, but the cold, fast-flowing river water, she thinks, is probably clean enough to drink. Her thirst will grow and become unbearable in the night. How is she to walk to the river in the darkness without light or lantern, her path crossed by the night predators of the forest? She unties her bundle and takes out a gray cotton smock that is damp, but not as wet as the dress she is wearing. She unwinds her kerchief, shakes out her hair, unties the woolen sash around her waist and hips and, reaching behind her back, unclasps the rusty hooks of her wet dress. Two of the hooks are already missing, and she knows that if she loses any more she will have to find some way to keep the dress from slipping off her shoulders. She will have to secure it with one of the scarves she has brought with her and wear her embroidered jacket over it, as if she were dressing for a village feast. She looks over to the window facing the men's barrack, leaning forward to see if any of the men might be peering in, but there is nobody outside the window and she quickly pulls the dress over her head. She bends over the fabric to see where the clasp has torn off. Her stomach tightens with a feeling of unease and fear. The rain has seeped through to her long undershirt and the breast band tied over it, but they are only slightly damp. She will change them in the night, she thinks, when the lantern goes out and the barrack is completely dark.

She feels more comfortable in the wide and loose smock, but her legs and arms are heavy with exhaustion. She is wearing her amulet and two thin silver chains with crosses, and decides to keep them on as they might be stolen if she leaves them in her bundle. She listens to the drumming of the rain on the roof. It's a comforting sound, though she is not sure why. Rain and water and mud everywhere. If she puts her tin bowl outside near the door it will soon fill, and she can take sips of clean water if she wakes up thirsty in the night. Thirst chases away sleep, and she doesn't want to lie awake for hours in the dark, her mind caught up in ever-tighter knots. She looks around at the haggard women in their frayed, wet dresses. Some, like her mother, are now wrapped in blankets, their soaked clothes hanging from hooks on the rafters. Two women are lying side by side on their backs, flushed and shivering in a fever, a girl of about ten fanning them. Maria wonders if they have caught a chill or if a disease has seized them. If the cholera breaks out in the barracks, everyone will be dead in a week. Fever and chills, she knows, are not signs of cholera. The illness swept through her village five years ago; eighty corpses lay wrapped in their soiled blankets in the meadow by the tea plantation. A wine merchant from Batum had brought the plague to the village, having come to buy barrels of wine with hot wet coins he kept hidden in his mouth. The toll- and tithe-men at the valley checkpoints would run their fingers over a merchant's body in search of gold, but few would think of looking under his tongue. The merchant had fallen ill and died in his cart outside the village, his horse walking on for miles after his soul had escaped his pestilential body, the sagging wheels of his cart creaking and clanking against the stones of the road. The vintner and his sons, who had sold him the barrels of wine and taken his pestilential coins, died as well. The first death in the village, that of the vintner, came in August, on St. Maria's Day, and the plague of that summer has ever since been known as Maria's Plague. The name unsettles Maria deeply. Everything that had belonged to the dead, or that the dead had touched, had to be burned. Impoverished villagers who secretly washed the pestilential clothes and blankets that they could not live without also died soon after. The church bell was ringing to chase away the plague, and the children of the dead walked through the village looking for food, knocking on locked doors that remained locked, including the church door, the priest fearing that the holy icons the dying would kiss in prayer would become pestilential.

Maria looks at the women who are still dragging their bedding this way and that through the barrack, arguing about where they will sleep, as if it matters. There is a stench of unwashed bodies and menstrual blood, and she decides she will swim in the shallows of the river at daybreak, even if it is raining and the water is cold from the melting snow in the mountains. She will wear her muddy dress in the river and wash herself and her dress clean. Some of the women have brought nothing with them. They have only the clothes they are wearing. If the weather turns cold, Maria thinks, they will be in trouble. The older children, too tired to play, are sitting hunched against the walls, and two boys, who are about ten or eleven and so should be in the men's barracks, are playing a counting game throwing nut shells. A barefoot girl of about six, wearing a potato sack with a large black "A" and a cross printed on the back, comes over to Maria and holds out a small gray stone. It is an ordinary stone, not much larger than a pebble. Maria smiles and reaches out to take it. The little girl quickly draws back her hand and runs off, looking over her shoulder with her lips in an angry pout. Maria beckons her to come back, but the girl runs to the door, where she stands looking out into the rain. Maria thinks that if the weather does turn cold again she might give her one of the scarves she has brought with her, though she knows her mother wouldn't allow it. Maria wonders what the "A" and the cross on the child's potato sack dress might mean. As the Greek Church is sending out sacks of potatoes to starving villages, perhaps the "A" stands for *Alleluia*, Maria thinks. That can't be it, she decides, realizing that exhaustion is making her mind wander, and she brushes the foolish thought away. She touches her cheek to see if she has a fever, but it's cold.

She feels a new and bitter sense of freedom. In the village she was a prisoner in her father's house, but its walls, which felt like the walls of a dungeon, now strike her as having been warm and sheltering. A strong gust of wind can knock down this flimsy barrack. As a little girl she played in the meadows, and followed her brothers, Kimon and Dionysi, and the sheep they were herding, up into the mountains. Back then her father treated her like a boy, showing her how to graft lemon trees onto orange trees, how to use the plow, how to slit the bark of pine trees to let the resin flow. He even called her Marko, a name he would have given a third son; at first he called her that for fun, because she was so boyish; then her brothers began calling her Marko too, and it soon became her nickname. She did the work in the fields and meadows that a boy her age, three years younger than Dionysi and five years younger than Kimon, would have done. By the time she was ten, the only person in the village who still treated her like a girl and ordered her around was her mother, who, as Maria knew even then, would have wanted her to have been a boy, or not to have been born; Heraclea had sometimes told her as much, not spitefully or in anger, just as a matter of fact. Cold words once spoken expire in the air but live on in your mind. And yet Maria's first memories of her mother were of her singing songs to her and kissing her cheeks. Her father and brothers must have been away, up in the mountains with the sheep. But when the boys were at home, her mother seemed to lose all interest in her. "I have two eyes," Heraclea would say. "Kimon is the apple of one eye, and Dionysi the apple of the other." She would say this to her sons, her husband, her neighbors, and to Maria. Heraclea prided herself in loving her two boys equally. She wove shirts and trousers in pairs, and with a needle thick as a nail sewed sheep-skin coats for them. But everyone knew that Kimon was Heraclea's real favorite. Heraclea said that boys were so much cleverer than girls. Were boys cleverer, Maria had wondered even back then. She could milk a cow and snub its horns quicker than they could, and she could sew raw goatskin sacks for cheesemaking, which her brothers couldn't. She played Five Stones Flying with the village boys, throwing pebbles into the air and then slamming them onto the ground with the back of her hand, often winning more points than the boys did because she was just as fast as they were and on top of that had the sharp eye of a girl. Boys were too rash and hasty.

Three years ago, in autumn, in the middle of a game of Five Stones Flying, her mother came out of the house, grabbed her by one of her braids, and dragged her inside. It was time, Heraclea told her angrily, that she start embroidering her dowry, or did she expect her father to feed and fatten her for the rest of her life? Maria didn't know what had happened, but a sudden change had come over the whole family. Her brothers were now cold to her as well, treating her like a girl: they would call out for a mug of water, or for bread and onions, and she would have to obey. Her brothers, her father, or her mother would look at her and say a single word and she would have to run. The first time her brother Kimon had called out an order she had spoken back to him, and her mother had slapped her hard across the face. Maria ran out into the yard and her mother followed and slapped her again and again. "Mothers are cold water," the villagers sang on feast days, and though Maria didn't know what that meant, she always associated wintry cold water with Heraclea.

Maria's childhood freedom was over, and a new life consumed by weaving, sewing, embroidery, and the many chores of the household began. She had to wind her kerchief around her face if she was going out into the yard to boil milk in the large pot or fill the goat-skin sacks with fermenting cheese; men from the nearby houses up the slope might see her. Not even her father called her Marko anymore. One day, when no one else was in the house, Kimon wrestled her to the ground, the way he would when she was still a tomboy and sometimes quick enough to dodge out from under him and pin his arm back, shouting, "I've won, I've won!" But now Kimon was a man, and she could not push him off her, and he held her down, his hips rolling and shoving against her as he whimpered—"It's just a game, it's just a game"—his tongue, rigid and red, darting into her mouth, his body shivering, and he jumped up, holding the front of his stained trousers. She looked at him, her eyes filling with angry tears, a bitter taste of tobacco in her mouth. "Don't worry," he said, "I didn't do anything to you, you're fine, don't worry." She began to cry. "Stop that!" he said, quickly looking at the door, though there was nobody in the house. "I kept my trousers up, so it was just a game, you hear?"

There was nothing she could do and nobody she could tell. If she told her mother she would not believe her, would say that she was an evil girl telling such lies about her brother; these were the kind of lies that whores told—what had Kimon done to deserve a whore like her for a sister, and what had she, Heraclea, done to deserve such a daughter? And if her mother *did* believe her, if she saw the stain on her dress and could not explain it away, then she would run at Maria with raised fists shouting that she had made Kimon do it, that she had ruined the family. When good boys did such things, and Kimon was a good boy, it was because they had been provoked—by a glance, by loosened hair, by a knee revealed on purpose. She knew what to expect from her mother, but she could not predict what would happen if she were to tell her father. Damianos the Potter, a kind and gentle man, had killed his daughter when she told him her brother had been with her; he had killed her for bringing disgrace on the family, for blackening her brother's name, for lying, for trying to poison his son's future and for ruining herself, as nobody would now marry her without her virginity. She had been found hanging in his pottery shack, and the village said that she had killed herself, though the village knew that she could not have thrown the rope over the high rafter and then yanked herself up off the ground on her own. Kimon had given Maria his stained trousers, and in the hour before dawn she went to the dark stream behind the house and washed them, along with her stained dress.

Her brothers soon left the village and were away for most of the year in the tea factories in Chakva on the coast, where a young man could earn in a week what he earned at the village plantation in a whole season. Maria was glad they were gone, a feeling of which she was somehow ashamed. Her home had turned into a house with four masters, her mother, her father, and the two boys shouting orders at her. Now that her brothers were gone for much of the year, she only had to do her mother's and her father's bidding. Her father had begun to look for a husband for her, and she knew that she would have to live this life until her wedding day, when she would exchange one form of slavery for another.

Maria's only escape was the hours between dawn and midday when she worked for Black Melpo, the old woman who had been mixing medicines for the village ever since Aphrodite the Witch had suddenly died a decade before. Maria helped Black Melpo gather the herbs, flowers, and beetles she needed for her tinctures and poisons, and on dark winter mornings Maria sat in Black Melpo's hut by a large oil lamp, filling pouches and glazed medicine pots. Remedies and poisons were sister potions, Black Melpo had told her, a single sting from a viper's fang chased away apoplexy, two stings brought on apoplexy and death. She cured ills, she said, with what caused them. Most of the potions were toxic: just touching the stem or the root of a white hellebore could be fatal, but Black Melpo showed Maria how to uproot and chop the plants, how to pick them up with long wooden pincers. Black Melpo lived beyond Maria's house, where the last shacks of the village were built against the steep rock that rose up to Saint Achilles Peak some eight hundred feet above. A narrow path wound from the back of Maria's house up to Black Melpo's hut, passing through the ruined precinct of an old mosque, the last witness of the village's forgotten Muslim past. Next to the mosque stood the ancient death house, now locked up to protect its rows of holy skulls, its walls round and its stones brown and red, and behind it were the tombstones of the abandoned cemetery; some were just simple slabs, others seemed like ancient tablets covered with strange letters and decorated with carvings of horses and sheep. Maria walked this path every day in the dark hour before dawn, her lantern lighting up the mud and stones. The minaret of the old mosque was still standing, miraculously intact, and her father and the men from the neighboring houses used the chamber at its base as a communal storage shed. On its roof, on a marble ledge, stood the sculpture of a two-headed bird that was twice the size of a man. One of its heads looked east, the other west. The bird stood there in the dark morning against the lightening sky, its wings open, ready to soar into the air. Seen from beyond the village square, the statue of the bird looked alive. Each head had a metal tongue with flute holes in it, and in the mountain winds they whistled like a cast of angry eagles. The sounds frightened the crows, and they stayed away from the village and its fields. On market days and church feasts, people from nearby settlements were always startled by the loud whistles that came from the old mosque, but Maria and the other villagers, who had grown up with these sounds, no longer heard them and could sleep through the loudest whistles in winter gales. Father Kyriakos, the village priest, said that a two-headed bird had descended from the sky many years ago when the Holy Virgin and the Infant Jesus had come to hide in the village during their flight from Egypt; the Virgin and the Infant were starving from their journey across the northern salt plains on their way to Mesopotamia, and the two-headed bird had saved their lives by feeding them strips of meat from animals it had hunted down in the plains. The birds of the village had offered up their feathers to the Infant so that it would stay warm, the saintly ancestors of the naked bats in the caves above the village, who fly only at night out of shame for their nakedness. Since those days, the statue of the two-headed bird has stood on its ledge next to the minaret, and even now, Maria thinks, with the village torched and destroyed, the old mosque and its whistling stone bird are probably still there.

Though Black Melpo was a robust old woman, she claimed she could no longer feel her feet, saying there was only air beneath her knees, as if she were hovering like a spirit over the meadows where she picked her medicinal herbs and flowers and caught vipers for their poison. She didn't seem to have any trouble walking, but she had told Heraclea that she wanted a young girl at her side on the mountain slopes, a girl like Maria, who could bend and crouch and kneel, plucking herbs, a child with good eyes who could spot among the tangle of grasses the beetles and dung pellets she needed for her potions. She would teach little Maria medicine mixing so that she could earn a living one day and support her parents in their old age, if they did not manage to marry her off. This prospect pleased Heraclea. A girl without a husband was like a dry and barren field—and yet from the day her daughter was born Heraclea lived in fear that someday Maria's dowry would ruin the family and cheat her brothers out of an inheritance that would secure them a good future. You can rob a girl of her rings and bangles, of her dowry of goats and sheep, yet you cannot rob her of her skills and trade. If the girl knew a trade, a bridegroom could be talked into a smaller dowry. How would she and Kostis live if they had to give Maria's future husband a vineyard and half their goats and sheep, if not more? Poverty was like a burning shirt, people said, and the shirt of poverty, Heraclea knew, burned even more fiercely in old age.

Black Melpo was not from the village, nor from any of the other villages in the nearby foothills. She never said where she came from, though the villagers thought it was a Greek settlement far away, south of the Arab lands. Selling mountain herbs and potions to the port towns was Black Melpo's main livelihood; the village women could only pay her with eggs and vegetables for her remedies and for the cleansings of the unwanted pregnancies she performed. The married women also sold her their hair, which hung eerily from rafter hooks throughout her shack, brown hair with brown, black with black, the precious blond and copper braids hanging separately by the pantry. She plaited and unplaited the hair, combing and curing it with smoke to kill the lice and nits, and in the spring she sold it to a Greek trader from Batum, who came to the village in a cart piled high with sacks of hair. Black Melpo taught Maria Greek letters so she could read out the weed and herb orders sent by the Greek apothecaries of Tiflis and Batum. Georgian letters too, which, before Maria knew what they meant, looked to her like worms slithering over and under one another. As there was no schoolhouse in any village nearby, Black Melpo and the village priest were the only people who could read. Father Kyriakos had tried to set up a schoolroom in his vestry to teach little boys at least how to spell their names and perhaps to write out the Lord's Prayer, but his venture came to nothing; in the first weeks some of the villagers had sent their boys, but soon fewer and fewer came, as they were needed in the fields and sheep pens. Once Maria knew the Greek alphabet, Black Melpo also had her read stories from Greek penny magazines to her while she crushed herbs and mixed medicines. "Read like you speak," Black Melpo had said, "faster, faster, I want to hear the story, like the storytellers tell their tales! Read just like you speak."

The stories in the magazines were always set in a Greece of golden palaces and dark forests, where princes with names like Aphrodisius or Erophilos were granted magic wishes for helping saints disguised as beggars and married the beautiful daughters of vanquished dragons. Black Melpo warned Maria not to tell her parents, or anyone else in the village, that she knew more than the alphabet; knowledge in a girl is like gold, Black Melpo said, best hidden from all eyes and used cleverly.

6

MARIA DREAMS SHE IS WALKING along a path, her shoes hitting against stones and falling off as she walks, the path coiling up the mountainside past the leper shacks and the ruined chapel of Saint Achilles and into the narrow lane that leads to the abandoned mosque and the death house next to it. The ancient stones of the death house are a reddish brown. Maria touches them but cannot feel them. The house is six thousand years old, the village priests have always said, the oldest house on earth, and it was built by Saint Adam with the red stones that Eve had carried in penance from distant Tabriz. The death house is round, with a large conical roof. Maria walks along the curving red wall, holding the three loaves of bread she seized as they fled the village. One loaf is about to fall, and she knows that if it falls she will die. The iron door of the death house stands open, the stone shelves inside laden with rows of skulls, the sons and daughters of Adam, all facing away from the door and upward to a fresco on the wall in which a row of headless bodies are running to escape the two-headed bird, twice the size of a man, its wings a faded gold, its talons reaching for the fleeing corpses. Cold fear pours through Maria as she runs past the cemetery and the abandoned mosque, past Blind Nektario's sheep pen and her empty house, until she reaches the village square. The village is silent; all the people have left, and though the wind is blowing, she cannot hear the whistle of the stone bird by the old minaret. She sees Black Melpo standing before her, waiting for her at the edge of the empty village.

Maria is awakened from her sleep by voices chanting outside and sits up on the straw sack, catching her breath. A few more seconds and Black Melpo would have spoken to her, Maria thinks in dismay, but then realizes it was just a dream. The lantern has dimmed but she can see that the barrack, now steeped in darker shadows, is empty except for a few sleeping women. The chanting outside grows louder. She gropes for her kerchief, quickly winds it around her head and across her face, and goes to the doorway, leaving her mother lying asleep. Twilight has turned into darkness, and in the rain she sees newcomers carrying lanterns that light up the wet stones and the broken shards along the path between the barracks. The Greek priest from Trebizond has arrived with his deacon and some muleteers, bringing provisions up from the valley. The priest in his wet cassock and tall hat is swinging his smoking censer, blessing the barracks where they will all be staying until they can leave for the Black Sea beyond the mountains and ravines.

Maria feels a light tap on her shoulder and, startled, turns around. It is the young woman with the cough.

"That's the priest," the young woman says eagerly. She looks feverish and is still wearing her wet dress. She is probably too ill to think clearly, and Maria wonders if her husband is still on guard duty.

"There are cauldrons and kettles at the back of the barracks," the woman says, "I saw them there, at least ten cauldrons, large ones, and soup kettles. Lanterns too, a whole line of them, and their glass isn't even smashed. Do you think I can take one?"

"Yes, I'm sure you can."

"I'll ask my husband." She coughs, holding her rag up to her mouth, and shaking her head smiles apologetically. "There must have been an army stationed here, or do you think somebody brought all those things? Just one of the cauldrons is big enough to boil half a deer. I wonder why nobody took them or stole them. All those cauldrons, so many of them! Perhaps nobody ever comes here. We must be really far from anywhere. On our way here we passed a dead village about two hours upriver, the village was on the side of the mountain, the houses were all abandoned, all rotting and crumbling. A plague village, my husband said. Everyone was dead. Since then there has been a spirit sitting on my shoulder, but it is a good spirit, it's telling me I must find some medicine."

"The blankets inside are nice and dry," Maria says. "You should wrap yourself in one and stay warm. You're wet, that's not good."

The woman nods.

"You don't want your cough to get worse."

"Should I ask the priest?" the young woman says.

"Ask him what?"

"If we should leave tomorrow."

Maria hesitates. "It would be better for your husband to speak to him."

The young woman nods. The folds of her wet dress are strangely heavy; there must be many coins sewn into the seams, Maria thinks, gold coins. Over her midriff and hips she is wearing a shawl-like sash woven of yellow and orange threads, the cloth thick enough to hide even more coins. The young woman looks lost among the others in their ragged and tawdry dresses. Maria glances at the priest and wonders what he might say to the young woman if she did speak to him. He looks quite different from the priests of Maria's village and the other villages in the valley back home: old men with long beards, their white hair tied in a knot at the nape. She can't tell if this priest is twenty-five or thirty-five, but the idea of a priest with full dark-brown hair and a short beard is new to her. His deacon, limping a few steps behind, is a more familiar figure; perhaps not much older than the priest, but withered, with a long face and sallow complexion, a man scarred by austere devotion.

"We will be leaving tomorrow," the young woman says to Maria, "we're not going to stay here. I need to get some medicine for my cold."

"In our village we burn bushweed and use the ashes."

The woman looks at Maria. "Bushweed?"

"Yes, you drink it. I think the ashes are mixed with water," Maria says, remembering Black Melpo crushing the burned bushweed into powder.

"Would your mother know?" the woman asks, turning her head to look back into the barrack.

Maria shakes her head. "We had a medicine mixer in our village. When you get to the town, the apothecaries will know. Ask them."

"Bushweed, bushweed, burned bushweed," the woman says.

The deacon is throwing handfuls of seed at the barrack walls, where the refugees are crowded. In the lantern light his face flickers yellow and gray like Bible paper. His eye momentarily rests on Maria, then he quickly looks away. With the voice of the true believer he shouts: "Let infidel thieves and brigands steal all your belongings, but only after they have counted every one of these seeds!"

"Amen!" the refugees mumble.

Maria turns around, but the young woman is gone. She sees a group of boys standing by the door of the men's barrack. Her kerchief has slipped, revealing her face, and they are watching her, not the priest or the deacon. One of them pokes his hand into his trousers, wiggles his fingers, and the boys laugh. Maria raises her kerchief, covering her face, and looks away.

"These barracks will be your abode for the time being," the priest calls out. "May they be blessed."

"Amen," the refugees mumble.

"Away, all vipers!" the deacon suddenly shouts, and the priest, his censer still swinging, looks back at him with what Maria thinks is impatience. "Lord God, hear our fervent prayers," the deacon goes on. "Draw the vipers to their lairs! Draw them away!"

"Amen," the refugees mumble.

•

Over the next few weeks, though the vipers do stay away from the barracks, swarms of orange beetles dart from every crack and scurry up the walls and over the roof beams, logs with thick shedding bark, burrowing into the bundles and boxes the refugees brought with them. At night the beetles swarm over the straw sacks, and Maria and her mother wake up in the morning covered with red spots. Heraclea is worried that they might ruin her daughter's complexion. Like her husband, she has always seen Maria's beauty as a hindrance, but now she thinks that it could become an advantage. They have lost their house and everything they owned; the girl has no dowry, and that makes her unmarriageable. She has no land, no sheep, no embroidered finery to offer a husband; who would want her? But Heraclea still has hope. The girl's remarkable looks might save them; now that they are away from the village and will never return, perhaps an older widower in whatever town they end up in might wish to adorn his empty bed. For a wealthy old man, a wife with a dowry is less important. He might take Maria and see to it that his new in-laws do not starve either.

Heraclea forbids Maria to touch the beetle stings, no matter how they itch. Marks can scar the girl's face, and she must not destroy the only asset the family now has left. Maria's hair is what the villagers call *miréa*, fatal: a mesh of tresses and curls that can entangle men. Heraclea plaits these tresses into severe braids. She winds them tightly over her daughter's head and covers her hair with a kerchief whose reds and blues have faded to a muddy gray so the girl will remain as plain as possible until it is time to parade her before a suitor: the evil eye can wither the whitest complexion and render a girl sickly and unmarriageable. To ward off this danger, Heraclea has small bags of salt sewn into hidden seams of her daughter's tunic, and beneath this outer layer Maria wears her bodice inside out and carries an amulet, a small silver cylinder, with a strip of Biblical parchment rolled up inside: "You have given me health, so let me live."

A warm wind blowing down from the mountainside sweeps the stench of the latrines into the barracks, and Maria, holding her kerchief over her face, hurries down the mud trail toward the river unnoticed as her mother and the other women are sitting on the stoop across from the men's barrack. She is barefoot, but is carrying her shoes in her bag, as they are valuable enough to be stolen. She can hear the women's voices and snippets of what they are saying, talking about Athens, where none of them have ever been, but which they imagine to be a city of marble and gold. She sees a few men standing guard up beyond the barracks, leaning on their rifles, but they are facing away from the river and talking among themselves. Three deer were shot the day before, and their heads—all that is left now—have been stuck downward into the fire pits and are slowly roasting, the smoke blowing toward the barracks. Skinned animals hang from nearby branches; their blood drips into tin plates. It is twilight, almost dark, and the women's voices grow fainter. Beyond the trees she hears the river clattering over stones but can't see it. A lynx yelps somewhere far inside the forest, and an owl, up on the mountain, screeches like a terrified child. She sits down on a flat rock and breathes in the fresh air. It is warm enough to sleep outside—she could curl up on the rock and fold her scarf into a pillow—but she knows that even though she is only a few hundred yards from the barracks, it is too dangerous. She is hungry, but there will be no food until much later: the deer heads have to roast a few hours longer. She can't smell the roasting meat, only the evening meadow and the river plants, and she thinks of her brothers far away, working in the tea factories of Chakva, carrying sacks and scrubbing the tea-drying platforms—the picking is done by little girls with hands small and nimble enough to nip off the best leaves. She has worked three seasons as a tea picker on the small plantation below her village, earning good food and a coin every day. Rows of little girls with fingers pecking at the leaves. Tea flowers in bloom! That is what this smell in the air reminds her of, and she looks around. She tries to picture her brothers' faces. Kimon and Dionysi are handsome men, like their father, but she can't quite make out their features, their faces blending with one another in her memory. Five months, she thinks, and I'm already forgetting what they look like. She is suddenly certain she will never see them again. During the weeks after he had followed her through the house that first time and wrestled her to the ground, Kimon followed her four more times. The first three times he had remained clothed, panting and whimpering as he writhed on her, but the last time he followed her he pulled down his trousers, his hand clamping her neck, pressing himself against her closed mouth, bruising her lips and cheeks, the salt of his skin staining her tongue. He only stopped when she said breathlessly that she would poison him, that she would drop Beelzebub berries into his food. Startled that she would dare say such a thing, that she would threaten him with death, he raised his hand to hit her, then lowered it; he was suddenly certain that she really would poison him if she thought her life was in danger, and her life would have been in danger if he had taken her virginity. Her wedding day would then have been her death day. The bridegroom, upon finding her without a maidenhead, would beat her, and before the eyes of the village she would have had to ride back to her father's house, her face and arms bruised, the mules and donkeys of her bridal procession carrying back her dowry in shame. What else could her father and brothers then have done but kill her for the honor of the family?

There is a rustling in the bushes, and Maria turns her head toward the sound; one of her braids brushes against her thigh, and she starts up. She thinks she would not have killed Kimon in order to stop his unnatural actions; she would have mixed only two Beelzebub berries into his food, bringing him deathly ailment but not death. Two berries every time he approached her until he stopped, weaning him off her like a mother weans a baby by rubbing bitter herbs on her nipples. She raises her hand to her cheek. It is quite warm, though she feels a chill creeping up her back. Perhaps a fever is coming. It will only be a matter of time, she thinks, before illness seizes the barracks. She looks down to the river, now black in the fading light, and the smoke trees standing guard by the riverbank. She feels her blood begin to beat. She takes her braid and brushes her finger over the soft ends of her hair. Black Melpo once told her that spirits rarely break through the wall that cuts their shadow world off from ours, a wall guarded by scorpions larger than oxen, and that only medicine mixers with their poisons can cross into that shadow world and return unharmed. Maria thinks of the song in which Medea wages war on a seven-headed snake that has emerged from the shadow world and devoured two of her brothers. If this snake suddenly comes out of the bushes, Maria thinks, she will run back toward the barracks before its tail can whip around her ankle. The song tells how Medea not only killed the snake, but the snake's shadow too, and how she found the bones of her murdered brothers in the snake's thumb. Maria gets up and inches away from the stone on which she has been sitting. She is sure she has seen something dark slither across the path, but then thinks how foolish she is to fear a monster from an ancient song. How strange the ancient songs are. What snake would have a thumb, not to mention a thumb large enough to hold the bones of two men? She has known the song ever since she can remember and is surprised that its strangeness has never struck her. She remembers sitting in the village square as a little girl, with her brothers and her father and all the other villagers on a warm evening, the smell of tea flowers in bloom, and an old man singing the song in a voice that came from deep in his throat, his lute mimicking the snake's moans and the hissing of Medea's golden sword in which a hundred sunsets glowed. The lute had the body of a fish, a long thin neck covered by many strings, and at the top of the neck the head of the Holy Infant with eyes that seemed to move and watch the listeners as the old man played and sang. He played his lute over the sick people who had been brought to the square and were sitting in a row under a plantain tree, the humming strings drawing the illness from their bodies. Kimon whispered to her that the lute was alive, that the Holy Infant was not the Holy Infant but an evil fairy, and that she should hide so that the fairy's eyes did not pin her down. Kimon was a fool, she thought even back then, but she pretended to be frightened and raised her hands to cover her eyes.

Kimon went bad in many ways, which was a great misfortune for the family, though nobody would admit it. As soon as he reached his teens he began taking things that were not his: small things, like a nail or a piece of rope that nobody would miss right away. Kostis wanted to beat sense into the boy, but Heraclea forbade it. He was her firstborn; he meant well, she said, he was just a prankster. Kimon grew into a charming young man everyone liked, stealing only if he could get away with it, until last summer, when he stole two sheep from his father's flock and sold them to a merchant in the village down in the valley. The two sheep, Kimon said, must have strayed when he took the flock out to graze; perhaps they had fallen into a ravine or been seized by wolves. But truth cannot be burned by fire or drowned in water. "I could have told him that he would be found out," Maria thinks, angry at both his foolishness and his deed. "I could have told him that in a few days word would come up from the valley that he had sold the sheep there!" By the following Sunday the whole village knew what Kimon had done. That such a handsome young man would do such a thing, people said—as if, Maria thinks, a man's appearance is somehow linked to his deeds. He must have a woman in town, people said. Heraclea had reacted to the news of the theft the way she always did when something unpleasant was said about her favorite son: she first refused to acknowledge that anything had happened and then, when it could no longer be denied, refused to acknowledge that

Kimon had done anything wrong. She told her husband it was his fault for not giving the boy enough money; things had changed—a boy needed coins now that there was a train in the valley that went to Batum. And Maria noticed that despite his anger her father was ready to yield to Heraclea and blame himself.

When the marauders brought fire and death to the village, almost all the young men, including her brothers, were away working in Chakva, unaware of what had happened. They still do not know; who would have told them? It will be many months before they return home on leave. She tries to picture Chakva, which her brothers have said was an eerie and forbidding place. There is a tall and ghostly cliff up the coast, they said, that falls the height of a thousand men into the sea. Maria looks back toward the barracks that stand out against the darkening sky and wonders if she and her parents should have fled north to the coast where her brothers are, instead of south to these poisonous lands. But the trains crossing the Caucasus are no longer running, not with rebels from the Gurian Peasant Republic digging up the rails and camping by the overturned locomotives until the Russians come and shoot them. Fleeing north would have meant fleeing toward danger. There was no other way for Maria and her parents to escape the burning village except south over the border, where they will still have to cross the last mountain passes to the Black Sea to find a boat to take them to safety and freedom.

•

Many of the refugees sit outside the barracks all night. Better darkness and the vapors from the ravine than the pestilential bites of the vermin. Maria's mother cooks up a mixture of boiling water and mashed oleander leaves and pours it through the cracks of the floors and walls, but still the beetles come. Maria knows that the oleander, despite its poison, won't help; the years she worked for Black Melpo gave her a better understanding of plants and their poisons than her mother has. But Heraclea would never ask her daughter for advice, and Maria knows better than to offer it.

"Your oleander paste is a waste of time!" Elpida the midwife says, as if voicing Maria's thoughts, and Heraclea looks at Elpida angrily. "Pouring that paste," the midwife continues, "is about as useful as climbing onto the roof to plow it!"

The other women laugh.

Heraclea rolls her eyes. "You'd do better to help me than to stand around giving advice!" she says.

"Helping you would be twice the waste of time!"

Turning to Maria, Heraclea whispers, "May that witch lie dead beneath a fallen wall!"

Maria looks at her mother in dismay. Though Elpida is gaunt and weak-bodied, there is something formidable about her. It is not just Elpida's sharp tongue; she seems to be one of those women who might hurt an enemy with more than words. But she is also to be pitied. Some months ago her husband and youngest son were shot during a skirmish in Tiflis. The women in the barracks whisper that they must have been carrying contraband, but Maria thinks that no matter how Elpida's husband and son died, they are dead, and Elpida is now alone with her bundle of dresses and sheets, her useless dowry from many years ago, and a plain, silent daughter called Karteri, who follows her like a shadow. Elpida has an older son as well, she has told the women, Alexandros, a strong young man who works on a Black Sea merchant ship based in Trebizond, which is where she hopes to go. But Elpida does not seem to be sure that her son really is in Trebizond, or what the ship he works on is called. What will Elpida do once she gets there? Walk through the streets of the port, asking people whether they know a young man named Alexandros? Elpida has already asked Father Andreas twice if he knows of her son, as Father Andreas is from Trebizond; the boy has dark curls, she told the priest, he is the kind of boy one would notice right away, a good Christian boy, and he would have been wearing his white fleece hat, a very tall and handsome hat. He has a scar on his cheek near his ear, the scar is as long as her little finger, she said, holding up her little finger for the priest to see.

7

FOOD IS SCARCE. THE RIVER flows too fast for any boats
or barges that the Greek Bishop of Trebizond might try to send
upstream from the coast. As the threat of famine begins to spread
through the Ottoman borderlands, the few sacks of food the bishop
can spare have to be carried on mules through ravines and gorges
all the way up to the abandoned chapel of Saint Georgios, a mile
from the barracks, where Father Andreas and his deacon have settled in a shack. That is as far as the caravan drivers will go. Every
morning Maria and her mother accompany the other women
along the river and up the winding path to the chapel. There, under
the deacon's supervision, the women boil soup and gruel, then wait
outside the chapel with their tin boxes for the rations the deacon
ladles out from a cauldron.

Maria's father never comes to the chapel. He and the other
men spend much of the day digging new latrines and fire pits. Each
afternoon Kostis and a young man called Homeros try to catch
fish at a bend in the river downstream, where the water is calmer.
Homeros used to work in the tea factory at Chakva and remembers Kimon, who was a little older than he. The Russian owner of

the factory had begun cultivating bamboo groves on the old mosquito marshes, land that was too wet for tea, and had built a workshop to produce lacquered bamboo chairs that he shipped to Saint Petersburg. Bamboo chairs were the height of fashion throughout Russia, and Mr. Popov, Homeros says, was earning almost as much from the chairs as from his tea business. Two days a week, Homeros and Kimon smeared layers of heavy black lacquer onto the bamboo. Kostis wonders why his son never told him about this, but he pushes the thought away: Kimon might not have wanted him to know about the extra money he earned because he was spending it in the bawdy houses of Batum Harbor. Kostis is delighted to have come upon someone who seems to have known Kimon quite well. He is aware that Homeros has noticed his daughter, however, which displeases him. It is a sign of the dangers and difficulties to come. The other men have noticed Maria too, but Homeros's glances worry Kostis more. Heraclea will have to talk to her, tell her to be on her guard, tell her what men and boys want from her, what they might do to her, and warn her of the shame and ruin it would bring to him and the family.

In other times he might have allowed Homeros to court her, his mother sending matchmakers and go-betweens; Homeros's family would not have demanded as large a dowry as some of the marriageable men who owned more land and sheep and had prospects in life—not that his mother and aunts would not have claimed as much as they could. "Take a dog from a sheep pen that is wet and cold, take a wife who is plain but has land and gold," the proverb warns. Maria's beauty would have been an obstacle when the matchmakers and parents met to discuss the dowry contract, which would list the land the future wife would bring to the groom's family, the number of pots and pans, blankets and towels, spoons and forks. But in spite of her beauty, which would lead to trouble in a marriage by drawing the eyes of other men, Maria was a strong girl who would have been capable of managing a household and serving her husband and his father, carrying out his mother's orders, weaving, sewing, washing, milking goats and making cheese, carrying sacks of grain to the mill for grinding, and bearing sons. Kostis would have looked for the bridegroom who could offer the most for the smallest dowry. Then his two fields, his vegetable plot, and his olive groves a half hour from the old village on foot would have remained for his sons. It was lucky that Kostis had only one daughter, for few men could scrape together more than one dowry. Now all this is gone, and all these considerations irrelevant. His house and land are in the hands of murderers who claim that the mountains are theirs, even if in ancient times the whole of the Caucasus and the lands beyond were Greek. Now his fields are laid waste, his olive trees burned, his flock of sheep slaughtered.

·

The women gather shortly after dawn for the daily trek up the rocky hills where the chapel and the priest's shack stand. Maria is walking with Lita, a girl from a village only a three-hour donkey ride from her own. Maria had never met Lita before their arrival at the barracks, but Lita was once to have married into Maria's village, to Mirtilis the locksmith. He was not really a locksmith but a locksmith's apprentice—though he was almost thirty—and he spent his days making iron spikes and coffin nails at Petro's smithy. Then Lita and Maria would have been neighbors. But Lita's father and uncles left for Greece a year ago and found work in Athens. After the winter snows melted, her mother packed up what was left of their household and set out on the long journey to Athens with Lita and her two little brothers, one of them still a baby. Her marriage came to nothing, which was good in every way, Maria thinks. She has asked Lita if she ever met Mirtilis the locksmith, and Lita laughed and said that she was quite aware of what fate would have had in store for her. But now destiny was pointing to Athens, a thousand miles away. A few days before the marauders had descended on the valleys, Lita's mother, Despina, had joined a caravan of carts making its way along the post road that led through the new Peasant Republic to the coast, where she'd intended to take a Black Sea steamer to Greece; but they had been caught in a skirmish of local peasants and Russians shooting at each other. Abandoning their belongings and cutting their horses loose, Despina and the children had run for their lives, joining the swarm of refugees fleeing across the river into the Ottoman lands. Losing her pots and pans, her blankets and finery, was a terrible blow for Despina— all she had managed to grab from the cart as they ran was a bundle of embroidered kerchiefs and smocks. For some reason Despina blames Lita for their misfortune, but Lita doesn't seem to care.

For Maria, the loss of everything her family had back in the Caucasus can only be a terrible thing. Gone is the life that she, her parents, and her parents' parents before them had led, with its rules, its joys, and its drudgery. It was a dangerous life, but everyone knew what the dangers were: the danger of raids in the spring and autumn, the danger of plagues and fevers in the summer. Yet despite the new fears and worries that haunt her in these pestilential barracks— where everything is filthy, where there is never enough food— not knowing what might happen next is somehow exciting. Father Andreas and his deacon could appear any morning and announce that they would all be going to Trebizond, or Constantinople, or perhaps Athens. It is the first time in her life that Maria can ask herself where she might be next week without knowing the answer. But beneath her excitement is a layer of dread. Her parents, particularly her mother, have always seen Athens and the other great cities that once belonged to Greece as beacons of hope, but Black Melpo told Maria that new village immigrants who could not learn the ways of city folk died of hunger in back alleys.

"I'm not sure I even want to go to Athens," Lita says, startling Maria, who for an instant thinks she has read her mind. Lita is carrying her three-year-old brother Dimitri. He tugs at her hair, and she winces. "I'll slap your fingers," she says to him, tapping his hand, and he laughs. "Athens, Athens, Athens," Lita sings, "who wants to go to Athens?"

"Where do you want to go?" Maria asks. "Back across the river? There's nothing there now, nothing."

"I'd like to stay right here," Lita says, pointing to her feet, and before Maria can step back Lita leans over to her and kisses her on the cheek.

"You want to stay here?" Maria says. "This is a terrible place. I'd rather drown in the river than live here!"

Lita leans over to her again, puckering her lips as if to kiss her once more, and Maria raises her hand to stop her.

"You'd let me kiss you if I was Homeros."

"No I wouldn't!"

"I'd like to stay here and go fishing with him," Lita says. "But only if you stay too."

Maria imagines Homeros sitting next to her on the riverbank in the sun, the cold water rushing past.

"You think Homeros wants to stay here fishing with us?" she says to Lita. "What do you and I know about fishing?"

Lita laughs, raising her hand to her mouth as if Maria has said something improper, and Maria steps forward and slaps her hand.

"We're going to have to leave here in the next few weeks whether we want to or not," Maria says.

"Oh yes? Without traveling papers?"

"With traveling papers or without. The vapors from the ravine and the rains will get warmer and we'll be cut down by fever, if the plague doesn't get us first. There will be clouds of mosquitoes, mosquitoes everywhere."

Lita frowns and hurries along the path as if she intends to leave Maria and catch up with the other women, but then she turns around and smiles. "I'm not frightened of fever or plague. If they didn't get me back in the village, why would they now? What I'm more interested in is who Homeros would want to marry, you or me?"

"Whoever has the larger dowry," Maria says.

"I don't have one and you don't either."

"That means he won't marry you, and he won't marry me," Maria says, unsure whether Lita is making a joke; she has a habit of saying outrageous things in a serious and solemn way, as if she were discussing something important.

"One good thing about being here," Lita says, "is that we're not hidden away in the house with the doors locked. If we're to be married off, the men can see us and we can see them. There'll be no surprises, like my father promising me to Mirtilis the locksmith just because Mirtilis was too much of a fool to ask for a real dowry." Lita winks the way the village boys do and crinkles her nose. She wears brightly embroidered kerchiefs and sashes, but Maria thinks she has the mind of a boy; she even looks like a boy, though in a pretty way. Her skin is reddened by the sun; she never covers her face the way the other girls and women do when they are outside, both to hide their faces from men's eyes and to keep their skin white. Lita doesn't seem to care, and she has plaited her hair beneath her kerchief into many braids, the way Turkmen girls do. She would never have been allowed to do that in her village, but in the barracks nobody notices. She now wears her kerchief around her neck, and when she runs the braids fight one another like long thin snakes. She spends most of her time taking care of three-year-old Dimitri, leaving her mother free to look after the baby. As they walk to the chapel, Maria and Lita take turns carrying Dimitri for the last stretch of the path up the hill.

"Homeros asked me about you," Lita says.

Maria stops and looks at her.

"He says he knows your brother Kimon—they worked together."

"He just came up to you and said that?"

"Yes."

"He can't speak to you just like that! What will people say? You were alone with him?"

"No, of course I wasn't, are you mad?" Lita replies. "He came up and spoke to me when I was outside the chapel with the other women."

"In front of everyone?"

Lita laughs. "He came out of the chapel with Father Andreas, and while the Father was speaking to the women, Homeros came over and told me about your brother. Nobody said anything." She leans forward to look at Maria's face. "I see your spots have gone. My arms are still covered, I'm itching all over—I hate those beetles." She scratches her elbow. "I wonder why he came to me to tell me he knows your brother."

"Don't scratch," Maria says quickly, "it'll only make it worse." She bends down and plucks some blades of grass, rubs them between her thumb and forefinger, and presses the green pulp on the spots on Lita's arm. "You'll see—they'll be gone by evening."

"I like Homeros," Lita says, handing little Dimitri to Maria and skipping a few steps ahead.

"I like him too."

"I know you do, and now that he knows your brother . . . but when we get back from the chapel, I'll ask him to marry me before you do!" Lita says, and Maria laughs. The women walking up the path in front of them look back and frown.

"A girl asking a boy to marry her!" Maria whispers to Lita, shaking her finger at her. "That's like a river running up a mountainside. You'll end up an old maid, a *very* old maid, if you start asking men to marry you."

Lita tilts her head, first to one side then to the other, and curtsies the way maidens do in old village songs. Maria laughs, holding her hand over her mouth so the women walking ahead of them won't hear.

"I don't think I'll be an old maid," Lita says, "not me! I want to get married. No, no, not me. I want to get away from my mother, I'd rather be a slave to my husband than a slave to her—at least with a husband you can talk back."

Maria has never met such an outspoken girl. She knows that men, especially new husbands, don't like women who speak their minds and are as forward as Lita is, and she knows that Lita's path will be hard and full of trouble: even if Lita's husband forgives her for her opinions, his mother and sisters will not; they will torment her. A girl's thoughts can be free, Maria thinks, but not her words. A woman's crown is her silence. All the mothers Maria has known act

one way with their daughters and another with their sons. And yet
Lita's mother has done truly bad things to her. Lita's way of forgiving her, or perhaps not forgiving her, Maria thinks, is to act in unexpected and undaughterly ways. For the first years of her life, Lita
was an only child—five of her younger siblings had been stillborn
or died at birth. By the time she was seven or eight, her mother was
calling her possessed, a *brother killer* whose jealous spirit withered
her father's seed. Her mother treated her coldly, and her aunts and
the women of the village became distant. When Lita was nine she
was still an only child, and her mother decided to drag the murder-
ous spirit out of her. She gathered the village women in the house,
where they seized Lita by the legs, turned her upside down, and
thrust her headfirst into the fireplace, passing her over the flames
that singed her hair and blistered her cheeks. "Will you allow brothers into this house?" the women chanted. "I will! I will!" Lita had
shrieked. "Will you love your brothers?"—"I will! I will!" The exor-
cism worked; a brother was born, little Dimitri, and then another,
little Theoharis. It took four years for Lita's hair to grow back and
for her cheeks to turn soft and pretty again. Lita told Maria about
the burning in passing, to explain why her brothers were so much
younger than she was, but Maria thinks that the fright must have
somehow scarred her.

8

IN THE FOLLOWING DAYS, MORE refugees arrive. The
melting winter snows in the mountains have swollen the border
river and people are drowning in the fierce waters. It is said that a
pair of children fell prey to a pack of wolves just after crossing into
Ottoman territory, and that their mother ran into the forest looking for them, though she knew they were dead. Some of the refugees have spotted wolves lurking beyond the ridge of the ravine,
thin tattered animals, their green and yellow eyes watching the barracks. The newcomers bring fragments of news: a revolution has
broken out in Constantinople; throughout the Ottoman Empire
Greeks are being slaughtered in Muslim villages, and Muslims in
Greek villages. As the newcomers made their way through the
mountains, rumors and hearsay turned into fact, and everyone is
now certain that Greeks are being killed throughout the Caucasus
and Turkish lands.

Maria sees that her father is no longer considered the leader of
the barracks, as he was when they first arrived. With so many new
refugees it is now every man for himself; the fish caught and the
game trapped are no longer shared. Kostis seems relieved by his

loss of authority. He looks like a leader, there is resoluteness in his manner, but he is shy. His natural impulse is to act alone. The barracks have become louder and more chaotic, there have been fistfights among the men, and now the only word of authority is that of Father Andreas. Kostis wants to leave with his wife and daughter before new refugees bring fever and plague. He will walk alone with Heraclea and Maria along the valley paths to the Black Sea if necessary, perhaps with one or two other men and their womenfolk, men with rifles and ammunition. Kostis speaks to Father Andreas and asks his advice. He still has ten rubles, he tells the priest, won't that be enough to board a ship for Athens with his wife and daughter? His wife has three gold talisman chains hidden beneath her tunic, and his daughter has an amulet and two silver crosses. "You would sell your daughter's crosses?" the priest asks. Kostis tells the priest that they must get to Athens. "But you have no papers," Father Andreas warns, "and these are troubled times. If you set out on your own without papers, you and your wife will be found dead by the roadside before you get to the port, and your daughter will be dragged away."

As the rains subside, an unseasonal, humid heat comes rolling up from the river, bringing with it swarms of large flies, their wings sparkling in translucent blues and greens. Everyone now avoids the barracks during the day. The women stay near the chapel, looking for trees with leaves and pods that can be eaten and gathering weeds they can boil. In the meadows by the forest, along a broad mud trail leading to the river, Maria notices wolf tracks, paw prints strangely crossed by the fresher tracks of a she-lynx, as if the forest cat had purposely stalked her predators. It is definitely a she-lynx, as the toes are stretched out softly, the paw print more wary and cunning than that of the male's strong footfall. A lynx will kill a single wolf, Maria thinks, if her kittens are nearby, and will fight a prowling pack to the death, ripping out the eyes of the leader and his consort, throwing the pack into confusion and sometimes flight. These cats are cunning and fast, their actions immediate and never wrong. But Maria cannot understand why these tracks should be crossing one another like a long braid all the way to the river, and she narrows her eyes, looking toward the water, almost expecting to see dead animals on the bank. The other girls have not noticed the tracks, and Maria doesn't say anything. The prints are dusty, and clearly not from today; the animals have returned to the forest. There are empty cartridges and rusting rifle bolts among the weeds from the border battles of the last century, and flowering goosefoot bushes beyond the mud trail, their white blossoms shimmering in the sun. Three women are squatting next to the bushes some two hundred yards toward the river, their ragged skirts hitched up. They seem to be discussing something while they relieve themselves; one of the women waves her arms and then reaches back into the bushes to pluck some leaves.

"Those women have no shame," Lita says, nudging Maria and frowning in mock indignation, "no shame at all."

"And even less modesty," Maria says lightly. "I'd like to see them try that back in the village."

Lita laughs.

At the first trees there are mushrooms and toadstools. The girls are not sure which ones to pick. Though Maria often helped Black Melpo gather herbs and beetles in the meadows, she knows nothing about mushrooms. The only ones she has seen Black Melpo pick are the white-foot mushrooms that killed insects and seemed to grow everywhere, and their deadly sisters, as Black Melpo called them, two toadstools that look almost alike—*medusitsa*, little medusa, and *medusoula*, baby medusa. They had purplish-red caps and looked delicious, but even a small bite of either toadstool led to nightmarish visions and death. Black Melpo would cut a few speckled shavings from the gills of these deadly sisters, small flakes that were barely visible, and use them as a narcotic that was so powerful she could slice off a man's gangrenous finger without his noticing.

Maria and the other girls wander farther out into the meadows, gathering whatever mushrooms they can find; the women will later sort through them and remove the dangerous toadstools, washing and rewashing the rest. Karteri, the midwife Elpida's daughter, is the oldest, though she is skinnier and shorter than the other girls and her fear of everything—shadows, insects, weeds— makes her seem younger; she follows a few steps behind Maria and Lita, with the youngest girls. She is plain and pale, with blistered, thin lips, but her yellow sandy hair, thick and almost colorless, is rare in the Caucasus. She is wearing a short waist jacket of velvet, like a rich girl from a town, and a wide fringe sash, but her shoes are men's shoes, hand-me-downs from her dead brother. It is remarkable how unlike her mother Karteri is, Maria thinks; a snake has snake children, people say, but Karteri is in no way like Elpida. They have the same slight build, but nature has made the midwife a skilled and capable woman with sharp and poisonous words, while Karteri is sweet, but convinced that she is unable to do anything, even the simplest chores. Perhaps that is the fate of the daughter of a mother like Elpida, Maria thinks, a mother who always does everything herself. Elpida is always a step ahead of Karteri, finishing everything her daughter starts, clicking her tongue and saying, "Useless girl! What have I done to deserve a daughter like you!"

A broken musket lies among the weeds, perhaps near the bones of the soldier who once carried it, and the girls move away to avoid stepping on the dead. Lita has found a ring of mushrooms by a snakeberry bush, picks them and drops them into her sack.

"We had a neighbor once," Maria says, "who ate a mushroom just like the ones you're picking. Poor Aunt Mirofora!"

Lita looks up. "*Poor* Aunt Mirofora?" She looks down at the mushrooms. "But they look like normal mushrooms," she says. "They look like they might taste good."

"To your mouth a mushroom like that might taste good, but to your stomach it's a poisonous spider," Maria replies, suddenly realizing that this is what Black Melpo would have said.

"A poisonous spider?" Lita asks.

"Yes, a poisonous spider."

Lita quickly takes the mushrooms out of the sack and tries to stick them back in the ground.

"What happened to poor Aunt Mirafora?" Karteri asks. "Did she die?"

Beyond the first bend in the river they suddenly hear voices—men's voices. The girls cannot tell if the men are speaking Greek. Maria and Lita look at each other and quickly tie their kerchiefs over their faces. They have wandered so far that they can no longer see the chapel and the men on guard duty. The girls run into the forest, pushing their way through the undergrowth, then crouch down low and peer out into the empty meadow. "Will they see us?" Karteri whispers. Behind them, from deep within the forest, comes the angry barking and chuckling of jackals fighting over carrion. One of the little girls begins to whimper, and Lita waves to her to keep quiet. There is a smell of decay and damp earth. The leaves rustle, a twig snaps, and then there is silence. Maria turns and looks into the forest in alarm. Insects hum and she hears a man's voice, and then another. The words are faint, and in the underbrush she can't tell what direction they are coming from. A viper darts out from under a buckthorn bush and quickly slithers away, its red and black scales shimmering beneath the leaves. Maria raises her hand to her cheek and touches her lips as if to hold back her breath. The leaves rustle again, again there is a sound of snapping twigs, but now she thinks it cannot be a man's footfall as she had first thought; it must be an animal, perhaps a boar, hiding in the underbrush. Red forest ants are crawling over the dry moss and fallen leaves. Lita touches Maria's elbow and she catches her breath in fear. She whispers something Maria can't make out. Two buzzards sail over a stretch of waist-high mugwort bushes and then disappear into them, chattering and barking. A third buzzard joins them, then a fourth. Something must have died there, Maria thinks, something large. Two of the buzzards suddenly flutter back up from the bushes, clawing at the mugwort and snatching at each other's beaks. The wind from the river carries Greek words that cut through the yapping of the birds, and Lita points to the riverbank, where a group of men are heading in their direction, toward the meadow, carrying dripping sacks. Maria shields her eyes and peers downriver. She recognizes Homeros, and then sees her father coming up behind him with some of the other men.

The girls come out from behind the trees before the men can see that they were hiding, and Lita runs toward the bushes flapping her arms; the buzzards squawk and fly up over the trees, spiral back down toward the bushes, then soar up again. The men are talking loudly; Maria can make out Homeros's voice, unfamiliar yet pleasant and self-assured. He is wearing a Russian cap she has not noticed before, which makes him look foreign and out of place. She notices that the sleeve of his shirt is torn. Walking in front, he comes up to the girls and stops beside Maria, holding out his bag to show her the fish he has caught. She leans forward to look at them with her kerchief raised to hide her face, uncertain how to respond, as he is a stranger and she must not speak to a man who is not a brother or a cousin. Her father is still some distance away, talking to one of the other men.

"I caught these myself," Homeros says to Maria. "I caught all of them." The younger girls titter as if he has said something indecent, and he turns to look at Lita, who is standing in front of them with her eyes lowered. He looks at Maria. "We'll all eat fish today," he says. "I like fish."

He is confident, she thinks, like her brother Kimon, something she finds unsettling. She wonders how well Homeros knew her brother, and if they ever went to the drinking halls in Batum together. He seems to expect her to say something, but she knows that it wouldn't be right for her to speak. She is unsure of what to do and looks at him directly, almost angrily, as if he were her brother Kimon; he lowers his gaze. She realizes she has been too forward, and as her father is approaching, she too now looks away.

"He's figured out how to catch the fish when they're sleeping in the afternoon!" Kostis calls out as he comes up, pointing at Homeros. Kostis seems angry that Homeros is speaking to the girls, but he clearly likes him. "A clever boy!" Kostis says. He grabs his shoulder and shakes him, his grip tight. Lita catches Maria's eye.

"I touch the fish on their bellies when they're sleeping," Homeros says, pointing back at the river. "The sun's hot, but the water's cold. But I don't mind at all."

Maria glances at him. Her brothers' friends are rough, Maria has heard, boys who drink and fight and go to houses filled with women who will lie back and raise their skirts. She can't imagine Homeros being like that.

"He rubs their bellies," Kostis explains. "Would you believe it? Like they're cats or something."

Homeros glances at Maria.

"That's how we caught so many," Kostis adds, slapping Homeros on the back again.

A short boy with muddy hair comes limping over to Kostis, his legs bowed and one of his bare feet deformed. He is wearing a torn jacket without a shirt, and lays his hand on his stomach to hide his navel. He has a black eye, and Maria looks at the other boys, wondering who might have beaten him. He holds out his fish sack. "I caught some too," he says. "This one here's a big one, big as a minstrel fish. I'm sure he tastes better than the small ones. Three people can eat him, and I'll be one of them!"

"We're getting good at this," one of the other men says bitterly. "Shepherds turned fishermen!"

Maria wonders at her father's rough friendliness toward Homeros. She can tell her father likes him, but also that Homeros somehow is frightened of him. Perhaps Homeros is not like Kimon after all. People say that crows and ravens fly together, but does Homeros's friendship with her brother necessarily mean that he is like him, a drinker, a man who goes after women in the port? Men have such strange ways with each other, she thinks. Her father's fits of rage at something one of her brothers had done might suddenly seem to subside and he'd slap him gently on the back, or grab the boy's chin and playfully shake it, but that seemed to frighten her brothers more than their father's anger had. Women are different, Maria thinks. If she did something her mother didn't like she got a hard slap across the face; no explanation and no menacing kindness.

"We'll be eating fish tonight," Maria's father says to her and

Lita. "We'll grill it over a fire. And we can grill some of your mush-rooms too." Kostis looks at Lita, his eyes lingering for an instant. Maria holds out her sack to show him what she has gathered, but he beckons to the other men and they all walk off toward the barracks.

9

THE SHACK THAT FATHER ANDREAS and the deacon have settled into behind the chapel is divided in half, the front part serving
as living quarters while the back is used as a stable for three goats
and a small flock of chickens. The animals accompanied the caravan of mules that brought the priest and his deacon through the
string of valleys from the nearby port by the Black Sea.

Every evening, after they have ministered to the growing number of refugees, the two men of the cloth sit alone in the shack
beneath a kerosene lamp hanging from a roof beam. The wooden
walls are bare except for a faded icon of Saint Xenophon, his wife
Saint Maria, and their two sons, whom they lost in a shipwreck but
through a divine miracle found again. The icon stands on a small
shelf, and in front of it is a glass cup with a burning wick floating in
oil, its smoke darkening the faces of the stern saint and his family.
The priest and the deacon drink cups of plum wine and play backgammon, licking at specks of the mad honey mixed with laudanum
that herdsmen from the mountains sold them in little clay pots. In
tiny dabs the poisoned honey brings happy spirits, in small spoonfuls visions and rants, and in larger amounts delirium and death.

The priest confines himself to tiny dabs, the deacon to small spoonfuls. Forgotten is the evil cholera that has gripped the Muslim refugees some twenty miles upriver; forgotten is the growing horde of refugees devouring the provisions that the Bishop of Trebizond tries to send every week by mule; forgotten are the unnatural heat, the beetles and rats, and the pestilence that is winding its bony fingers around the necks of the old and weak.

Along with the sacks of food, the Bishop sends newspapers, sometimes a week or two old, which bring the attractions and concerns of the distant capital to this forsaken edge of the Empire. Mademoiselle Cotopouli, the Sarah Bernhardt of the Greek stage, is appearing in Constantinople. Father Andreas reads that her troupe performs special matinees for ladies on Wednesdays: the Ottoman dowagers and their unmarried daughters and retinues can arrive at the Théâtre des Variétés in their veils and unveil themselves in the loges, revealing Parisian dresses.

"La Cotopouli will be in Constantinople for the whole month," the priest tells the deacon, as if proposing that they attend a performance. He looks at the date of the paper. "Last Wednesday she appeared in *Oedipus*," he then says, "and on Thursday in *Just Three Kisses*, and this weekend she is performing in *Enough, Madame Prime Minister!*" He puts down the newspaper and looks at the deacon. "We Greeks gave light to the world!"

"Yes, but the world took the light and left us in the dark," the deacon mumbles.

Father Andreas looks at him and then picks up the newspaper again. Trouble is brewing in the capital. Perhaps more than brewing, he thinks. The Sultan, from what he can gather, is under siege in his own palace. This is incredible. The ruler of an empire stretching from Bulgaria to Mesopotamia, from the Mediterranean

Arab lands to holy Mecca and beyond, has been left with nothing but his harem as a shield! From what the priest can tell, a revolution is underway. The rebels have cut off all supplies to the palace, and His Majesty's starving guards have fled, along with all his servants. The newspapers are not specific, nor do they seem particularly concerned. Aside from the cultural news from the capital, the lead story is about the murder of a French-Egyptian lady on a Turkish steamer. Madame Claudius Bey has been found dead in her cabin, her pearls stolen. *Murder on the High Seas*, the headline reads. Father Andreas narrows his eyes and reads the sensationalist article with interest. But it is worrying that the newspapers are avoiding the real story.

"Listen to this!" he says to the deacon. "It's a letter to the editor from His Imperial Highness Prince Burhaneddin." He clears his voice and changes his tone, as if in imitation of a young Ottoman royal: "'I ask you, sir, to denounce all rumors about my person, including the rumor that I have joined the revolutionary forces besieging my father's palace.' What do you say to that?"

"I say the prince has joined the revolutionary forces."

The priest mistakes the deacon's comment for an unexpected witticism, but when he looks up from the paper sees his drawn, humorless face.

"Sons against fathers, fathers against sons. A sign of the times," Father Andreas says. "But we are in a terrible predicament. You, me, the poor people under our care, the Empire, the provinces. We can't march down to the coast, an army of refugees. There are guards at all the passes, we'd all be shot on sight. And the cholera is creeping down the river and will be upon us if the barracks get any filthier. We can't leave and we can't stay."

The deacon dips his spoon into the honeypot and licks a dab

of the golden poison. "Behind us unclimbable mountains, before us the raging sea," he says.

Father Andreas licks his honey spoon too and nods glumly. As the sweet poison seeps through their veins, the two men of the cloth start a game of backgammon, throwing the dice with increasing vehemence until the deacon becomes too disoriented to play.

"Behind us unclimbable mountains, before us the raging sea," the deacon says again, pointing out the window into the darkness, where he imagines the sea might be.

"Along with the supplies," the priest says, "I received an interesting letter. It's been on my mind all day. A proposal that might make the raging sea before us much calmer."

"Ah," the deacon says, as if he has remembered something he wanted to say, but then sits waiting for the priest to continue.

"You could call it a marriage proposal."

The deacon smiles and begins to chuckle.

"No," the priest says with a strained grin, "the matchmakers aren't knocking at *my* door. Heaven forbid!" His subordinate's insolence should annoy him, but the mad honey gives even his darker thoughts a touch of mirth. The idea of his marrying is amusing: perhaps a wealthy matron from Trebizond, a widow with hennaed hair, he thinks, her plump body struggling to break free of a tight corset.

"What proposal?" the deacon says, licking his honey spoon again.

"A gentleman from Constantinople, a reputable personage with connections in the highest circles . . ." The priest falters, suddenly worried what the deacon, though his junior, his servant in a sense, will say to this proposal that is as troubling as it is heaven-sent. "A proposal from a personage with the highest connections, even in the palace." He thinks of the beleaguered Sultan and sees him cowering in a mahogany-paneled room, shielded by his young wives, all from Caucasus villages just east of the mountains beyond the river that the refugees have crossed. A very old man, surrounded by very young women. Father Andreas realizes that the honey is clouding his thoughts and pushes the pot away.

"Did you know that Prince Burhaneddin's mother was from one of the villages near here?" Father Andreas says to the deacon. "On the other side of that mountain over there. A two-day ride, once you've crossed the river, perhaps three days, but not more."

"What marriage proposal?" the deacon repeats.

"And all of Prince Reshad's wives too. Except for . . ." Father Andreas pauses. "Except for his third wife, who was born near Constantinople. That's never happened before, a Turkish girl in a royal harem. We're living in a new era," he adds, trying to remember in his haze of poisoned honey where he has heard about Prince Reshad's wife.

The deacon stares at the priest.

"The proposal is being conveyed by a Turkish man traveling in these parts," Father Andreas says, managing to gather his thoughts again; he suddenly feels wide awake. "The man is aware of our predicament here in the barracks."

"He is?"

"Yes, he is," the priest says resolutely and then quickly adds, "and he's prepared to help. Some of his connections in the capital are seeking wives—good, kind girls from beyond the border who have been well brought up and are ready for marriage. Young enough to bear many children. His connections will pay us well, so that the girls' families . . . and everyone else, the two of us as well . . . can make our way to the port and take a ship to safety."

"You mean he's a matchmaker?" the deacon asks.

"Not exactly. This gentleman is from Constantinople, not from some mountain village."

"He's offering money? A Turk buying Greek girls?" The deacon's voice cracks.

The priest watches in alarm as he scoops up a whole spoonful of honey and swallows it, and then feels a wave of anger.

"*Buy*?" he shouts at the deacon. "What do you mean *buy*? The future bridegrooms this gentleman is representing are all wealthy men, Ottoman gentlemen who intend to provide for their wives' families! No one is buying anything!"

"The Turks want to buy the girls!" the deacon shouts back. "They want to buy girls the way they've always done!" The animals in the stable on the other side of the wall begin to stir, the chickens fluttering their wings in alarm. "The Turks will choose the prettiest girls," he continues shrilly. "They will pay for them and take them into their houses with their other wives and concubines. That's what they'll do! It's slavery! Nowhere in the world is there slavery anymore, not even in Abyssinia! Just here, in this godforsaken land!"

Father Andreas is amazed at the deacon's outburst and listens blankly to his ranting about Turkish ways, Turkish wives, and Christian girls turned into Muslim slaves. The deacon has taken too much of the mad honey. Father Andreas looks at the icon of Saint Xenophon and his family, his wife and somber sons holding large crosses, their eyes menacing and filled with divine light, the faded gold of their halos a brownish yellow. The floating wick in the glass bowl in front of the icon is beginning to tilt; he will have to pour in more oil, he thinks, or the light will go out in the night. As the deacon continues to shout about the evil ungodly ways of the

Ottoman Empire, the priest's ears begin to ring. He staggers out of the shack and hurriedly makes his way to the chapel, where, leaning against the wall, he catches his breath. He can still hear the deacon ranting inside the shack. There is a sharp sound, and he imagines that the crazed man has hurled his drinking cup against the wall.

Father Andreas sits down on the ground and closes his eyes, resting his back against the rough chapel wall; he feels both serenity and despair, a sort of happy sadness. The evening air is pleasantly warm, and the nocturnal insects seem to have retired to the river.

·

The next morning the priest is awakened by the women who have come to prepare the daily rations. Inside the shack the deacon is lying on the floor in watery excrement with his eyes closed. The women hurry to the river to fetch water to clean him, leaving his soiled clothes in a pile next to the latrine, mumbling spells at the bad omens that cross their path: a spider skimming across a pool by the riverbank, a yellow butterfly on a yellow flower.

They come back to the shack with buckets of water. Heraclea wraps her shawl tightly across her chest so it will not brush against the deacon's body and, crossing herself, begins to wash him, running the cold wet rag over his thighs. There is excrement on his chest too, and even on the silver amulets around his neck, which Heraclea carefully picks up with her rag and rubs clean. The priest watches the women lift the thin, shivering deacon to his cot, apparently unconcerned by his nakedness and stench. Heraclea takes a strip of sackcloth and begins wrapping it around the deacon's hips as if she were swaddling an infant, while the other women roll him from one side to the other and lift his legs. She raises her hand to her eyes, picks up the deacon's member, points it downward, and wraps the sackcloth tightly over it. "We will burn his shirt and trousers," she says, turning to Father Andreas. "They are too soiled—we can't wash the illness out of them."

10

LATE IN THE MORNING MARIA and Karteri are down by the river, beating the dirt out of heaps of clothes in a knee-deep pool. They swing their sticks like cudgels high over their heads, bringing them down on tangles of shirts and kerchiefs, the cold water splashing, and their hands black from the ashes they have rubbed into the clothes to wash out the dirt and mud.

"Let's stamp on them—it'll be easier than with these sticks," Maria says.

"Astrakhan, piki-piki rann," Karteri sings, jumping up and down on her pile of clothes. "The cup is called Miss Chasha, the monkey's called Natasha." She throws her stick onto the riverbank. Her kerchief slips back, revealing her rich, yellowish hair. "My schoolteacher was called Miss Natasha," she says eagerly. "She came to our village because the Russians said that now that the Caucasus is a real country, even girls had to learn to read and write."

Maria stops and looks at her. "The Caucasus has always been a real country," she says.

Karteri takes off her kerchief and shakes out her hair.

"What pretty hair you have," Maria says, surprised it isn't in braids.

"I should have braided it," Karteri says quickly, glancing at Maria, and then looking away. "I know I should have."

"Your kerchief is long enough—nobody can tell your hair's hanging loose. It's all hidden. I've never seen hair like yours before."

"My mother says it looks yellow and dirty, like Russian hair. And that only women who sell themselves in the port wear their hair loose."

"Really?" Maria shakes her head. The midwife in her own village and those of the nearby villages were kind women—healers and bringers of life—who always had words of comfort on their lips. But the words of Elpida, Karteri's mother, are always angry and unforgiving.

"My hair is yellow, the color of dust," Karteri explains. "My mother says my face is yellow too, that I'm yellow all over, chicken-yellow, and that no man will marry me."

"That's not true!" Maria says angrily, and Karteri looks at her in surprise. Maria reaches out and touches one of the long strands. "Many men would marry you just for your hair!"

"But I don't have a dowry."

"Me neither," Maria says, shrugging her shoulders.

"But you are different. Even my mother says that you are beautiful."

There is a burst of birdsong as a flock of olive-speckled songbirds flies up from the smoke trees. The girls begin stamping on the clothes again.

"We need to get some soapwort flowers for the scarves," Maria says. "Soapwort," she repeats slowly and Karteri looks at her blankly. "The ashes are too rough."

They leave the clothes soaking in the pool and walk along the bank to the bend in the river where the stones end and the mud begins. Black Melpo would have loved these meadows, with their medicinal weeds and flowers, all left unplucked as there are no villages nearby: the apothecaries of Batum would have paid a fortune for them. Maria and Karteri have ventured quite far from the barracks again; if there is danger, they can't call to the men standing guard duty, and the others, fishing downstream, are even farther away. Some of the men have gone into the forest to dig pitfalls to trap stags and other large game, but the forest lies on the other side of the barracks, away from the river.

"My father always said that the Greeks will come and take back this land, and the land beyond," Karteri says, shaking her head and pulling her hair back. She has left her kerchief with the soaking clothes, and her head is bare. "Even the Sultan's palace will be Greek."

"The Sultan's palace?" Maria laughs.

"My mother says the Russians want to build a road of iron," Karteri continues, "all the way to Athens. Even farther. A long, long road of iron."

"A road of iron?"

"Yes, chug-chug."

"Ah, rails, rails," Maria says, nodding. When Karteri speaks fast she doesn't always understand her. The Greek spoken in the far-flung Caucasian villages, which have been cut off from each other for many centuries, has splintered into almost entirely different languages. Some of Maria's words are a mystery to Karteri as well. The women in the barracks treat Karteri as if she is a simpleton, but Maria thinks that Karteri is cleverer than she seems: she is the only girl in the barracks who has been to school; most of the villages don't have a schoolhouse. The real school, villagers say, is the pasture and the mountainside. A schoolmaster cannot teach a boy what plants to keep his goats and sheep away from, or what mountain weeds make a goat's milk richer. Schoolhouses ruin boys and make girls useless in the house. Maria knows that if it had not been for Black Melpo, she herself would not have learned to read.

There is a broad mound rising some fifty feet above the water with clusters of amaranth growing on its slopes, and covered on top with soapwort bushes. Maria sees two wolves some distance across the meadow, thin animals with reddish fur creeping through the grass. They have spotted the girls and are moving away toward the forest. Maria takes Karteri by the hand and they clamber up to the top of the mound. A flock of shrieking birds flies up from the trees by the river, and Maria, startled, wheels around.

"I'm scared," Karteri whispers.

"There's nobody here—just us."

"We shouldn't have come this far," Karteri says.

"We'll get some soapwort and go back down right away."

An eerie silence has descended over the meadows. Maria sees a circle of hawks flying high up above the mound. There are six of them, perhaps seven. They could come shooting down from the sky to attack, but they would only do so if their nests were in danger, and hawks would not be nesting here, among lion's claws and amaranth bushes. Looking down to the water flowing past the mound, Maria is startled to see two men kneeling on the riverbank, facing each other. She steps back and grabs Karteri by the wrist. The kneeling men are right at the bottom of the mound, only a hundred feet away. She crouches down and pulls Karteri with her. "Quiet," she whispers, "quiet, they're close enough to hear us." The two men are just kneeling there, face to face, shivering, as if they are waiting to be beheaded. They are wearing shirts, but no trousers, and Maria can see their bare thighs. They can't be mountain villagers, she thinks, for why would they have come here without their trousers; they must be from the barracks, boys who have come for a swim, but she can't see their faces. One of them moves, and she recognizes Homeros. The boy opposite him leans forward and their mouths press together, but Homeros pushes him away, his hand resting on the boy's shoulder to keep him from leaning forward again. Karteri turns to whisper something into Maria's ear, but Maria quickly puts her finger to her lips, and the girls begin crawling backward. Maria sees Homeros sway as he kneels, his hand rapidly tugging beneath his shirt as if he is punching himself. Maria and Karteri run down the slope to the riverbank on the other side, back past the mud flats to where the stones begin.

"We weren't supposed to see that," Maria says, panting as she runs.

"He kissed him!" Karteri says, pointing back toward the mound, stopping to catch her breath. "I've seen a naked boy before," she quickly adds, as if she is apologizing for something.

"We mustn't tell anyone, not even Lita," Maria says, and Karteri nods. "We tell nobody."

In Maria's village, one of her brother Kimon's friends had been caught kneeling before him in the meadow. Nobody had mocked Kimon, for what man would not allow another to kneel before him, but the boys and men of the village cat-called after Kimon's friend wherever he went, "Be my whore, suck me too!" They knocked off his cap and spat into it, telling him he should wear his sister's kerchief instead. His name was Oresti, Maria remembers, he was fourteen, a year younger than she is now. One day the village boys caught Oresti on the path that led to the abandoned mosque behind her house, pushed him to the ground, and lay on his face, their trousers unbuckled, their hips pitching and shoving. Returning home bruised, his clothes torn, Oresti had found his father's door bolted; not even his mother would open up. Black Melpo hid him in her house and then gave him the money to go to Baku, where it was said he found work in the oil pits. There'll be more work than he can handle in those pits, villagers joked, kissing oil diggers beneath the belt. It had all been her brother's fault, for her brother had told all the men that Oresti was good at crotch-kissing, as good as a whore from Batum.

"My mother says that boys do things that are strange when it is time for them to get married," Karteri says.

"I think your mother is right."

Karteri is about to say something, when Lita and little Dimitri come hurrying down the bank with a sack of fresh ashes.

"Come take a look! Quick!" Lita shouts, and little Dimitri joins in, "Quick, quick! You won't believe this!" The birds in the pines start singing again, and Maria and Karteri can't hear the rest of what Lita is shouting to them. Lita must have seen Homeros and the other boy, Maria thinks in horror. Maria sees Karteri glance at her and wave her hand before her face, a sign Maria doesn't understand.

"Come quickly!" Lita shouts. "You won't believe it. You'll never guess!" She drops the sack of ashes she has brought and scrambles up the steep path to the cluster of pines. Beyond the rim of the ravine there is a procession of local Greek villagers who live a day's ride upriver. The tired donkeys and mules are climbing out of the canyon by the barracks, with the men in the saddles and the women trudging in front in their dusty finery, tugging at the beasts and coaxing them up the steep slope. The animals are wearing mud-spattered garlands of field flowers plaited around cloves of garlic to ward off the evil eye, and polished glass splinters and thorns to prick the grasping fingers of demons. The ribbons and tinkling bells around their necks ward off the impish spirits of the air, Satan's evil handmaidens. Children in embroidered feast-day jackets with muddy hands and dirty faces are running up the hill, flapping their arms and shouting to one another. The arriving villagers wave and call out greetings, and the girls wave back, not sure what to make of the gaudy procession. In this desolate border region they haven't seen anyone except for the other refugees for weeks. The men look like village Turks, their reddish caps wound with gray, muddy cloth, but they are wearing silver necklaces with Christian crosses, and the words they are shouting to each other somehow sound Greek. The women's kerchiefs cover their faces almost entirely, leaving only a slit for the eyes.

Maria sees her mother and Elpida come out of the barrack, followed by a group of women chattering excitedly, and wonders where the men are. She looks beyond the barracks, but cannot see anyone on guard duty. If these people were marauders, she thinks, everyone in the barracks would have been killed already, the sacks and bundles with their last possessions dragged away. But Elpida's and Heraclea's kerchiefs are tied back; they are matrons who have nothing to fear from these strangers. They make their way over to the arriving villagers, and Elpida, raising her hand welcomingly, or perhaps menacingly, brings the procession to a halt. Maria can see her mother standing firmly but nervously next to Elpida: they almost look like old friends, perhaps sisters-in-law who have come out of their houses after a morning of cooking, milking, and weaving. The old man on the first mule jumps down from the saddle, walks up to Elpida, and says something. Elpida seems uncertain for a moment, looks at Heraclea, and then answers. It is clear that the man cannot understand her, and she cannot understand him. When Heraclea speaks he smiles with what seems like relief. From a woolen bag slung over his shoulder he fishes out some large oranges. Elpida and Heraclea quickly take them, their heads bobbing as they mumble their thanks. The mountain villagers bring out more oranges and give them to the women crowding around their procession. Elpida bows and attempts a friendly smile, tucking another orange into her apron, and then another.

11

MARIA, KARTERI, AND LITA TIE their kerchiefs across their faces and make their way with little Dimitri in tow over to the caravan of villagers. The last of the donkeys and mules are now laboring up the ridge, snorting and braying as the village women tug at their bridles. The girls hold out their open hands to one of the limping dust-covered women, who stops and quickly points to the man sitting on the mule behind her, calmly smoking. He is unaware that beneath their drab kerchiefs the girls are young and pretty and so does not pay them any attention, only opens his sack and throws some oranges at them. The oranges roll down the path, and the girls scramble after them. The man laughs, and calls out, "*La-dzu*—come here," beckoning and nodding. Maria hurries over, and he hands her another orange.

"So you'll eat that orange, or just stand there?" he says in his strange tongue, eyeing the wet seams of her smock and her bare feet, still red from the cold river water.

"You've been standing in the river?"

Maria looks at him.

"Are you from over there, over the mountain?" he says, pointing toward the Caucasus.

Maria looks at the mountain and nods.

"Are you a girl?"

Maria understands the word for girl and takes a few steps back, surprised by his question. Who would mistake her for a boy, dressed and kerchiefed as she is? But then, as he tugs his reins lightly and the mule walks toward her, she realizes he is asking whether she is a young girl or an older matron. "You've got girl feet, not woman feet," he says. "You're a girl, you're fourteen, are you? Sixteen? Call me a Mohammedan if you're seventeen, twice a Mohammedan if you're eighteen!" He raises his index finger and wiggles it. "I can tell your hand doesn't touch what married women must touch." He takes his foot out of the stirrup and, grabbing hold of the mule's wither, leans forward in order to swing his leg over the animal's rump as if to dismount. Maria steps back, her kerchief slipping, and the man, seeing her eyes and lips, winks at her. "Ah, for you I'd sin, I would, as God is my witness!" he calls out, tugging the bulge at the front of his trousers. He then says something about a heart and a flying dove— but the woman who is walking in front of his mule looks at Maria angrily, lowers her kerchief and spits, and Maria runs down the path to catch up with Lita and Karteri. "*Fos da matia'ss!*" the man shouts after her. "Light unto your eyes!"

•

"So here you are!" Lita's mother calls out, hurrying toward the girls, carrying her wailing baby. "They're handing out oranges, and you're playing around in the dirt?"

Lita's eyes narrow. "Yes, I'm playing around in the dirt, but I've already got two oranges." She holds them up for her mother to see.

"Look after your brothers," Lita's mother says. "I'm going to the chapel with the others to get the blessing, and a blessing I need with a daughter like you."

Lita gives her mother one of the oranges. She takes it and hands her the baby.

Behind the chapel, the men from the barracks and the newly arrived men from the villages are sitting around a fire, roasting coffee beans on a broad tin platter. The hot beans crackle on the scalding tin, and Kostis flicks the roasted ones from the pan into a stone bowl, where, with a round stone, he hammers them into a fine powder. Father Andreas and the deacon are too sick to leave their shack and greet the visitors who have come, as they do every year, to celebrate Saint Georgios's Day at the saint's abandoned chapel. The men are chatting in rudimentary Tatar and snippets of village Greek, and though they smile and pat each other on the back, it is unclear how much either side understands the other. The tongue the villagers speak is primitive and wild, a mixture of half-forgotten Ancient Greek, Tatar, and local Turkish. Their speech neuters everything it touches, turning the Virgin Mary, Jesus, and even God Himself into an "it"—a mere object—the greatest of blasphemies.

"We must leave here—*munda, munda!*" Kostis says to the villagers, loudly repeating the Tatar word for *here*, and then saying it slowly in Turkmen, in case they perhaps know that word.

The villagers nod eagerly, and Kostis looks at them anxiously.

"Should we go upriver? Downriver? Where? *Kaida, kaida?*" Kostis asks.

The village elder, a lean and agile man with white ringlets spilling from beneath his cap and turban, replies with a fast stream of ancient words, of which Kostis and the other men of the barracks understand only "town," "Black Sea," "is," and "Russians." Speaking to these villagers is like drilling a hole in water; their language has also abandoned all its tenses: it is a tongue with no past and no future, just a present. Are the Russians now in the town by the Black Sea? Are they attacking the town? Have they attacked? Would they attack? Will they attack? Kostis wonders how these people can communicate in such barren speech, in a language that is like a skeleton without flesh. These mountains were long ago the land of Colchis, where Jason came for Medea and the Golden Fleece. The fleece had probably been hidden somewhere nearby. Medea's palaces lined the great river that flows past the barracks, their halls and hanging gardens now lying in heaps of ancient rubble and debris. In those days the river was filled with so many gold flakes and nuggets that fleeces dipped into it came out golden. These villagers in their gaudy costumes, with their garlanded beasts, are Medea's wild descendants.

"The end!" the village elder says, when he sees that the men of the barracks are puzzled at his words. "The end, the end!" He points all around, smiling with encouragement, and the mountain villagers laugh and slap their thighs in applause.

Father Andreas emerges from the shack, pale and gaunt, his black, ankle-length cassock fluttering against his thighs. He has tried to wake the deacon, who since the night of plum wine and mad honey seems to have sunk into a poisonous sleep and is lying stretched out stiffly on his cot. The priest suddenly remembers the Turk's letter and the financial offer that could save him and all the desperate people in the barracks. He looks with dismay at the haggard women waiting for him by the entrance to the chapel. One of the two goats the visiting villagers have brought is dragged to a post by the entrance, facing the mosaic of Saint George and the Dragon inside. Turkish herdsmen have gouged out the saint's eyes: not out of Muslim malice, as the priest has assured the refugees, but in terror of the saint's austere gaze. The head of the dragon, inlaid with green and gilded stones, lies meekly at the saint's bare feet, its large and docile, cowlike eyes left intact. The young nun who has been freed from the dragon's jaws by Saint George is kneeling in prayer before him, dressed in the flowing robes of a Byzantine princess. Purling water made of blue and turquoise stones cascades past the subjugated monster. Next to the mosaic is an empty niche as wide as a door and rising all the way from the floor to the ceiling; the wall inside the niche is a yellowish gray, and there is a mangled iron grate in front of it. For centuries the niche housed the dragon's shoulder blade, three times the height of a man, which had been dug up from the slope leading down to the river. But some twenty years ago, during one of the border wars, a Russian major pried the iron bars apart, a terrible sacrilege, and took the holy bone across the river as a war trophy.

Father Andreas walks over to where the goat is now tethered, holding a knife behind his back, and slits the animal's throat. The women crowd around to watch the spilling blood spread out in crimson shapes.

"*Kundar!*" Elpida says, seeing the shape of the saint's spear forming in the blood on the rough ground. She looks up, sees the village women's blank faces, and whips her hand through the air above her head as if she were casting a javelin.

"*Pudari!*" Heraclea shouts, seeing a leg, catching Elpida off guard. Elpida looks at Heraclea and slowly nods.

Father Andreas eyes the blood, feeling a wave of nausea as the remnants of the evil honey trickle through his veins. The mountain men who sold him the delicious poison must have mixed it with mushrooms, for his visions have been perilously exhilarating. He thinks of the deacon still lying in his deathlike sleep in the shack.

He can hear the rhythmic banging of the sharp stone on coffee beans coming from behind the chapel, for the men have little interest in these rituals. Then comes the aroma of boiling coffee, and the priest thinks how just a few sips will set him right. He hears Kostis's voice saying something about hot coffee and fire, something indecent that Father Andreas can't quite catch. The men laugh, and someone says that coffee and women are best when they're boiling hot.

The goat's blood is spreading into further patterns.

"You are right," Elpida says to Heraclea. "There's a spear, and there's a horse's hind leg. We shall all go far."

"Yes, good signs, very good signs," Heraclea says, surprised that Elpida is agreeing with her. Heraclea sees Elpida cross herself and bow before the image of the saint, and she and the other women begin crossing themselves and bowing too.

They put tin bowls filled with water beneath the mosaic in honor of the horse that stood by its master. Father Andreas dips his finger in the goat's blood and with it marks the children's foreheads and cheeks with the sign of the Cross. The goat's carcass is carried around the chapel three times before it is skinned, its meat cut into chunks and boiled in the cauldron of gruel.

12

THE FOLLOWING DAY THE DEACON dies without having
regained consciousness. A week of heavy rain follows his death, and
a cold wind sweeps away the insects plaguing the barracks. There
is water everywhere; the riverbank is too muddy for the men to go
fishing. Some of the refugees disappeared the night after the Saint
George's Day feast, and the rumor in the barracks is that they must
have followed the trail of the mountain villagers upriver. But Father
Andreas knows that the mountain villagers will not have welcomed
them in their walled settlements, for though they are good people
who follow ancient traditions of hospitality, they bolt their doors
to strangers who come intending to stay. He thinks they must have
then headed downriver to the port, a foolhardy enterprise without
papers or travel permits, with checkpoints at every pass.

That evening, alone in his shack and imprisoned by the heavy
rain, the priest thinks back on his relationship with the dead man.
The deacon, working at his side for almost a decade, was a valuable helper; but now that Father Andreas has time to think, he realizes that he never particularly liked him. It is an uncharitable and
unsettling thought, but nevertheless a true one. The deacon was an

old-fashioned Ottoman Greek—browbeaten but defiant—not a new Ottoman man of the world, like the big-city Greeks. In a single generation there had been a great change in Greek ways, but though the deacon had been raised in elegant Smyrna, a city of trams, cafés, and theaters, all that change had somehow passed him by. The priest realizes with surprise that he knows very little about the man with whom he spent so many years. His Christian name was Haralambos, "shining with joy"—which the deacon had certainly never been—and his family name was Spatharios, "sword-bearing knight." He was a simple man, but a zealot, peculiar in his ways and with a harsh dogmatic streak. He was one of those vocal Christians, not literate enough to read the Bible since most Greeks no longer understood its ancient language. Men like the deacon know only the phrases from the Bible that they hear in church, words that can be dangerous in the ear of a zealot, and believe them with unques-tioning fervor: phrases like *There are eunuchs who have made them-selves eunuchs for the sake of the Kingdom of Heaven.* Father Andreas smiles bitterly and shakes his head, as if there were an onlooker in the desolate shack who could appreciate how destructive this bib-lical pronouncement has been. So many saints and martyrs have reached for knives to cut away the flesh that kept leading them to sin. There are peasant monks and nuns across the river who have villagers neuter and spay them as if they were livestock and then live together in cold, barn-like monasteries in utter virtue. What is the point? How is one to renounce the temptations of the flesh if there is no flesh that tempts? How can one abstain, if there is noth-ing to abstain from? The deacon never married and never showed any interest in doing so; but celibacy, which wasn't even necessary for a deacon, was an unrelenting torment for him. The more he tried to fight his urges, the more they consumed him. In his zeal he was certain that the Bible's words were giving him guidance in his battle against himself. When he first became a deacon fifteen years ago in Trebizond, he pressed a knife against his member in the latrines behind the dormitories, but at the first sting of pain and the first drops of blood, he ran weeping through the cloister to the infirmary. Father Porfirios administered laudanum, bathed the deacon's member in spirits and, taking pity on him, gave him a formal dispensation, once a week, to rub his member with as much vigor as was necessary to achieve relief. Only once a week, Father Porfirios said; the Lord will look the other way.

The wind is blowing down the mountainside, whistling through the rain into the chinks in the walls. Streams of cold air come through the windows, and the flame before the icon of Saint Xenophon and his wife and sons flickers as the wick tilts in the oil of the glass cup. Saint Xenophon is staring at Father Andreas with yellowing eyes; he is an old man with furrowed cheeks and a white beard, but his wife, Saint Maria, is young and beautiful; she seems to be smiling, her lips moving in the flickering light, her robes those of a Byzantine queen. Father Andreas throws some brushwood into the fireplace and lights a fire. The logs sputter, the flames brighten the room, and he begins to feel better. There would be no fire over in the barracks, but they have the wool blankets the bishop has sent, in which they can wrap themselves.

The deacon's family will have to be told of his death, Father Andreas suddenly thinks, and wonders how they are to be found. There must be an address or a name in the old ledgers of the bishopric. The deacon's three silver amulets will have to be sent to them. He dips his spoon in the honeypot and licks a small dab, promising himself that this is all he will taste of the deadly nectar for the evening, just enough to brighten his mood. He is pleased that the Bishop of Trebizond has sent more newspapers with the supplies: without them his imprisonment in the shack during the days of rain would be unbearable. Before they were sent, the newspapers had been read by the whole bishopric, making their way down the hierarchy from the bishop to the toothless janitor, who, despite his lowly position, is a well-known local poet who writes sullen, carefully metered verse in archaic Greek. It is the janitor who has meticulously refolded the newspapers—a large stack by the end of the week—and packed them into the saddlebags. In all the years Father Andreas and the deacon have traveled throughout the province, ministering to small Greek communities in the mountains, supplies and newspapers have always been sent to them.

Father Andreas is a man who likes puzzles. Mechanical puzzles, mathematical puzzles, puzzle boxes with hidden locks that seem impossible to open. The Ottoman press sparks the same excitement in him, for on every page there are vital clues to hidden meanings, even in the smallest notices. In the newspaper on the top of the pile, he reads that the British consul in Trebizond, Sir John Longworth, has taken the Tuesday steamer to Batum. That is all the notice says, and it is followed by another that says that the British representative in the town of Samsun—Mr. Papadopoulos—has taken the same steamer to Batum, as has the American consular representative, Mr. Stephanopoulos. The notices are in the form of society items, and between them is an announcement that Dr. Halsian, obviously an Armenian, has married the delightful Miss Ik... —he can't read the name, as someone, probably the janitor, has smudged the ink with his dampened finger. Why, Father Andreas wonders, are all the consuls leaving for Batum in the Russian Caucasus, outside Ottoman territory? A longer piece, also in the form of a society item, claims that the Empire's former Grand

Vizir, Kiamil Pasha, and the current Minister of Public Works, Gabriel Noradunghian—another Armenian—have met with the Austrian ambassador for a series of interviews. "Interviews?" the priest mumbles. "A series of them? What can that mean?" There is a picture of the three men, all wearing fezzes, and Father Andreas wonders which of them might be the Austrian. In the *Osmanli* newspaper, he reads that the General Director of the Imperial Ottoman Bank has returned from Paris, but that the Orient Express had had to stop outside Constantinople because military trains have commandeered the tracks. It is left to the reader to imagine whether the director managed to enter the capital or whether he had to take temporary lodgings in one of the outlying villages.

The priest puts down the newspaper and looks at it. It is trying to tell him something, but his mind, dulled by the honey and the constant drumming of the rain, is not alert enough to understand. Is the newspaper saying that the Empire is now undeniably under siege, and that the foreign consuls and representatives are fleeing the larger towns to the safety of Russian territory? Has Russia finally invaded the Empire, snatching up the great Ottoman cities that stretch like a priceless pearl necklace along the Black Sea coast all the way to Constantinople? Is the port town now in Russian hands? "Pearls!" Father Andreas remembers and turns the page, looking for more news about Madame Claudius Bey, who, as he remembers reading a few days ago in an older newspaper, had been murdered at sea for her necklace. A second-class passenger had been arrested, "a turbaned man 35 to 40 years of age," he reads with interest, "whose countenance was by no means reassuring." The murderer, the newspaper says, had been seen outside her cabin during the night of the crime, "evidently in a state of wild excitement." He quickly opens a more recent newspaper. The wild turban-wearer, the later newspaper says, has been released, and an Algerian merchant, a fellow first-class passenger, arrested. This murderer had moved in the best circles, as had Madame Claudius Bey, whom he might have known socially. "Known? Socially?" Father Andreas thinks. The newspaper explains that the murderer probably needed the pearl necklace to pay off his gaming debts, and that he was a fine figure of a man in a well-tailored suit. On the following page Father Andreas reads the headline: "I AM THE NEW COMMANDER OF THE BELIEVERS!" The brash headline is in bold type, snatching at the eye of the reader. The Sharif of Mecca, the article says, is proclaiming an Arabian Caliphate in defiance of the Sultan, who is the one and true Caliph of Islam; but for how long, Father Andreas wonders. His eyes narrow. What if the Sultan is toppled? What if he has already been toppled? The Sharif of Mecca would only dare to proclaim himself the new Caliph if the Sultan has fallen. The headline cannot be missed, but the proclamation, a great blasphemy, is not on the front page where it most certainly would have been if this rogue Caliphate in a rioting Ottoman province was to be taken seriously. Father Andreas rereads the article and surmises that it is unclear whether the Sharif of Mecca has actually made the proclamation or is only thought to be preparing to do so.

There is a slow and careful creaking sound. Father Andreas starts and catches his breath. The sound is from the door on the other side of the shack, where the animals are kept. Someone is opening it slowly, stopping every time the hinges rasp. The hens cackle, and there is a sound like a spray of gravel being thrown at a tin. He hastily blows out the lamp on the table before him, but realizes that the burning brushwood and logs in the fireplace are casting flickering shadows through the room. His own shadow wavers and spreads monstrous and deformed over the wall as he crouches to move out of the light. If only he had a rifle, he thinks; even a priest needs a rifle here in the wilderness. He should have told the men in the barracks to give him one of their rifles. He cautiously walks over to the wall that separates his side of the shack from the animal pen, his shadow following him.

"Who is it?" he calls out in alarm. "Who is it?" He feels a stab of fear in his stomach.

"Hello!" comes from the other side of the partition.

"Yes?" Father Andreas says. "Yes?"

"Sorry if I woke you—I've come to feed the animals."

"Who are you?"

"It's me, Homeros."

"No, you didn't wake me, it's too early to be sleeping," Father Andreas calls out in relief. "You didn't need to come all the way here in the dark and the rain."

"I'll be over in a minute," Homeros replies, and the priest again hears the sound of thrown grain and the excited chattering of the hens. Lightning flashes and the rain begins to beat down harder on the shack. The door opens and Homeros comes in, muttering greetings, putting his wet lantern on the floor and shaking the rain from his hands.

"You look like you fell in the river!" Father Andreas says. "I'm surprised your lantern didn't go out."

"We were worried back at the barracks because we haven't seen you since . . . since . . ." Homeros can't bring himself to mention the deacon's death, and he is too tired and wet to remember the ways one might speak of a dead man respectfully without mentioning him. "The women sent me to say they'll come and cook tomorrow, even if it's raining."

"But it's foolish for you to come out like this in the rain and darkness, very foolish," the priest says. "What would you have done if your lantern had gone out? You would have been in the wilderness with ravines before and behind you!" He goes to the fireplace and pulls a burning stick out of the pile to relight the lamp on his table.

"I started out earlier but the gully was flooded, so I followed the mountain path to the other side—but then I couldn't find the way up here."

"You're soaked!"

"I'll dry my things in front of the fire if you have a warm blanket for me. I can wrap myself in that."

"Those blankets are good and warm," Father Andreas says, pointing to the deacon's cot.

Homeros stares at them.

"Don't worry, they're not the blankets of the departed, may God embrace his soul. The blankets are mine."

13

THE BUYER OF GÍRLS IS to arrive at the chapel in ten days to run his eye over any marriageable maidens among the refugees. *Marriageable,* Father Andreas knows, means beautiful, or exceptionally beautiful, and *maidens* means fourteen, fifteen, maybe sixteen. Older girls, even if pretty and unspoiled, are not considered malleable enough to begin a new life without traces of the old. He knows that Maria will certainly be chosen, and perhaps her friend Lita too; if only Lita were not sun-browned like a boy. But it has been raining all week, so it is quite possible that by the time the buyer arrives Lita will be pale enough to be viewed.

Father Andreas looks at Homeros, who is still asleep on the cot across from him, huddling under the blanket, his clothes now dry in front of the fireplace. Last night's fire is a heap of cold ashes. Father Andreas has spent the night on the deacon's cot, aware that Homeros, a young and simple villager, would be terrified of the dead man's spirit. The priest now lies half asleep on the deacon's deathbed, weighing his next moves with drowsy clarity. It is just before dawn, still too early to be awake. The rain has stopped, and soon some of the women will arrive to cook the gruel in the large cauldron outside.

If the girls are purchased, he thinks, there will be enough money to secure a passage for all the refugees out of these borderlands, with their miasma and disease, and there will be a significant amount of money for the families of the purchased girls; more money than they could earn in a lifetime of herding sheep in the Caucasus. He has sent a letter to the port town inviting the buyer to come, accepting his proposal with elegant words. All that now remains is for him to inform the refugees—but he isn't yet sure how; finding the right words is vital. A thing can be presented this way or that; the sale can be a godsent salvation—or a fire-and-brimstone calamity. What is a blossoming orchid: is it a beautiful flower that can grace an imperial garden, or a festering parasite sucking life from all the trees around it?

Will you sell your daughter to a Turk? Such a question would spark outrage among the Greek refugees. Men and women would storm the chapel with stones and cudgels, shouting accusations of unchristian evil and Mohammedan devilry. They would lynch him, tear his cassock, and drag his body to the river.

Will you sell your daughter to a Turk?

That is not the right question. The reality—a cold reality—is that a man representing a certain gentleman in far-off Constantinople is going to bring salvation. Though money will be proffered, it is not a question of buying or selling girls. In the Greek settlements of the Caucasian mountains, and in every Greek village by the Black Sea and the Mediterranean, a girl has to have a dowry if she is to be married off into another family, into a life of drudgery. She is then the property of her husband, the slave of her mother-in-law, and the servant of his jealous sisters and sisters-in-law. Hers is then a life of hard labor through all the day and into the late hours, when the sheep are sent out for night-grazing. Her husband mounts her, like beasts mount beasts, and she bears child after child. She eats whatever scraps she can find in the kitchen, for though she serves at table, it will be years before she is permitted to sit and eat with the others. Her family has given the bridegroom's family as much money and land as it could afford, and often more. Does that mean they have purchased the bridegroom? the priest thinks, and grins sourly. If the bride survives the many childbirths and constant toil, she will one day, when her own sons are grown, turn into the hard and unforgiving matron of the family, feared and served by her sons' frightened wives.

But in the Turkish lands, the wealthiest Turks—from governors to royal princes to the Sultan himself—insist on acquiring the poorest brides, brides from other lands and other religions, young girls who speak no Turkish and know nothing of Ottoman ways. "The master of the house is begotten," the old Turkish proverb says, "the mistress of the house is bought." A Turk of standing does not want a woman with pedigree in his harem who might raise her head to him in defiance, or call upon her influential father or brothers whenever she does not get her way. What difficulty the Sultan himself has had in finding husbands for his many royal daughters and nieces, despite the excellent connections that a marriage to an imperial lady brings with it! Only a man rising through the ranks, a young man of great ambition, would want to compromise his freedom within his own household in exchange for such rank and power in his public life. In the Greek high society of Athens, Odessa, and Alexandria, sons of grandees marry heiresses who speak French and are brought up to entertain at banquets and feasts. But foreign brides brought into the Ottoman Empire by Turkish gentlemen are expected to know nothing, nothing at all. Only once they are being groomed for the status of concubine or wife will they then study deportment, poetry, and elegant Turkish. This prepares them to entertain their master in the seclusion of his harem.

Homeros turns in his sleep, and Father Andreas wonders what kind of husband he will one day be. Probably like any of the other Caucasus Greek villagers, he thinks, riding his donkey to the field while his wife trudges behind him carrying hoes and shovels.

His mind returning to the purchase, Father Andreas thinks how different the Ottoman world is from that of the Greeks beyond the borders of the Empire. As an Ottoman Greek himself, whose family has lived for many centuries as subjects of the Sultan, he finds the antiquated ways of these people from the Caucasus strange, even unfamiliar. For the refugees this is a new land where right is left and left is right. They don't know that the poorest girl in a borrowed cotton shift stands a far better chance than any high-born princess of marrying the wealthiest men of the Empire, even His Majesty the Grand Sultan himself, the descendant of Oghuz, grandson of Noah. He thinks of the great Sultan, who is now, the newspapers say, trapped in his own palace, with Constantinople under fire, his nephews, perhaps even his sons, leading the rebels outside. A terrible fate, when your own flesh and blood turns on you. Supplies will have been cut off. All His Majesty has left is his harem, now probably full of frightened, starving women. There have been Circassian, Greek, and Russian royal wives; and all the wives of the current beleaguered monarch were brought from the Caucasus; purchased, in fact, Father Andreas thinks. No wealthy girls, no well-bred girls, no girls with connections: that is not the Ottoman way. He shakes his head as if to dispel his tangled thoughts and gets up.

It is after dawn already, and outside in the yard he sees Heraclea and a very old woman he hasn't noticed before busying themselves about the cauldron in which the daily gruel is boiled; the old woman, he thinks, must be one of the more recent refugees. Heraclea lifts a large sack onto her shoulder and begins emptying it into the brew. She must have dragged the sack out of the storeroom next to the animal pen, he thinks, surprised that he didn't hear her. Heraclea is a mannish woman, her roughness the result of relentless hard work; she has worked from morning till night all her life, and can carry a mule's load on her back. The older woman pours water into the cauldron from a bucket, peers carefully over the rim, and then pours in more. Her movements are quick and lively. She is one of those grandmothers with a very old face but the thin, light body and movements of a girl.

Seeing the two figures hovering by the cauldron, Father Andreas suddenly realizes how he can tell the refugees about the impending sale without triggering outrage in the barracks. He is suddenly wide awake. He will take one of the women into his confidence: Heraclea, the mother of the girl whose remarkable beauty means that she will certainly be bought. Once he has won the mother over, she will do the rest. She will know how to tell the others. He will say to Heraclea that he has found the perfect bridegroom for her daughter—which indeed he has—a man wealthier than she can imagine, a man seeking a virtuous, unspoiled girl, a girl like Maria. The bridegroom, the wealthy gentleman from the capital, will not ask for a dowry, and is in fact even prepared to give the family enough money to buy a large house in Athens, where they will be safe, and there will also be money to buy land, and still more for her sons. Heraclea will gasp and clap her hands. He will call the rich Turk "the bridegroom," "the gentleman," "the man of influence," "the wealthy man"—and only then, when her mind is aglow with images of a future life in Athens, her sons at her side, will he refer to the bridegroom as "the Ottoman gentleman," perhaps even "the Turkish grandee." *Grandee* is a word that will eclipse the problematic word before it; a word is like raw leather—you can mold it into any form you want. *Grandee* means riches, and the greater the riches, the blinder the eyes of the beholder. Heraclea will not ask the obvious questions: "But my daughter is Christian, how can she marry a Turk? Will he not want her to become a Turk too and turn her back on our God and our Mother of God?" By then it won't matter. Heraclea will understand the problem, but her nimble mind will already be seeking the words with which she will win over her husband, how she will tell him of their godsent luck. The good man, the good bridegroom, Father Andreas will tell her, wants to help the others here too. The matchmaker he is sending to bring him his bride will find brides for his friends too, all wealthy and wonderful men. They will help us all. They will provide everyone passage to Trebizond and Athens.

He approaches the two women, who bow and greet him, stepping away from the cauldron as if finding it unseemly for him to catch them at work. They try to take his hand and kiss it, but he waves and makes three quick crosses in their direction as a morning blessing.

"Once the gruel is boiling, I'll see to the animals," Heraclea says, still bowing, rubbing her hands down the side of her dress as if to dry them. She is remarkably ugly, he thinks, a large-boned woman who manages nevertheless to look shrunken in her dress—the sparse bowls of watery gruel and boiled weeds have clearly withered away her curves. He notices dainty patterns embroidered along the seams and hems of the dress, beautiful and delicate threads spattered with mud. As she prepared to flee her burning village, she, like so many of the other women, threw on her best dress, scooping up her good shawl and kerchief as she ran, fleeing in her Sunday finery, now tattered and worn, the bright colors faded.

"Don't worry about the animals," Father Andreas replies. "Homeros is here. The boy can do it."

"The men are all fishing; he might want to go too," Heraclea says apologetically, hesitating to contradict the priest.

"That's true," the little old woman eagerly chimes in. "The beasts will need to be rubbed down, and I can also let them out to graze." She squints up at the sky, and then looks at the priest with a smile. "It doesn't look like rain."

The door of the shack opens and Homeros comes out sleepily, still draped in his blanket. Seeing the women, he waves to them awkwardly, and Heraclea calls over to him that he can either look after Father Andreas's animals or go fishing with the men, but then raises her hand to her mouth and bows uncertainly in the direction of Father Andreas, realizing that she has spoken out of turn, that it is for the priest to tell the boy what to do. But Father Andreas seems preoccupied and has not noticed her forwardness.

"I'll see to the animals right away," Homeros calls back. "I'll see to them now. The fish can wait," he says. "They can wait."

Heraclea smiles at the priest. "He's a good boy," she says.

"I want to talk to you about something very important," the priest says to her. "When you are finished here, find me in the chapel."

14

HERACLEA KISSES FATHER ANDREAS'S HAND. They are standing in the chapel in front of the mosaic of Saint George and the Dragon. She is weeping with joy, and the priest is watching her with relief. He has lit candles, and the green and gilded stones of the monster's head in the mosaic glisten in the dim light, its cow-like eyes watching him. Heraclea's sturdy body heaves, and he wonders if Maria will one day become a rough, strong-armed woman like her. He wonders why a handsome man like Kostis would have married such a plain, even ugly, woman, and thinks she must have had cunning matchmakers and a very good dowry.

Heraclea tries to speak but can't.

"You understand, I'm not saying that we *have* found a wealthy bridegroom for your daughter," the priest repeats, concerned that he and she both might be setting their hopes too high. "The matchmaker will arrive next week, and then we'll know for sure."

"Thank you, Father, thank you," Heraclea whispers, reaching to kiss his hand again. She bows over it and raises it to her forehead. He feels his hand grow unpleasantly wet with her tears.

"I'm almost certain the matchmaker will be pleased with Maria," he says, despite himself.

"Thank you, Father, thank you!" Heraclea says again, trying to bow and curtsy at the same time.

"Maria is a good girl, from a good home," he continues. "What bridegroom wouldn't want a girl like her to be the mother of his sons?"

Heraclea shakes her head vehemently, and Father Andreas hesitates, then realizes she is merely indicating that she cannot imagine any man not wanting Maria to bear him sons.

"The bridegroom," he says, "is quite concerned about your predicament here, and will provide for all your needs."

She nods energetically, then, suddenly mortified at weeping so openly before the priest, turns away and stares at the young nun in the mosaic whom Saint George has freed from the dragon's jaws.

Heraclea is a woman on the brink of desperation, Father Andreas thinks, a drowning woman being offered a branch just as she sinks beneath the water. She has lost everything she has spent all her life toiling for, and though a wooden door has fallen shut on a past filled with hardship, a golden one is now about to open. He looks at her rough, scarred hands, and then at the blue and turquoise stones in the mosaic—the cascading waters heralding the demise of the dragon—and realizes that her future seems more certain than his. If he and the refugees managed to leave these godforsaken mountains, what would they find in the flatlands by the sea? How long would the nearby port town last, how long Constantinople, how long Trebizond where he was born? Where would he go if Trebizond were ransacked by new conquerors? Though his blood is Greek, he is an Ottoman. Would he leave the great Empire and go to Greece, a small, poor, struggling land? He feels dark thoughts descending upon him. He would stay in Trebizond, he thinks, come what may, for the stones of one's native town are warmer than all the hot springs of Babylon.

"All will turn out well," he says to Heraclea. "We must have faith in God."

She nods again eagerly and crosses herself three times.

"The kindhearted grandee, the Ottoman gentleman from the capital," he continues, briefly pausing for effect, "will secure a wonderful future for your family and your sons, if his choice falls on Maria."

Still sobbing, Heraclea continues expressing her thanks, and Father Andreas sees clearly and with relief that she has understood that "grandee" means that the man will be rich enough to buy a whole Caucasian village and more, and that "Ottoman gentleman from the capital" means that the man is a Muslim and a Turk. As she continues in a calmer voice with her Caucasian Greek words of gratitude, Father Andreas understands that she will do what is needed. She will see to it that her husband is pleased with his daughter's impending marriage, and she will tell the other women that the priest will be bringing a wealthy matchmaker to the barracks for some of the girls, a great matchmaker who, if the girls please him, will help everyone leave these plague-ridden mountains.

•

Hurrying back to the barracks, Heraclea thinks how lucky and how unlucky she has been in the children she has borne and not borne. In the first two years of her marriage she had two boys. Fate smiled upon her. Philolaos, the village cooper, now some ten years dead, had had two sets of twins, all girls, and then another two girls. A house with sons is a fertile field, a house with daughters a cemetery. His family was utterly ruined. He had to give away all his land

and possessions for just two dowries, leaving all his other daughters to be destitute spinsters. Aphrodite the Witch had examined Heraclea's swelling belly and foretold each of the boys: her belly was pointed, and she had dreamed of tigers and knives. People said that the spirits of two blackbirds sat on Aphrodite's shoulders, one on each side, weighing her down but whispering knowledge into her ears. She consulted them in whatever she did, and she always did their bidding. Aphrodite the Witch had studied Heraclea's face, breasts, and nipples: women carrying boys flower out, women carrying girls become drawn and pale. With her first son in her belly Heraclea had blossomed, and with her second too, but with her third pregnancy her face withered, a terrible blow, as she had hoped that she was one of the bearers of boys, a queen in the village hierarchy. With feathers and eggplant stems, Aphrodite the Witch cleansed her of that pregnancy, and of the following two as well. All those babies would have been girls. When Heraclea, now a definite bearer of girls, became pregnant with Maria, she dreamed of needles and fruit, and her belly was round, undeniable signs that a girl was once more on the way. Aphrodite the Witch again plucked a turkey feather and crushed herbs and lemon in her mortar, but this time the cleansing was not to be. That very morning, Aphrodite, bending over the shallow stream where she was washing rags, fell in and drowned, though the water was only a few inches deep. She had fallen face forward, and lay with her head in the water, her hands angrily slapping the muddy bank again and again, until she gave up and lay still. Women came running. Why hadn't she just turned her head to the side? Why hadn't she just looked up out of the water? The witch was a strong woman of fifty: even a bedridden crone could not have drowned in such a trickle, they later said; the blackbird spirits must have weighed her down, held her head under. And yet, Heraclea now thinks, as she scrambles up the path on her way back to the barracks, if Aphrodite had turned her head to the side that day, there would have been no Maria, no future prosperity for her sons, for Kostis, and for herself. It was God who had drowned the witch before she reached for the feather and potions. God stood by my side, Heraclea thinks. After Maria's birth, the new village witch, Black Melpo, told Heraclea that she would henceforth bear only daughters. Black Melpo rubbed her with salt and lemon every week and gave her tiny clay fire cups to heat and place on her lower back, to repel the girls that kept entering her womb. She has borne no more children since then, and had been thankful until now, when, in a mesh of golden thoughts, she wonders what even greater heights of wealth she and Kostis might have reached if she had borne more daughters like Maria to sell to bridegrooms in the Ottoman capital. Fate has dealt her a sweet but very bitter card, she thinks.

15

THE FOLLOWING MORNING FATHER ANDREAS walks through the women's barrack, surveying the girls sitting silently on their dirty straw sacks beside their mothers in whatever finery they managed to salvage as they fled the Caucasus. The women have cleaned the barrack as best they could, but the putrid stench from the latrines is unbearable and he breathes through his mouth, the foul air coating his tongue. He wants to cover his face with the sleeve of his cassock, but knows that he can't do that in front of these women who have to live and sleep here. These barracks were not built to hold so many people, and for so long. The miasma of illness hangs in the air; it is only a matter of time before the deadly bacilli will spread. Where will he quarantine the sick, he wonders.

He looks at the girls. They are even thinner than they were when they arrived—some of the younger ones look like little boys in threadbare cotton dresses and kerchiefs. Who would want them as concubines or wives, or even servants? Girls can be fattened up quickly, but buyers prepared to pay significant sums expect quality, not potential. A prominent Ottoman physician in the capital has written a lead article, much like an official proclamation, explaining that twelve-year-old girls can, biologically and medically, be considered women, and consequently brides. Five years ago the physician's article would have passed unnoticed, but now a group of free-thinking Muslim women, veiled but unprepared to bow to men, have retaliated with articles of their own: "By Allah, what can a twelve-year-old girl understand about the essence of marriage? What can she know about running her part of a household? What is she to do if she gives birth?"

"By Allah, indeed," Father Andreas thinks as he walks through the barrack. The Empire is unraveling; the Sultan's censorship office is clearly losing its grip on the press; and the newspapers, running free, are publishing everything under the sun—everything, that is, except what is actually going on. But the Ottomans have ruled these lands for five hundred years, he thinks, and will surely rule them for another five hundred; they are some of the wealthiest men in the world, and they will see to it that their world remains intact.

He walks slowly back and forth past the women and girls. He considers quickly stepping outside, as if he had forgotten something, to breathe in some fresh air. But he doesn't.

He imagined that the women would crowd around him, asking questions about their marriageable daughters, entreating, shouting, perhaps even attacking him for proposing that they give their Christian girls to Turks; but his idea of relying on Heraclea to inform the others has worked. She has obviously presented matters to them in the best possible light. For the first time he sees a glimmer of hope in the women's eyes.

Elpida is sitting next to her plain daughter, who is wearing an old, richly embroidered dress that was clearly part of her mother's dowry. Over the girl's waist and hips is a wide apron sash that seems to be made of silk, and instead of a kerchief she is wearing a small beaded hat, round as a coffee saucer, of the kind rich women wear, in order, Father Andreas realizes, to display her thick yellow braids, her only asset. He remembers the girl's name: Karteri, "the stoic one." It is a fitting name for the girl, who seems to endure her overbearing mother in frightened silence. He knows she will not be bought, despite her yellow hair, and feels sorry for her; but plums do not grow on almond trees. She might be taken into a house as a servant, where she could work for a plate of food, but fate will offer her nothing more, probably not even that, as she does not seem particularly strong. But the sale of her prettier friends can bring Father Andreas a large enough commission to secure papers for all the refugees, and sea passage to Trebizond, perhaps even beyond, if more than two girls are sold. Karteri might one day be married off to a hardworking man, a Christian Greek, and toil for him and bear him children. Is that a better fate for refugee Christian girls than turning into wealthy Muslim matrons? The deacon would have said yes, as would his brother priests and the formidable Bishop of Trebizond. And yet the year before last, a Greek girl in Trebizond— she was fifteen, like Maria—was abducted by a Turk, a city councilor three times her age. Greek girls in Trebizond go out into the streets unveiled, for all the world to see. The councilor had seen her and seized her. He made her his—tenderly, as he was later to say— and locked her in his house with his two wives; but the girl escaped and made her way to the bishopric to seek refuge. And what did the Bishop of Trebizond do? He sent her right back to the Turk, with an escort of deacons to make sure she did not escape again. "The Bishop," Father Andreas thinks, "despite his pontifications, is as much of a realist as I am." The girl had been despoiled. Her family would not have wanted her back, unvirgined and unmarriageable. Her brothers might even have killed her for the shame she had brought on them. Better a living and prosperous Muslim wife than a dead and defiled Greek girl, had been the Bishop of Trebizond's verdict.

"Good morning, Father," Elpida ventures, noticing with a flicker of hope that he is looking closely at her daughter. Father Andreas, startled for a moment, unaware that he has been staring at Karteri, smiles, raises his hand in blessing, and walks on.

He has received another letter, sent via a private messenger on a mule, confirming that the buyer will arrive for the inspection and purchase within a week. This is the one item of reliable news the priest has encountered since arriving at the barracks, and to an extent it has calmed his fears. If Constantinople is indeed in flames and the Empire on its knees, the buyer of girls would hardly be coming here, to the end of the world, seeking foreign maidens for the wealthy households of the capital.

Father Andreas concludes that there are no more than six or seven girls who can in any way be considered marriageable. As the letter from the buyer has established, the girls are to be between thirteen and sixteen, but the priest is resolved that he will not present any girls under fourteen. Maria, along with Lita, ought to be among the first to be presented to the purchaser for viewing. Father Andreas is surprised to see that these two are not sitting on their straw sacks along with the other girls and women, despite his having asked all the womenfolk to assemble. Lita's mother is there, gaunt and careworn, her baby asleep against her breast, and little Dimitri dozing next to her; but she seems distracted. Father Andreas is about to ask her where her daughter is, but thinks better of it. He doesn't need to evaluate Lita or Maria; they are clearly marriageable.

Feeling a wave of nausea, he makes three quick signs of the Cross in the direction of the women and girls and walks out of the barrack and down the path to the river, away from the stench of the latrines.

He hears the excited chattering of the women as the door falls shut behind him. He can't see the river beyond the smoke trees, but he can hear the echoing sound of water rushing over stones. There is a loud chirping and twittering from the trees—birds angrily battling for branches—and a tangle of animal calls from the nearby forest. The sky is gray, the clouds gathered in strange, face-like formations. The Greek mountain villagers who live upriver have different words for different clouds; perhaps the forgotten names of primeval gods, pagan words that should be forbidden. He feels feverish and wonders if it is from the stench of the barracks or the diseased vapors rising from the ravines. He looks around, disoriented. He sees Homeros by the river, holding one of the sacks he has given to him for his fish. He is talking to Maria and Lita, the three of them alone, how can that be? He feels a wave of anger, its vehemence taking him by surprise. Homeros has clearly sought out the girls. He is dangerous. Two beautiful girls and a beautiful young man. Lita is speaking animatedly to Homeros and pointing at the river, but Homeros is looking only at Maria. The priest hears Maria's voice calling a greeting to him through the twittering of the birds. She seems relieved to see him, and he raises his hand and waves. She waves back and shouts something about washing clothes. It seems to be a question; perhaps she is asking whether he wants her to wash his things. Homeros also calls out a greeting to the priest, but quickly leaves with his sack, his eyes lowered. Is he embarrassed to have been caught alone with the girls? Maria and Lita bow to Father Andreas and go back past the smoke trees to the riverbank, where Maria begins wringing out shirts and laying them on the bushes to dry while Lita watches, still carrying her baby brother. Father Andreas takes the path leading to the chapel and his shack and climbs up the slope. The weather has turned hot again. Better too much heat than springtime snow, the refugees and he as well freezing to death. The mud along the path has dried and become hard and brown, which is good, as the path was impassable during the rains. The sun is strong, and he wishes he had thought of bringing his umbrella.

Without doubt Maria is the most marriageable of the girls, he thinks. He remembers the deacon's outrage and bitter words about selling Greek girls to Turks. Though both Father Andreas and the deacon were citizens of the Sultan's empire, the deacon had simply not understood how the world worked. Are the Greek Christians kinder to their wives than the Muslim Turks? In the villages Greek wives carry heavier loads than mules and camels, while their husbands doze in shady olive groves. In the towns Greek wives toil in their houses, toil at market stalls, toil at sewing and cooking, while their husbands gather on the square to smoke pipes and drink coffee. Once a girl like Maria or Lita is bought by a wealthy Muslim man, she will start out as what the deacon had called a *pallakida*, a concubine, pronouncing the Greek word as if it were a curse. Father Andreas prefers the more refined Turkish words. If the girl pleases her master, her future within his household is assured; if she gives him sons, even more so. And if one of the master's four official wives should die or be sent away, the former refugee girl, who has not had a single brass coin to her name in her whole life, might suddenly become a wealthy man's wife, her son groomed to be the next master, and she the ruling dowager of the house. These were opportunities that only the Ottoman Empire offered.

Too tired to feed the cackling hens, he goes into his side of the shack. He lies down on the cot to rest for a few minutes, intending to get up and see to the animals, but is overcome by sleep.

16

ON THE FEAST DAY OF Saint John the Theologian, the buyer of girls comes riding up the canyon with his four guards. Ply a needle or lift a pitchfork on the Theologian's Day, and the saint will send hail and bolts of lightning to ruin your crops. The refugees no longer have any crops, but having been raised in fear of the Theologian, they sacrifice the lambs that the local Greek villagers from up the river had brought them as presents. They spend the morning roasting the meat on fires in the meadow beyond the chapel, and the early hours of the afternoon eating it. No transactions must take place on such a day, but Father Andreas knows that he has to receive the buyer of girls whenever he chooses to come, and his letter said that that would be today. It is early afternoon when he arrives; his head bobs above the rim of the canyon as his horse stumbles up the stony path, its hooves clacking on the stones. The refugees leave their food and line up in the sun to greet him, their faces drawn, wet, and greenish: the rich meat, to which they are no longer accustomed after months of hunger, is tearing at their insides even as they are hungry for more.

Despite the heat, the Turk's face seems cool and rosy, that of a well-fed man, and Father Andreas notices that he bears a striking resemblance to Ahmed Djemal, the young general who is bringing change to the Empire. Ahmed Djemal's handsome face is in every newspaper and progressive pamphlet, and there is no Ottoman citizen who does not know it. The buyer of girls has a magnificent mustache, just like General Djemal's, and a clear, pale skin unusual in a grown man, a handsomeness that perhaps conceals a coldness and brutality. The refugees huddle by the path in front of the priest's hut and begin shuffling forward and pushing each other like beggars outside a mosque, and Father Andreas, alarmed that the Turk might be offended by such a welcome, nervously motions them back and hurries toward him, calling out pleasant Muslim greetings: "May the peace and the blessings of Allah be upon you!"

"And upon you too," the Turk replies, unnerved at the sight of a Greek cleric in a long black cassock running toward him uttering pious Muslim words. The priest reaches him and starts tugging at the horse's halter to help it up the last few yards of the slope; the Turk's guards hurry to assist him. At the wall of the chapel he elegantly dismounts. He has ridden many hours through the canyons in the heat, but there is not a bead of sweat on his forehead, or any trace of fatigue. He approaches the priest and bows in greeting, and the priest bows back.

"We ran into some brigands along the way, which is why I never travel without these men," he tells the priest, pointing at his guards, who, despite their strong bodies and scarred, sunburned faces, seem to be boys rather than men. The darkest of the four, who is doubtless from one of the Ottoman provinces south of Syria, nods and smiles timidly, then with sudden violence jabs his rifle in the direction of some bushes.

"These are dangerous mountains," the priest agrees, ignoring the boy, "very dangerous."

"And dangerous times," the Turk adds. "This heat, this heat, it's not natural this early in the spring."

"It is very unnatural," the priest agrees, "very unnatural."

The women of the barracks are wearing kerchiefs and caps over their tight braids, their faces thin and worn; the men have slicked back their hair with river water and are wearing frayed hats and whatever feast-day sashes and jackets they have. Some of them are wearing cartridge belts and bandoliers across their chests and carrying pistols in their belts like ornaments. A swarm of ragged children are running around the meadow, shouting loudly to one another. As the Turk draws closer, he eyes the women's sallow complexions and tattered finery.

"May we invite you and your guards to partake of our meal?" Father Andreas asks, knowing that the Turk will decline, even though he is almost duty-bound to accept their hospitality.

"I thank you for your gracious invitation," the Turk replies, "but traveling always unsettles my stomach. I can never eat when I travel, I become quite ill; it is a curse."

Flies are buzzing and an air of pestilence hangs in the afternoon heat, emanating from the open sewer by the meadows beyond the shack. The Turk approaches one of the women and she quickly turns her back to him just as a spluttering green stream pours from her mouth against the chapel wall. He tactfully looks away. The refugees quickly bow their heads to the Turk and offer him the Tatar greetings they all know from their villages, the rough words assailing the Turk's Ottoman ears.

The priest has felt it politic to keep the five girls who are to be sold hidden from view. They are now sitting quietly on the step behind the chapel, in tunics that have been boiled and scrubbed. Their hair hangs free and unbraided. In the morning, Heraclea piled Maria's hair into two elegant domes in the fashion of the wealthy young ladies of Batum, the way she would have done in the village if a matchmaker or prospective mother-in-law came to visit. But the priest thought that such ostentation might offend the buyer, particularly if he were a religious man. The Prophet of Islam once expressed displeasure at what he called "women with hair styled like the tilted humps of camels." Such women would never enter the Muslim Paradise—not even its fragrance would reach them, the Prophet said. And yet, though the buyer of girls might be offended by modish humps of hair, it is important that the girls do not appear too plain. Twice this morning the priest slipped back into his shack to flick his tongue over a spoon of mad honey. Just a few specks on the tongue, for inspiration. He had considered having the girls wear garlands of spring flowers, but then felt that this too might offend the Turk. Had they been Turkish maidens, their hair and faces would have been hidden beneath veils; but then, had they been Turkish maidens, they would not have been put up for sale. They were Greek girls, and he would present them as such. A gazelle needs no ornaments to be beautiful; the girls' beauty would stand out better unadorned.

Father Andreas leads the Turk around to the back of the chapel, while his guards remain with his horse, one holding the bridle, the others standing on either side, eyeing the waiting refugees coldly, as if they might steal the animal. None of the refugees are to be present during the viewing of the girls; a sour look or haggard stare could spoil any transaction. To the priest's surprise, the Turk's name is in fact Ahmed, like the dashing young general, and the Turk confides with undisguised delight that he is often mistaken for General

Ahmed Djemal, particularly when he rides out with a retinue. Father Andreas wonders what kind of retinue he might ride out with, but, preoccupied with the impending sale, he does not ask. As they walk through the grass and weeds they hear giggling from behind the chapel; one of the girls says something and the others laugh loudly. The Turk looks at the priest. Things aren't going well, the priest thinks in dismay. As the two men reach the back of the chapel the girls quickly stand up and lower their eyes, as they have been told to do. Father Andreas tries to figure out who has misbehaved, but the girls stand looking sullenly at the ground. Maria has assumed that the matchmaker from Constantinople would be a woman, as all matchmakers in the Caucasus are, and suddenly feels alarmed. They are to be looked over by a man, and she cannot understand how that can be. The Turk walks up to Lita, who is first in line, and leans his face close to hers. He stares at her silently. Her lips begin to twitch and she steps back, raising her hand to her mouth and laughing nervously. She is as taken aback as Maria that the Turk is not a woman and is frightened by his unseemly familiarity. Maria wants to peek at Lita but doesn't dare turn her head.

Father Andreas is surprised that there are to be no preliminaries or small talk before the formal viewing, and feels a slight rush of nausea, afraid that Lita's ungirlish behavior might already be compromising the sale. This is not a good beginning; he now wishes he had placed Lita last in the line. He had not wanted Maria to be viewed first: it was never prudent to present one's best merchandise right away. People say that the eyes of the buyer are in the hands of the seller, and therefore a good seller, the priest had thought, offers a passable item first, then a mediocre one, and only then his prize commodity, followed by more mediocre items. And yet Father Andreas sees that the Turk has already noticed Maria.

He probably already knows whom he will buy. Professional buyers are that way; they walk into a bazaar and know within seconds what they want. The Turk's face moves closer to Lita's, and she leans back, peers at Father Andreas, and laughs again, confused that the priest is allowing the stranger such forwardness. The Turk does not seem to notice, and raising his finger touches her lower lip and then gently pulls it downward. Lita grasps his wrist, which takes him aback, but she doesn't push him away. She just holds it gently, as if she were holding the hand of a friend, while he prods her teeth, narrowing his eyes and bringing his head even closer. He taps her shoulder as if checking something, and Lita, now no longer surprised by the strange things he is doing, looks at him coldly. He moves on to the second girl, a short, doll-like creature with very white skin and jet-black curls who doesn't look to be much older than eight or nine, though she is fourteen.

"She is fourteen," the priest quickly says, worried that the buyer's obvious lack of interest might be because he thinks she is a child.

The Turk nods and smiles, but it is quite clear that he will not buy her, even though the priest is certain that many men would find her childish looks appealing. The Turk's face now approaches Maria's, and she suddenly feels fear stifling her breath. Back in the Caucasus she would never have been looked over by a matchmaking man, but these are other lands and other people, she thinks. The Turk is young—surely younger than her father—and clearly a wealthy man, as his clothes and manner show. She notices a gold ring on his finger, with a ruby in it, and then sees that he has seen her glancing at it. She raises her eyes and looks at him, which she knows she is not supposed to do. She sees his eyes rest coldly on the two silver crosses she is wearing; her hand moves, she wants to lay it on the crosses to cover them but does not. She glances at Father Andreas, who is watching; she can tell he is nervous, but he has clearly not noticed the crosses and the Turk looking at them. She again glances at the Turk; even seen from so close there is no trace of sweat on his forehead or cheeks. His fez is no longer quite red— the sun has bleached it to a strawberry pink, and she remembers a Russian sugar candy that her brother Dionysi had once brought her as a gift, which tasted of strawberries. The Turk motions for her to open her mouth. Again her fear returns. She opens her mouth, noticing the short locks of hair jutting from beneath his fez, and she sees the edge of a crimson silk ribbon that runs along the bottom of the rim. He inspects her teeth, and suddenly sticks out his tongue at her. She smiles awkwardly, mistaking his gesture for some kind of joke, but he quickly motions that she should stick out her tongue the way he did. "Tongue up," his fingers sign, "tongue down!" He looks into her throat, narrowing his eyes and raising his eyebrows as if trying to peer deep inside.

"Foo, foo!" he says, his hands beckoning for her to blow at him, "foo, foo!"

She blows, and he sniffs at her breath.

"Virgin?" the Turk asks, turning to the priest.

"Of course," the priest says, louder than he had intended, offended both by the implication that he might be trying to trick the buyer, and that these girls under his care might be impure.

The Turk turns back to Maria and notices her startled look. She must have understood, he thinks, and she has, for the word is the same in the Tatar songs that everybody in her village knew. "A virgin pure, untouched by man, waiting by the fountain green."

"Can you speak Turkish?"

She understands the question but does not respond.

"The man wants to know if you know any Turkish," the priest prompts in Greek. He knows she has understood the Turk but hopes she will not break into a flood of mountain Tatar.

"From my diamond palace by the emerald lake," she says in Tatar, "I flew to you with golden wings from lands where snow lies sparkling white."

The Turk is startled to hear the half-familiar, ancient Tatar words, so similar to Classical Turkish, and Maria looks at Father Andreas and sees that he seems even more surprised, perhaps even alarmed.

"She must have learned those verses in the Caucasus," Father Andreas says apologetically. "They always sing the ancient Tatar songs, since they don't have any of their own, though I doubt they know what they mean." He wonders what would have made the girl speak out of turn in such a way and suddenly say these verses; he has warned the girls not to admit to knowing anything but Greek. Is this some sort of rebellion on Maria's part, or has she just spoken the words in panic? It must be the latter, he thinks. "She doesn't know Turkish," he says, smiling disingenuously at the Turk, his eyes darting back to Maria, "but I am sure she will learn it in no time. She is as clever as she is beautiful."

"That is good," the Turk says. "I wouldn't want to acquire a girl who knows Turkish. 'Lands where snow lies sparkling white'— that's beautifully said, a perfect line of ancient verse. I just hope she doesn't know too much Tatar."

"Oh no," Father Andreas says quickly, "she knows hardly any— just a few old songs!"

"Do you speak Tatar?" the Turk asks Maria despite Father Andreas's assurances, and she points back toward the chapel, aware that nodding or shaking her head would be equally dangerous, but that a meaningless gesture might be her best response.

"She doesn't know any Tatar," the priest repeats coldly.

"That is how it should be," the Turk says. "You see, we need to start from alpha, as you Greeks say." He pauses for effect. "If you start from omega, you can only go backward, but if you start from alpha you can go forward with a clean slate. A girl with some Turkish, with bad Turkish, with barbarous Tatar Turkish, is of no use to us. When we buy we want a clean slate."

The priest nods sullenly. Such base words of trade and commerce had not been used until now, and he wonders if the Turk might somehow be trying to insult him. But the Turk has lost none of his affability. *"Lands where the snow lies sparkling white?* I will certainly take the clever one with the green eyes."

17

FATHER ANDREAS IS RELIEVED THAT the buyer of girls has made his choice so quickly: no questions, no haggling, no long discussions. The transaction has taken no more than ten minutes. This is an unusual way of doing things, very modern, he thinks; the Turk is clearly one of those new Ottomans who have adopted the ways of the Europeans. But Father Andreas is disappointed that Maria is the only one of the five girls who will be purchased. He had thought that the Turk would at least have bought Lita too, though it was hard to imagine her as a docile presence in a rich man's house.

The priest and his guest walk across the meadow toward the riverbank, away from the refugees, who have noisily returned to their roasting lambs. A band of little boys runs toward them in a game of catch, shouting in high-pitched voices, and Father Andreas shoos them away. "And don't run down to the river!" he calls after them as they run down the hill toward the riverbank. "The sun is too hot for this time of the year," he continues, turning to the Turk.

"It brings vapors," the Turk says, pointing back toward the ravine. "We rode through there quickly, we didn't stop."

"One must ride through such ravines without stopping, such heat so early in the year brings pestilence, and if you stop, the fever seizes you." The priest raises his hand and snatches at the air.

The Turk tells him that he plans to cross the river into the Russian Caucasus that same afternoon. It will be cooler there, he says, perhaps even cold, as the land rises high into the mountains, though the rise in the path is so gradual that one would not notice. "You're up in the snows before you even realize it," he says.

Though the priest has nowhere to put the Turk up for the night, he politely and insistently urges him to stay, a gesture that is expected of him as the host and which he knows the Turk will turn down. Surely, Father Andreas says, he would not want to ride on after dark with robbers and rebels at every bend in the path; he must stay, he insists. But the Turk tells him that as much as he would like to stay the night and enjoy the food and company, he has urgent business to attend to across the border, and so will spend the night at the Zeheb Inn, only an hour's ride into the Russian lands. The Zeheb Inn is a good place and the owner a good man, a Greek he has known for years, the Turk adds as if to appease any worries the priest might have on his account. Father Andreas smiles, and so does the Turk. Having exchanged the obligatory pleasantries, the Turk turns the conversation back to the details of the transaction. He will return in two days with a caravan of mules and horses, and at that point he will pay half the priest's commission for brokering the sale. He will arrange travel passes, he says, and the priest and the girl's father can then accompany him to the port town, where the magistrate will witness the finalizing of the sale papers. That way everything will be in order, and the buyer and the seller will have a legal document.

The papers are mainly for the benefit of the girl's family; a family always feels better knowing that things are being done officially. In all his years as a middleman, he says, he has never had any problems on the buyers' end—it is always the sellers who cause trouble: It's not enough money! Their poor daughter! They want guarantees! They want, they want, they want!

The priest thinks of the looming pestilence and the restlessness of the refugees, which after weeks of their being herded together in the barracks is beginning to turn into unruliness. "We come from Allah and to Allah we return," he says to the Turk, who for a moment wonders whether such words are not subversive in the mouth of a Christian cleric, or perhaps mocking. The priest is angry, he thinks, that he is only purchasing one girl. Smiling affably, he tells him almost apologetically that he would have liked to have taken more than one girl, because they are all prime maidens; however, his current Constantinople account has specific requirements, and the girl with the green eyes is the only one who matches them. He tells the priest that in two days, when they set out for the port, it would be a good idea to take along the four other girls, as they can be shown to other middlemen who might be able to place them well. The girls will then be shipped out in first-class cabins on vessels heading for the capital or other Ottoman cities, chaperoned by matrons, as the purchasers would want only the best for maidens destined for their households. The Turk tells the priest that they can also take three or four boys down to the port, handsome twelve- to fourteen-year-olds, if there are any. For a lesser sum, they too can be placed with wealthy buyers: craftsmen or merchants, under whom they will serve, in a sense, as apprentices. The chances for suitable sales are good, the Turk says, and pitchers must be filled when the water is flowing. The boys will spend ten years or so with their masters, and then be released from their indentures with a nice sum of money to start businesses of their own. They will grow up to be successful Turks, with new Turkish names, completely unencumbered by their Greek pasts. And occasionally the masters love the boys under their charge like real sons, in which case the brightest futures are in store for them.

18

TWO DAYS LATER THE JOURNEY down to the Black Sea begins. Maria watches the Turk's fez bobbing lightly as the caravan descends the wide mountain path into the valleys beyond the chapel. The Turk is riding on his sturdy horse, a honey and brown chestnut, while his guards in their dirt-spattered fezzes are walking in front of him, pointing their rifles at bends in the path. Maria is riding sidesaddle on a silver-gray horse draped with Persian saddle blankets. The horses are well groomed and well fed, not like the thin village horses in the Caucasus; these are the horses of a rich man, Maria thinks. The priest is riding beside her, from time to time calling out a witty response to the Turk. Lita and the three other unsold girls are riding quietly in single file behind them, while the boys destined for indenture walk behind the pack animals that are laden with carpets, bales of cloth, and sacks of coffee and grain.

Maria has heard that the Turk's name is Ahmed, like Saint Ahmed the Calligrapher, whose feast is on the day before Christmas, and she is surprised that the Turk has the same name as the pious Christian martyr. A red scarf is wound across her face, and she is holding above her head a light parasol with gold trim and tassels, a present from the Turk, who wants her skin to remain pale—even a touch of sun can affect her beauty in a way that is frowned upon in the capital. He is talking with his guards, and Maria listens to the stream of Turkish, trying to follow.

As the Turk had only managed to secure traveling passes for the children, Kostis was not able to travel to the port with the caravan to complete the paperwork for his daughter's sale. This relieved both the Turk and Father Andreas, for neither wanted to risk his having a change of heart once they reached the port. Kostis, too, was relieved that he was not to join the caravan: some of the boiled weeds he had eaten had affected him badly, and he felt as if his stomach was filled with stones. This should have been the happiest day in his life, he thought. His daughter was to be married off to a man wealthier than any he had ever heard of, and instead of having to give away a fortune for this privilege, he was receiving one. The marriage was a godsend, a celestial blessing. It was a match he never could have hoped for. It was as if a holy saint had descended from Heaven in his hour of need to grant him deliverance. And yet, as always happened in the old tales when a saint or god granted someone a magic wish, a dark and foreboding "but" inevitably followed. "Everything you touch will turn to gold, but . . ." "You will marry the most beautiful woman in the world, but . . ." The "but" in Kostis's deliverance, he thought as he lay recovering in his dark corner of the men's barrack, was that he could not meet Maria's husband face to face, as he was supposed to, that he could not decide for himself if he was the right son-in-law. He would never set eyes on Maria's husband—not before the marriage, and not after. He would know nothing about the man who would be marrying his daughter, not even his name. The sheer greatness of the sum, Kostis knew, would have to be a sufficient guarantee of this man's character and trustworthiness. Kostis asked if Maria's sale could be postponed until he was no longer ill; the priest said no. Then could the priest finalize the contract for him? The priest said yes.

"Obey your future master and give him many sons!" Heraclea told Maria, uttering the formula that the mothers of her village had spoken to their daughters for centuries as they left for their new husbands' houses. Maria took off her amulet and the two necklaces with the silver crosses and gave them to Heraclea, who took them and put them in her bag. Heraclea turned and continued to mash resin with wild hyssop leaves in her bowl, rubbing the green paste with a smooth river stone: the concoction would calm Kostis's burning insides, and she seemed more preoccupied with grinding the paste than with her daughter's departure. She was worried about her sons. She had hoped that Kostis would travel to the port with the priest and the Turk so that he might send them a telegram, since they still did not know that their village had been destroyed. The boys wouldn't be returning from the tea factory for another few months, and she wanted to let them know as soon as possible that their future was now bright and lay in Athens. She asked Father Andreas to send them a telegram from the town; just ten words: *Village destroyed STOP Wonderful news STOP Traveling to Athens STOP Will send tickets STOP.* To her relief, the priest immediately agreed, without even asking her for the money for the telegram. She knew that the boys would be puzzled by the message, but it was better that they should be puzzled than alarmed.

Heraclea's thoughts had not touched on the prospect that she would never see her daughter again: the shock of the unexpected gold coins that Kostis had already received from the priest as a down payment—an enormous sum—had overwhelmed her, triggering new dreams and worries. But as Maria packed the few possessions she would take with her, Heraclea was seized by the fear that her husband's food poisoning might kill him. It was not the boiled weeds that had upset his stomach, she thought, but all the meat he had eaten at the feast two days ago. Her uncle, who had died a few years before her marriage, had been taken captive by the Russians for carrying contraband and starved to a skeleton: when the Russians released him, a kindhearted village woman took pity on him and gave him nine eggs. In his hunger her uncle had eaten them all at once and, writhing in agony, died. If Kostis were to die now, what would she do? Heraclea's mind wandered as she continued crushing the resin and leaves while Maria folded her barrack blanket for the last time. However tall the dark mountain, Heraclea thought, there is always a path down to the sunny valleys. If her husband died, she would take the money from Maria's sale and travel to Chakva to find her sons on the plantation. She would not have to steal across the river in the night and trudge over mountain passes; a wealthy widow, she would travel in a ship, but sleeping with her bundles down below in the steerage, her gold coins sewn into the seams of her skirts and coats. She would give the money to her sons and they would all sail to Athens, where they would buy the house that she and Kostis had talked about in the two days since Maria's sale. In this house she would preside over her sons, her future daughters-in-law, and her grandchildren.

Clouds cover the sun, thin clouds like pools of milk spreading over the sky that will grow heavier and bring rain; Maria folds her parasol, resting it across her saddle. The path is uneven, and the horse's hooves slide, scattering loose stones. She is wearing a long embroidered dress, hot and heavy in the midday heat, a wedding dress that one of the refugee girls who had drowned in the river had intended to wear. The girl and her mother must have spent many months embroidering the patterns. Maria hadn't known the girl, who had come with one of the later groups of refugees that tried to cross the river during the rainstorm. Maria imagines the rushing flood and the pelting rain, the girl gasping and shouting soundless words as the cold river pulls her under and her mouth fills with mud and yellow water. No magic fish, large and golden, the bewitched maiden of the old village songs, comes to save her. For a minute, perhaps two, the girl thrashes and kicks as the river pours into her mouth, and then her spirit leaves her lifeless body. It is dangerous to wear a dead woman's dress, and more dangerous to wear one that had been intended for a dead woman's wedding. In the Caucasus, destitute itinerant peddlers dig up dead women and girls to rob them of their dresses and finery, which they then sell, wandering with their sacks from village to village. Whoever wears the ill-fated clothes does not have long to wait before Satan comes to knock at her door. But the priest bought the dress from the drowned girl's mother with rations of meat and olive oil, mumbled incantations, and gave Maria special dispensation to wear it. Heraclea then laid out the dress on the stones of the riverbank and passed her talisman chains over it, south to north and east to west. These are difficult times, the priest told Heraclea, who, despite the measures she and the priest were taking, was worried that the dead girl's dress would draw evil to the family. These are bad times, he continued calmly, but they are about to change into the best of times. When the music changes, the dance changes too, he said, and this dance will be one of wealth and abundance; there will be plenty of food in all their futures—no rats and no pestilence. Maria could not set out to meet her new master in tattered clothes; she had to wear the dead girl's wedding dress until the grandee she was destined for provided her with garments that would outshine any that Heraclea had ever seen. The spells of the Caucasus would weaken and fade as the girl traveled farther and farther away. Nobody need fear the old beliefs.

In the meadow among the tall grasses, Maria sees broken marble columns, an ancient temple Xerxes destroyed to free the gods trapped inside. She unwinds the scarf from her face and turns to look back at Lita, who is staring down into the ravine, where the river is rushing loudly over rocks. Lita's horse is an orange-brown bay, with a black mane and tail; it too is struggling over the stony path, though Lita doesn't seem to notice, steadying herself with one hand on her saddle's pommel, shaking the reins listlessly with the other. Maria can't tell if Lita is happy or sad, and she is not certain how she herself feels. She runs her finger over the soft fabric of her parasol. This is her bridal procession, on its way to meet her husband, who lives in a faraway place. This is supposed to be a happy time, and yet there is fear inside her, fear she is worried might grow and spread, the fear she has heard that every young bride feels as she rides away from her parents. It has not yet struck Maria that she will never see her parents again. Only two days have passed since the buyer of girls chose her. Maria knows that she has been chosen and Lita has not; her mother told her that among all the unmarried girls in the barracks, she alone was picked for a husband, a great man who wanted a good Greek girl. Tears begin to run down her cheek, and she raises her parasol in case the priest or the Turk might turn and look back. She and the other girls have been raised with the hope that by the time they were fifteen or sixteen they would be married off and sent to the house of a husband their mothers had proposed and their fathers chosen. The husband's house might have been a few houses away, or a few villages, or a few mountains, and the girls would have ridden there in a bridal procession of horses and mules, just as she was doing now; except that the mules would have been packed with their dowries of linen and spoons, and perhaps carved boxes or chests filled with provisions and presents, not with the sacks of coffee, grain, and bales of cloth that these mules were carrying.

Over the last two days Maria's mother kept kissing her cheeks as if she were a cherished infant, and her father looked at her with the same pride and pleasure with which he had looked at his sons when they brought back gold coins from the tea factories in Chakva. A lifetime of worry about husbands and dowries that would ruin the family was over, as was the newer fear that they would all starve in a distant foreign land. A future that had seemed bleak now shone in a golden light. Maria's father spoke of nothing but Athens, and how the family would move there with the money the Turk was paying for his daughter. In Athens gold grew on the trees, he said, emeralds and rubies sprouted in the meadows, and diamonds poured from every fountain. He had heard that many Caucasian Greeks had made fortunes in the liberated lands of Greece, and now he was to be given a fortune in gold coins before he even arrived in the Promised Land. And coins beget coins, the money from his daughter's sale would beget more money, that money would in turn beget land and cattle. Once in Athens he would send for his sons, who would travel to Greece from the plantations of Chakva like gentlemen. They would have a berth on the Russian ship that they would board in Batum, and not sleep down below in the crowded steerage. In Athens there would be many wealthy brides for the boys to choose from. It would be a life of abundance and ease. Heraclea could make money by washing clothes in Athenian houses, and in the evenings, sitting by a lamp that could turn night into day, she would sew and embroider. Her nimble fingers could crochet costly tablecloths, or she could make boxes and pretty knickknacks to sell to wealthy gentlemen. They would have a garden where she could grow tomatoes, cucumbers, green peppers, and rows of beans; whatever they or the boys didn't eat she could sell in the market. And Kostis would buy a cart and rent it out, and then buy a second and a third, and rent those out too: "Kostis Varsanis & Sons."

The dead girl's dress clutches at Maria's neck, the embroidery tightening over her breasts. To her right is a sheer drop into a chasm through which the fast-flowing river pours. If the spirit of the dead girl should soar from the river and snatch at the dress that was once hers, Maria's horse would stumble over the edge and she and the dress and the parasol would fall into the rushing waters. She sees her bloodied face being dragged over sharp rocks by the raw torrent, fish darting through her hair, her blood spreading through the cold water, the spirit of the dead girl tearing at the dress, the widow Manthena and her murderers lying in wait among the weeds in the deeper waters.

The Turk turns to look at Maria and smiles. Maria smiles back.

19

THE CARAVAN COMES TO A bend in the path, and Maria ties her scarf across her face again and re-opens her parasol to fend off the sun. She wonders what her husband will be like and feels a knot of fear in her stomach. She watches the Turk riding in front of her, his fez gleaming a reddish orange in the sun, and wonders if her husband might be someone like him. In the old village songs, ancient heroes are given as a prize the beautiful daughters of the dragons they kill. The heroes live with these wives happily ever after, but the songs never say if the wives are happy with the husbands to whom they have been given. Every marriage begins with tears, people say: the bride's tears. She looks back at Lita, who raises her scarf over her nose and comically shakes her head from side to side in an impersonation of a veiled harem woman. Father Andreas also looks back, and Lita dutifully ties the scarf across her face as Maria has done. Lita seems to be enjoying the ride.

The path has become narrower, and the priest is now riding a few paces in front of Maria. She is watching the two men from under the rim of her parasol, trying to follow what they are saying. Father Andreas seems somehow frightened of the Turk; perhaps not frightened, she thinks, but wary, the way a high-placed servant might be wary of his master. This is strange and unsettling. The priest does have the manner of a man of the church, but she thinks the Turk has more authority. Back in her village, the word of old Father Kyriakos, who had been priest since before her mother was born, weighed even more heavily than that of the village elder or the great lady of the tea plantation. But who is the Turk, she wonders. Is he really a matchmaker? The only matchmakers she has known of were old and poor women, usually widows or spinsters. But the Turk is an elegant and wealthy man with guards and a caravan. Why would he have come from so far away to arrange a marriage between her and the great man in Constantinople? Perhaps he is a friend of her new master? But what friend would travel through a whole empire to arrange a marriage? When Black Melpo cast the entrails of an animal to see what was in store for the man or woman to whom the animal had belonged, the entrails always pointed, Black Melpo would say, to a fate that could not be escaped or changed. Perhaps Maria is destined for the great man in Constantinople, and the Turk is the go-between who will see that the will of Fate is done.

Across the river, on the face of the cliff that rises out of the water, are ancient figures carved into the gray rock, a long procession of thin maidens, their outstretched hands holding bows with arrows ready to fly. Beneath their feet lie rows of men with pierced chests. The maidens are walking behind a regal woman in a tall headdress that seems to be a garland of cloth and gems. She must be Queen Medea, Maria thinks. The figures are high up on the cliff wall—they could only have been cut into the stone by flying men, hovering like hummingbirds. She feels hot and thirsty in the sun and drinks from her water gourd. The water is warm and tastes of river weeds; there are grains of sand on her tongue. She looks back at Lita, who smiles and points at the foothills in front of them and then stretches out her hand, mimicking an expanse of rolling waves.

Maria sees something moving on the ridge across the river. A flash of light, a sunbeam on polished metal, and a man's head appears from behind a rock above the sheer drop down to the water. She thinks the man must be running, but then realizes he is on horseback. A second head appears, then a third. Now Father Andreas notices them too, and Maria sees alarm in his face. An echo of galloping hooves comes across the river, mingling with the sound of the rushing water. The horsemen are carrying rifles. She can't see the Turk's face, but she can see him lean forward and motion to his guards with a gesture she doesn't understand. She catches her breath in fear and looks back at Lita, who has dropped her parasol. The horsemen disappear behind some trees, only to reappear in a clearing, where they dismount.

"God have mercy on us!" Father Andreas mutters.

One of the horsemen raises his hand and calls out something, but his voice is muffled by the sound of the river. He calls out again. The cliffs are yellow in the glare of the sun. One of the Turk's guards raises his rifle; the Turk turns and looks at him in horror. A shot comes from across the river, followed by a second. The guard drops his rifle and falls to his knees.

Maria thinks he has been hit, but he just kneels there, then raises his hands in the air, his shoulders shaking.

"You fool!" the Turk hisses. "You'll get us all killed!"

The guard jumps up and runs past Maria's horse, away from the river and toward the roadside where there are rocks he can hide behind. There is another shot and he falls forward, facedown, and lies there, his arms and legs stretched out and quaking. Maria's horse takes a few quick steps forward, but then abruptly stops, clacking its hooves, unsure whether to bolt or stay. Maria sits still in terror, stiffly holding her parasol above her head. Her hand begins to cramp, but she does not move. The guard is crying and spluttering like a frantic infant. Maria's horse stamps its hoof, and Maria knows that if her horse bolts she will certainly be shot. The guard suddenly falls silent. Out of the corner of her eye she sees that his legs and arms have stopped shaking. She has the urge to jump off her horse and run toward the rocks, but she cannot move.

"Everyone stay where you are!" the priest calls out to the children, without looking back toward them, as any movement might bring another deadly shot. "This was an accident. There will be no more shots if you stay where you are. Just stay where you are!"

The cavalryman on the ridge across the river shouts the same words to the Turk he shouted before. The Turk still can't make them out, but he raises his hands and calls out, "We have papers! Papers! Constantinople!"

The cavalryman shouts something back and, lifting his rifle up in the air, he and the other men mount their horses and ride off. The Turk sits motionless in his saddle, a fixed smile on his face as he waits for them to disappear.

20

IN THE LAST VALLEYS BEFORE the Black Sea the river widens, its banks lined with stagnant pools where the water has overflowed and been trapped on the gravelly shore. A forest of oak and chestnut trees covers the higher slopes on either side of the river, and the meadows below are filled with clusters of the yellow-flowered bushes whose nectar the mountain bees turn into their mad deadly honey. Father Andreas is carrying a little pot of it in one of his saddlebags, but since the shooting he has felt too hot and perturbed to dip his spoon into it; nor does he have a parasol, as the girls do, and the sun is stinging his cheeks. He wants to discuss the killing of the guard with the Turk, but the Turk clearly does not want the incident mentioned. Father Andreas's body is aching from the hard saddle and the horse's jolting steps, and he feels a sudden anxiety. The valley is wider now and there is no more danger of snipers, but the caravan will soon be coming to the army checkpoints, and his mind begins to conjure up confused images of soldiers stopping and searching them, robbing them of their horses and belongings, and dragging off the frightened girls and boys. He suddenly hears birds twittering loudly in the trees, and with a shake of his head dispels the thoughts that are assailing him. The sun is affecting him he thinks and peers up at the sky. He leans down to his saddlebag to fumble for the honeypot but is worried that the Turk might look back and see him licking the spoon. But if he doesn't use the spoon, he will not be detected if he opens the saddlebag quickly—he can pull out the pot and lift it to his lips at an opportune moment. His fingers fumble with the tight leather knot that secures the bag's flap; he tugs and pulls at it. The knot comes undone, and he grabs the pot, uncorks it, and quickly flicks his tongue over the sticky rim. He feels a flash of sweet, liberating poison.

As the path nears the riverbank, Maria imagines dipping her ankles and knees in the cool water, which has lost its menace now that its torrents are no longer wild; the pools along the banks seem too shallow to conceal the spirit of the drowned bride. She wonders if the spirit of the dead guard is now following them instead; but it must still be lingering by his grave, his body lying in a shroud of worms and beetles. Maria sees herself sinking into the water, the coolness seeping through the fatal wedding dress, dissolving its magic as she lies down to rest on the smooth green stones at the bottom. She wonders how long it would take her body to dissolve if she were to lie in the water and let the current carry her down to the Black Sea. When Adam lived in these lands, he ordered Eve to stand in the river for thirty-six days to repent for her sin, and she entered the water, bringing with her a stone to stand on so that she would not drown when the currents rose with the melting of the snow. She stood in the cold river for six days, her body softening and darkening, and death was descending upon her; but the serpent saved her life, dragging her out of the water, and laying her on the riverbank, her body brown like a rotting apple.

Maria is tormented by thirst, but her water gourd is empty. She touches her cheek. It is hot and damp with sweat. The dress has already become dusty, and the polished gold beads of the slippers the Turk has given her are cutting into her feet. The unsold girls ride sidesaddle behind her in wide, billowing peasant smocks that seem more comfortable. The parasols the other girls are holding look like oilskin umbrellas; they are as practical as her gold-tasseled parasol, but not as elegant.

One moment the guard was alive, the next moment he was dead. He must have been her brother Kimon's age, she thinks, and wonders if she will live to be that old. Since the sniper shots, none of the unsold girls have said a word. The pretty, doll-like girl, who is fourteen but looks eight or nine, is sitting on her saddle with her lips pressed together.

The path descends toward the pass leading out of the valley, and Maria sees clusters of stone and wood hovels huddling beneath a mountain ridge. On either side of the village stand crumbling stone towers and a stockade made of wood packed with mud. There are men sitting on the top of the towers; Maria can see their heads in the distance and the metal of their rifles flashing in the sun. She holds her reins to her chest, as if they could shield her from a bullet; she is not frightened or alarmed, though she knows she should be. She feels nothing except for the ache of her body after the many hours in the saddle.

A herd of cows is standing in the shallows of the river, their horns snubbed off, the stumps painted a reddish yellow that shimmers in the sun like gold nuggets. The cows watch the approaching caravan blankly through a cloud of tiny flies that dart and spin above the water in the afternoon heat, flitting in zigzags, trying to lay their deadly eggs in the soft skin of the cows' underbellies; if they succeed, the cows will be dead within a year. How clever the cows are, Maria thinks, to be aware of the danger and to wait placidly in the water until the swarm retreats downriver in the late afternoon sun.

Alongside the path to the village, withered sticks have been hammered into frames over which sheep's innards are stretched like rock-hard drum skins blackened in the sun, totems to ward off the evil eye of strangers. Women in dark red caftans, with kerchiefs wound across their faces, are kneeling by the pools along the riverbank, pounding dye into coarsely spun yarn and then dipping it into hollows of reddish-brown water. The rims of the hollows are inlaid with colorful glazed shards of broken pottery. Little girls, lifting their skirts above their knees, stamp the dye into the yarn with reddened feet. The dyes ooze out of the hollows and spread over the river like blood. The women stop working and stare at the newcomers, ready to run back toward the village if they have to.

The bank is covered in smoke and steam from cauldrons of dye, and a dour woman, at least two heads taller than the others, is shoveling red beetles, roots, and tree bark into the brew, her face turned away from the noxious steam. A group of men with rifles appears by the line of houses beyond the dye pools. A pack of thin, snarling dogs comes running up the path from the village, barking and yelping, the guards swinging their rifle butts at them. The women eye the caravan as it descends the path toward the riverbank. When they see the priest they begin waving, bowing, and crossing themselves: "*Selam, selam, Pateramis!*" He waves back, making quick small crosses in their direction, shouting blessings at them in what sounds like a mixture of Turkish and Ancient Greek.

"So you give sermons in Turkish too!" the Turk says. "Not that one can really call the babbling of these women Turkish. You haven't been converting Muslim villagers, have you?"

The priest shakes his head, uncertain if this is a pleasantry or some kind of censure. "I am not a missionary!" he quickly replies. "These people are not Turks, they are Drungi and Christian."

"Drungi?" the Turk asks, looking with distaste at one of the totemic frames of stretched sheep innards he is riding past, leaning as far away from it as he can. There is a slit in the hard brown skin stretched over the totem sticks, and the Turk realizes with disgust that it probably comes from the animal's hindquarters.

"The Drungi were some sort of Roman legion that settled here when the Romans occupied Colchis," the priest says, "though they always spoke a strange kind of Greek."

"Colchis?"

"That's what this land was called in Greek before it became Ottoman."

The Turk looks at Father Andreas blankly, and then nods at the village women, who begin clapping and waving.

21

FATHER ANDREAS FOLLOWS THE WOMEN in the red caftans up the path leading toward the first stone huts of the village beneath the ridge. The men standing guard in the stone towers call greetings and fire shots of welcome into the air. Only the tall dour woman remains by the steaming cauldrons of dye, shoveling beetles and tree bark into the red brew. A few days ago the mayor of the port town was assassinated by insurgents, and the women say that Kurdish soldiers are now searching the area beyond the pass. Patrols have come to the village twice seeking fugitives today, and new reprisals against the rebels are expected.

The Turk orders the horses and mules to be unpacked, and Maria and Lita watch the men heave the sacks off the animals' backs, untie their saddles, and lead them to the riverbank to be watered. Lita hands Maria her drinking gourd, and Maria takes a few quick sips of the warm and musty water. The Turk and the muleteers confer for a few minutes, pointing to the village and to the path leading down to the valley, and then unroll their small prayer carpets, raise the tips of their fingers to their ears, and in unison begin repeatedly kneeling, bowing, and standing up again.

Maria and Lita stand alone, Maria holding her parasol up against the sun. There is a loud buzzing of flies.

"I thought those riders were going to kill us too," Maria says. "I've never seen anyone die before." She fights back her tears and remembers the widow Manthena covered in mud, how she was pushed into the ditch by the marauders in the village. Maria didn't see her die, but she is sure that she saw her just seconds before her death.

"I also thought they were going to kill us," Lita says. "Killed by bandits and left unburied and unblessed—were they bandits, do you think?"

"In uniform?"

"You're right," Lita says.

"I wonder how many more narrow escapes there'll be," Maria says.

"You mean before they actually get us?

"No," Maria says, thinking Lita is making a joke, but she sees right away that she isn't. "I mean before we get to wherever we're going!"

"I wonder where that is."

"As long as it's not here," Maria says. "This is a terrible place. Look at all those magic sticks and animal skins."

"These people must really be afraid of the evil eye."

Maria looks at the crumbling village. "I'd like to know what the evil eye can ruin in a place like this," she says.

"Better seven wolves than staying here," Lita says.

"I'm sure we'll meet seven wolves if we stay here," Maria replies. She and Lita watch three women in muddy dresses dragging a thick tree trunk that is trussed with heavy ropes up the path to the village. One of the women has an infant strapped to her back, its head lolling from side to side as she tugs at the ropes.

"I'm not used to riding so long," Maria says, shaking one leg and then the other. "My bottom's sore, I don't think I can sit."

"I'm sore all over," Lita says. "I don't think I can sit or stand. I wonder how many days we'll have to ride like this."

"Where are those dogs that attacked us?" Maria says, looking around. "If they come for us again we'll have to throw ourselves into the river."

"Dogs can swim," Lita says. She turns to look at the cows that are standing upriver in the shallows. "What pretty little gold horns they have. Do you think they'll bite us if we go over to them?"

Maria smiles but frowns as well. "Didn't you have cows in your village?"

"No, just goats and sheep," Lita replies. "But I *have* seen a cow before." She rolls her eyes and smiles.

"They're clever animals, very clever," Maria says, turning and looking back up the river at the cows. "I don't think we can go to them. Father Andreas would be angry."

"I suppose he would," Lita replies.

Maria looks at the other unsold boys and girls playing noisily by the pool with a crowd of ragged village children, beating the water with sticks and splashing each other. They seem to have forgotten the killing of the guard already. She thinks of his shaking arms and legs, and that strange childlike wailing; a terrible sound that she tries to push to the back of her mind. Two village boys of about sixteen are wrestling by the mud banks, trying to push each other into the river, laughing and glancing at Maria and Lita. Some of the younger village children are throwing knucklebones onto the ground in a peculiar counting game, and Maria notices that the unsold boys seem to have already figured out its rules and are echoing the same strange words the village children are calling out. A thin little boy with a swollen belly throws a mud clot at Lita but misses; she stamps her foot at him and he runs away laughing. The Turk and his guards and muleteers, oblivious to the noise, continue to pray. The pungent smell of an animal that has crawled out of the river to die in the bushes mixes with the stench of the steaming dye from the cauldrons. Maria and Lita watch the praying men.

"If we walk to the bend in the river," Lita says suddenly, "we can run up the bank and head back to the barracks. Nobody would know we're gone until it's too late."

"And then what?" Maria whispers.

"We can climb back up the path, and if we walk all night we can be at the barracks by tomorrow. It won't be dangerous at night if we walk by the side of the path by the bushes—nobody will see us. No brigands and murderers, and I'm not scared of wolves and forest cats."

"And then when we get back up to the barracks? You think they'll want us back after we've been sent off on our bridal procession? What bride ever returns once she sets out?"

"This is your bridal procession, not mine," Lita says, narrowing her eyes against the sun. For the first time since Maria has known her there is no playful undertone to her words. "I haven't been promised to anyone, so why shouldn't I go back?"

"But Father Andreas said he'd also find you a husband who'll make your father and brothers rich, like my husband."

"There'll be no husband like your husband," Lita says lightly, her good-natured humor returning.

"Anyway, we can't go back," Maria says, imagining her father's face if he saw her coming up the path from the ravine. She would never be forgiven, not by him, not by her mother, and not by her brothers. Her father would beat her for the dishonor she was bringing upon the family. All his hopes and plans would be gone with the sack of coins for the sale that he would have to give back to the priest, who would have to return the coins to the Turk, who would have to give them back to the grandee in Constantinople. He would cast her out, and she would have to drown herself in the river. She now belongs to her new husband and master. If she returns to her family, the promise that was made to him will be broken. And yet, though Maria is afraid of turning back, she is just as afraid of what tomorrow and the day after might bring, though she is not prepared to admit this to Lita. Black Melpo once said to her, "Tread calmly along the path that has been chosen for you, even if it is a path of nettles and thorns." Maria decides that she has to stay calm. Fear will come and fear will go, but it would be best to keep it to herself. As long as she does what is expected of her by her father, her mother, and the priest, whatever happens will surely be for the best. Her master, everyone said, was a good man, who was saving her parents and brothers and all the people of the barracks. His deed of saving so many people is more than good, she thinks. Who would do such a thing? A king? A saint? But still she feels afraid. She wonders what advice Black Melpo would give her. "A new bride always trembles," Black Melpo would have said, "until she knows at which end of the field she is supposed to piss." And Black Melpo would have been right. People were always afraid until they knew what a new situation would bring, what would be expected of them. She smiles at the memory of Black Melpo's coarse proverb, and Lita, thinking Maria's mood has changed, smiles back.

"You know something, Maria? You're old for your years. Has anyone ever told you that?"

Maria looks at her. "Now that I think of it, so are you."

"You're pretty and clever," Lita says to her, and then adds, "you always think things through."

"But you're full of surprises, and I'm not," Maria says. "I wish I could be full of surprises. I can maybe think surprising things, but I can't do them."

"And I can maybe do surprising things, but can't think them," Lita says, more in fun than seriously.

Maria reaches out for Lita's hand, and the two girls walk up the path toward the tall dour woman by the steaming cauldrons. Her face is not covered like those of the other women; her kerchief is tied at the back with two big knots. She looks like a strong man who by some strange chance has walked into the fields in a woman's caftan. She pushes a clump of brushwood under the cauldron, pokes the fire with her shovel, and then walks toward the girls, eyeing Maria's wedding dress.

"Health to you, daughters, blessed your arrival," the woman says roughly, her voice surprisingly shrill. Her greeting sounds to Maria more Greek than Tatar, but is neither.

"Greetings," Maria and Lita reply in Greek.

"Who you belong to?"

Lita glances at Maria.

"You his wives?" the woman says, jutting her chin in the direction of the Turk kneeling in prayer, surrounded by his guards. She puts down her shovel and quickly reaches over to one of Maria's sleeves and tugs at the material, rubbing it between her fingers, her eyes narrowing. Maria steps back, horrified that the woman's blackened fingers might stain the dead girl's wedding dress, but they do not.

"*Laa dhaka!*" the woman suddenly says, which Maria recognizes as "come here" in a wild, half-forgotten Greek.

The woman reaches into her apron, pulls out an apple, rubs it on her skirt, and hands it to Maria, who wonders where she could have found it at this time of year. She then takes out another apple and gives it to Lita, not bothering to rub it.

"And don't spit out the skin," she says. "The apple's heart is in its seeds, but its soul is in its skin."

Maria opens her mouth to say something, but the woman begins a long monologue, unconcerned whether the girls understand Drungi. The woman is worried that her brew has become too hot—the insects need to be simmered, not boiled, otherwise the rich reds turn into useless browns and you might as well drag the yarn through the mud and be done with it. There are enough Greek and Tatar words mixed into what the woman is saying for them to grasp the gist. Maria bites into her apple, avoiding the area with a wormhole. "No, eat that bit!" the tall woman shouts, pointing at the apple. "It's the best part! And if there's a worm in it thank Saint Penelope; its bitter entrails have medicines that will make you bear boys, many boys, and your master will want you all the more!" she says, pointing at the wedding dress. "A man wants his family to be filled with men, not women!" She wrinkles her nose in disgust. "Daughters are worthless, and their dowries eat up a man's sheep and fields! I was one of five daughters, and my father died in an empty sheep pen!"

Maria and Lita nod.

"But when it comes to making dye, it's only womenfolk who count!" the tall woman goes on. "Seeking a man who knows his dyes is like seeking cow dung in a field without cows." She lifts the hem of her caftan, baring her strong brown knees, and with it grabs the hot rim of one of the cauldrons. She tips it lightly to the side so that some of the dye, which is threatening to boil over, will pour out onto the earth. "Only womenfolk! We make the dye, and these beetles are she-beetles! Only she-beetles! Mix just one man-beetle into the brew and your color turns foul."

The woman looks down the slope at the Turks, who are rolling up their prayer carpets.

22

THE VILLAGE ELDER LIVES IN the last house beneath the ridge, beyond the reach of the marauders who once roamed the valley and are sure to again as the Sultan's hold on his eastern provinces weakens. On the ridge above the house, two granite pillars point obliquely into the sky like slanting minarets. The village elder says that they were once the frame of a catapult with a hurling arm and heavy ropes, the holy catapult with which Nimrod hurled Abraham into a great bonfire burning in the valley. There is also a hoofprint in the stone beneath the pillars that was made by the Virgin Mary's donkey when she visited the village on her way to Mount Ararat and rested in the shade of the holy catapult.

The village elder's house cuts into the side of the mountain and is surprisingly large inside. On the lower level are the barn and stables; above, a single spacious room is separated into two sections by a partition of cloth hangings, and the walls are gray and black with centuries of smoke from the hearth and the chimney. The men's section is on the outside, with narrow, deep-set windows looking out over the valley and the winding river. The sequestered women's section is deeper inside, its floor covered with musty carpets and cushions, its windows all on one side, facing an inner yard. A large wooden shed for the maidservants has been built as an extension onto the women's area. From the yard that curves around the house like a horseshoe come the sounds of girls' voices and clattering looms.

The village elder, along with three of his grown sons, is sitting with the priest and the Turk, hidden from view in the men's section of the house, talking and smoking flower-scented tobacco rolled into rough brown paper cigarettes. An odor of smoke and rancid milk is seeping through the cloth hangings. Maria is sitting silently on a straw pillow in the women's section, surrounded by bowls of lamb pilaf and tiny goblets of thick, bitter coffee, while Lita and the other unsold girls are outside in an open shed by the looms. She hears Lita talking and laughing, but can't make out what she is saying. Lita always manages to enjoy herself, wherever she is, Maria thinks; she would prefer to be outside with her, to see what the girls are weaving, but knows that, as the Drungi women have mistaken her for an honored guest, she has to sit with them, tasting whatever they serve her.

The elder's wife, a small leathery woman, picks up her coffee goblet, takes a long sip and, tilting her head back, empties the thick grounds into her mouth. She chews the grounds, her teeth and lips brown, nodding and smiling at Maria, "*Kep klessa, kep klessa!*"—"So pretty, so pretty!" She waves to Maria, encouraging her to drink her coffee, and Maria takes a sip, the grainy liquid spreading over her tongue like poisonous mud and sand. She feels an uneasiness in her stomach. Unlike the tall dour woman by the cauldrons near the riverbank, the elder's wife seems convinced that Maria can't understand anything she says. Five other women are sitting on broad cushions, crushing and rubbing herbs and roots for dyes. Two small girls and a little boy, all wearing long dresses patched

together from bright goat-hair cloth, are shredding onion skins
and tiny purple cabbages with what look like miniature axes. The
whole household seems to be preparing dyes. Village women come
visiting, their hands red with dye, some standing in groups by the
wall, others sitting down on cushions by the village elder's wife.
The women discuss how much Maria must have cost, and they call
out numbers to one another in liras and kurush. The elder's wife
notices that Maria is watching the children chopping the pink and
purple vegetables. "Tell her that those are for our reds," she says to
the other women, leaning toward them but still smiling at Maria
and bobbing her head. A plump woman, with a goiter that she is
trying to conceal under rows of coin necklaces, cranes her swollen
neck toward Maria and, like a mother teaching a new word to an
infant, rounds her lips and slowly mouths, "*red.*"

Maria repeats the word and smiles.

"She understood you!" the elder's wife says with delight, clapping her hands together. "Ask her how much her sandals cost."

"How much did your sandals cost?" the plump woman with
the goiter repeats slowly.

Maria looks at her.

The woman points to one of the coins on her necklace. "How
many coins did the sandals cost?"

Maria shakes her head. She sees that three small crosses have
been tattooed with black ash into the side of the woman's goiter to
halt its growth.

"Ask her how much that thing over there cost," the elder's wife
says, pointing at Maria's parasol, which had been folded and laid
across a pillow like a valuable ornament.

"How much?" the woman with the goiter asks, pointing
eagerly. "How much . . . how many coins? Coins?"

The elder's wife pushes a bowl of purplish olives, large as plums, toward Maria, who takes one. The olive is surprisingly rancid; alcohol pours over her tongue as she bites into its fermented flesh. Maria's instinct is to spit it out, but the women are watching her. The fingers of the elder's wife root among the oily olives in the bowl for the largest one, and she pops it into her mouth, then does the same with another, her cheeks puffing out as she chews. She spits the pits into her fist and places them by her foot on the carpet, wiping her mouth with the hem of her smock. She smiles encouragingly to Maria, points at the olives, and holds her hands out before her chest as if she is cupping large and heavy breasts, "They'll give you good milk, milk." She purses her lips and makes the suckling sounds of an infant. The woman with the goiter leans forward to pull the olive bowl closer to Maria, but Maria quickly shakes her head. The elder's wife then picks up two slices of meat, waves them over the plate to shake off any drippings, and holds them out to her, nodding her head in encouragement, and Maria takes them. The women begin discussing berries, nuts, and roots, and debating different dyes. Maria smiles at them when they turn to her. She finds that she is getting used to the strange way they speak. Their language is not really Greek or Tatar, she decides, but a funny jumble of both, in which words often start in one language and end in the other. The elder's wife is saying that a group of Zaza women on their way to the port town told her that they boiled dandelion roots for the deep pink in their skirt patterns. The elder's wife says she doubts they would manage to make their way safely through the roadblocks and past the soldiers hunting down rebels. It is foolish for women to wander about when desperate, womanless men are on the march, she says, and foolish for Zaza husbands to allow their wives to travel alone and unveiled in pink and purple dresses, more foolish than holding a lighted candle in the sun! She begins clapping her hands and singing in a strange, high-pitched voice: "The Armenians are fleeing to their Russian lords, but victory lies with our Sultan's swords." The other women clap their hands to the rhythm and join in the refrain. They stop singing as abruptly as they started and continue their conversation. "Women have no business going about on their own at any time," the woman with the goiter says, leaning over to Maria, forgetting that she might not understand. "If the Turkish men don't get you the Armenian men will, and if the Armenian men don't get you the Kurdish men will, and if they don't get you, there are all kinds of men behind every bush and tree, every rock and bend in the road! Men have wild eyes and lusting manhoods." She lays her hand on her coin necklaces as if to protect them.

The women discuss the widow Koftena, who was raped by four men from across the mountains early one morning while she was bringing in the sheep from the night-grazing pastures. She was almost fifty but became pregnant all the same. Koftena had tried to stop the pregnancy with salt and ash baths, feathers, and spells, but nothing worked, and the seed of the four men turned into a boy. She had known she would have a boy since she dreamt of knives and wild animals, and had seen a full moon in her sleep. For nine months she craved honey cakes and dried fruit in syrup. Boy cravings are sweet, the women said, and girl cravings are sour. Brown nipples mean boys, pink nipples mean girls. Dream of a string of beads, and you will bear a string of girls. The boy is now five and has Kurdish eyes, like the men who raped the widow Koftena, the women say; the boy's eyes are bright and brown like almonds, like polished bronze.

The village elder's wife nods her head gravely, and the women again begin discussing the Zaza women's dyes. Do they use hemlock bark or elderberries for their darker purples? Wild raspberries or grapes? Cloudberries or whortleberries? Maria sees a baby rat run along the edge of the carpet and disappear in a gap between the hangings that separate the men's and women's sections of the room. The elder's wife reaches back and smooths down the carpet as if the rat had rumpled it, and then pats the dust from her hands.

On the other side of the hangings the men are discussing the sleeping arrangements for the night. The Turk tries to place two large coins in the elder's hand to pay for his hospitality, but the elder refuses them. The Turk insists, says the coins are a gift for his kindness, but the elder keeps protesting that he and Father Andreas are honored guests. The main question is where Maria is to sleep. That she will sleep in the elder's house—the best and most secure in the village—is understood. And yet, even though this Christian household is divided into a men's and a women's section like a Muslim house, what is to prevent one of the elder's sons from getting up in the night and, in the drowsy confusion of slumber, pushing aside the hangings and deflowering Maria? No male over the age of five can be allowed to sleep anywhere on the premises where she will sleep. Maria's sale papers are to be finalized the following day down by the port, and her future will be as ruined as the Turk's finances if, after all the negotiations and down payments, she has to be sent back to the barracks in disgrace. The elder says that the men of his household will sleep on the roof, as they do in the hot nights of summer, while Maria sleeps inside the house with the women of the elder's family. The hangings would be raised, and the women would have the whole house to themselves. That way the matrons could also act as guards for the night. Lita and the other unsold girls could sleep with the elder's serving maids in the shed. The Turk and the priest would camp in the horseshoe-shaped yard in front of the two entrances, and the unsold boys and the muleteers of the caravan would camp in a nearby meadow.

The elder's wife, who has been following the men's conversation on the other side of the hangings, nods and smiles at Maria, then turns abruptly to the other women and says, "Tell her she will sleep here with us."

The woman with the goiter again leans toward Maria, her coin necklaces tinkling. She points at the carpet in front of Maria and slowly, mouthing the words as one might to a deaf woman, says, "You will sleep here with us."

Maria nods.

A sallow but strangely beautiful young woman, not much older than Maria, comes in from the yard and sets a coffee pot to boil over the large flame of a porcelain lamp. She does not acknowledge Maria's presence but cowers near the lamp, waiting for the water to boil. She keeps her head turned away from the other women. The lamp is glazed in beautiful blues; thick Greek letters have been painted on its base with the simplicity of a child's writing, spelling out words in a wild, disintegrated Greek: *Patirim pou esti sto ayera,* "My Father who is in the air." *Pou na elthi i Vassilia ss,* "O, if only Your Kingdom would come." The pestles, mortars, and polished metal jars lining the floor along the walls also bear Greek letters. There are Greek letters everywhere, but they mostly spell strange and Greekless phrases from east of the border. The sallow young woman's hands move quickly and nervously, throwing coarse black coffee powder into the water and stirring it with a long, bone-like stick. She approaches Maria and pours some more coffee into one of the goblets. Maria catches a glimpse of her eyes and sees that they are a bright, almost unnatural blue, the color of the evil eye. Maria looks away, as do the other women.

At the far end of the room, the part that has been cut into the mountain, there is a small alcove with a stone altar. An unusually large icon of the Holy Virgin stands at its center, her thin, yellow face staring into the room with unforgiving eyes. There is no infant Jesus, which puzzles Maria, as she knows that the Holy Virgin must never appear without him. She is pointing enigmatically at a lamb that is standing stiffly before three large ears of wheat painted in shining gold. The icon seems ancient, perhaps from the days when the Drungi served the Roman rulers of Byzantium, but the golden ears of wheat look freshly painted, still glistening and wet. If Maria knelt before the Virgin and kissed the icon, she thinks, the wheat would gild her lips. Along the front of the altar, flickering wicks float in glasses of sooty yellowish oil; beside them stand bowls of grain and uncured olives. Two large milk-white stones, almost identical in shape and as round as ostrich eggs, stand on either side of the icon.

The sallow woman goes up to the altar, bows before the icon, places a goblet of coffee next to the bowls, claps her hands once, and mumbles something.

"Wife! More coffee!" the elder's voice barks from across the carpet partition, and to Maria's surprise the sallow young woman bows toward the partition and replies, "Yes, Master!"

Maria looks at the leathery old woman who was presented as the elder's wife, suddenly wondering who she is, and who the other women are. The old woman addressed them each as "sister," but looking at them now Maria realizes that their difference in age is too great for them to be siblings. The idea suddenly strikes her that they might all be the elder's wives, and she wonders if, like the Prophet Lot, the elder has married his daughters and granddaughters, a terrible and frightening thought.

The sallow young woman covers her face with her scarf, places a large silver canister and glasses in metal holders on a platter, and carries the platter to the carpet partition where she kneels, pulls one of the hangings slightly to the side, and, averting her eyes, slides the tray across the floor into the men's section of the room.

23

THE CARAVAN IS TO SET out after the priest's morning service, which is to be held outside the burned-out chapel at the edge of the village. Last winter a leaning candle set the chapel's wooden lattices alight, destroying the ancient icons in front of the altar sanctuary, though the villagers managed to carry out the other icons lining the walls. These are now kept in a granary near the elder's house, their silver and gold darkened by smoke and soot, and the elder's kinsmen bring them in a solemn procession to the ruins of the chapel for every Mass.

Maria wakes up feeling slightly ill, the heavy food from last night souring her stomach. She drinks from a jug of unpleasantly salty water, still warm from having been boiled, that one of the women must have put next to her straw sack while she was still asleep. She can hear animals snorting and stamping in the large stables and pens that make up the ground floor of the house, and there is a sour reek of milk and smoke coming from the hearth. The village dogs and the wolves in the nearby forest are yelping and howling; the wolves seem close enough to the village to seize the sheep that have been taken out for night grazing, but the women don't seem concerned. She sees a stream of ants scurrying across the musty sheepskin blanket that lies folded next to her, and she sleepily brushes them away with her hand. At first light the disheveled wives of the elder—it has become clear that they are all indeed his wives—are already bustling about the room, talking loudly and dragging pots of milk to the fireplace, while Maria, exhausted from yesterday's long ride, drifts in and out of sleep. The woman with the goiter, who took off her coin necklaces only after she lay down for the night, and is now wearing them again, is carving thick slices from a chunk of cheese that has been fermenting in a sheepskin sack and slapping them loudly into a large bowl. The sheep had been skinned and the skin turned inside out so that the raw milk and rennet poured into the hairy inside would mature; the woman with the coin necklaces now darts her knife into the bowl, flicking out the dead animal's hairs. As she crouches by the sack, her palm shoots out to squash any beetles that scuttle past, which she then flicks under the carpet.

•

Neatly kerchiefed and dressed, the women start climbing the hill toward the burned-out chapel. In the morning mist the gray shell of its nave looks like the skull of a dead man, the two blackened holes of its doors staring down on the village like hollow eyes. Maria follows the women, the muddy path soiling her new slippers. The ripped-open body of a cat lies in the mud by a patch of weeds, and Maria sees the pack of wolfish dogs that must have killed it milling about farther up the path by a refuse heap. A gust of wind brings the stench from the open sewers, yellow and brown spume flowing from the houses down to the river; she covers her nose with her kerchief. She wishes her mother was with her, though she knows that her mother would not have been a comfort. The villagers jostle one another and crowd into the chapel's yard, and Maria, pushed to the side, cranes her neck trying to find Lita and the other unsold girls; she peers through the crowd of people but can't see Lita anywhere. Father Andreas begins chanting the Mass, surrounded by men holding the icons that the elder's kinsmen have brought. Two villagers next to the priest are holding a large icon that shows Adam preaching from a golden pulpit to kneeling angels, while God, gray headed and gray bearded, blows the first words of man into his body. The words are Greek. Maria looks at God's face; it is expressionless and brown, the face of an elder burned by the sun. She has never seen such a huge icon before: it is taller than a man. She notices that some of the angels have three wings, some even four and five; the higher the angels' rank, the more wings they have, and she wonders how an angel can fly with three wings, tilting and pitching across the sky. As Father Andreas chants, the villagers begin calling out prayer responses, seemingly at random, crossing themselves and clapping their hands together before the icons. They seem to be conducting their own pagan service alongside the priest's Orthodox Matins, and Maria looks at Father Andreas, expecting him to stop chanting and call the unruly congregation to order, but he does not seem to notice. Maria begins to make her way through the crowd. She does not see Lita outside the chapel precinct either. It only becomes apparent that she has disappeared when everyone gathers after the service and the Turk's men begin saddling the horses and packing the mules.

Father Andreas's face turns gray. He speaks a few words to the Turk, and then, with the elder in tow, hurries up the path toward the pasture.

"What happened?" Maria calls out to one of the unsold girls, who steps back and raises her hands to her face, as if she is afraid Maria will hit her. "What happened?" Maria repeats. "Where's Lita?"

"We thought she was with you," the girl says, and begins to sob. "Do you think we'll all be sent back?"

Maria hugs her and pats her hair. "Don't worry, we won't be sent back," she says, and then realizes that the girl is hoping that Lita's escape means that they can now return to their parents in the barracks. The other girls begin crying too, and Maria steps back, unsure of what to say. A crowd has gathered, women and men calling out in a jumble of Drungi and Turkish where they think Lita might be. Maria looks around but can see neither the Turk nor any of the elder's wives. The boys seem to have disappeared too, but then she sees them playing near the pools of dye farther up the path. Their hands will turn red, she thinks; it will take much scrubbing to wash away the dye. She is surprised that she would think such a thing at a time like this. The villagers are convinced that Lita has wandered in her sleep over the night pastures into the forest, where demons and tongue-snatchers lurk. At night, they say, devils roll through the forests like wheels, seizing maidens who walk among the trees. "The poor girl, the poor girl," they keep saying. The Turk's muleteers and guards, who have finished loading the animals, begin pushing the villagers away.

Father Andreas and the village elder come back down the path without Lita, and Maria can see that the priest is struggling to contain himself and not shout oaths and recriminations. The Turk appears, carrying his prayer carpet, and Maria hears him and the priest exchange words—the priest agitated, the Turk calm. The villagers insist on forming a search party to venture into the forest, and Father Andreas, after trying first gently then almost angrily to stop them, finally gives his blessing. It is clear to him that Lita is not in the forest but has returned to the barracks, and he knows that the Turk will not permit a further delay. Maria has to be brought to the port in time for the papers of her sale to be prepared and for the Trebizond steamer. The unsold girls and boys are, as Father Andreas knows, of little importance to the Turk, who has offered to find buyers for them more as a favor to him, though the Turk will obviously be paid a commission if they are sold. Lita is capable enough of looking after herself; if she is lost, she will sooner or later come to a village or settlement. It is agreed that if the Drungi villagers find her, the elder will look after her until the priest returns after Maria's sale has been completed.

24

MARIA AND THE PRIEST ARE riding side by side behind the Turk and the guards, who again point their rifles at every bend in the path—but more anxiously this time, Maria thinks. The Turk has taken along three young Drungi men as extra guards, not in fear of the dangers that might lie ahead, but to impress the soldiers and sentries at the barricades and checkpoints: the more guards a man travels with, the more important he is. She notices that the Turk is wearing a new fez and an elegant shirt. He has purchased several Drungi carpets, which hang in tight rolls on his pack mule with the sacks and small leather boxes. The Turk has also bought Maria a billowing red caftan, its bodice heavily embroidered, since the sleeves of the dead girl's wedding dress were short and wide, and slipped up to expose her elbows whenever she raised her parasol. The wedding dress now lies safely packed away in one of the saddlebags, and Maria is resolved never to wear it again. She has been given coarse woolen stockings that make her slippers feel tight, as have the unsold girls on the horses behind her, who were barefoot yesterday, but are now wearing the stockings and Drungi sandals made of goatskin and straw: soon the caravan will reach the first military checkpoints, manned by the Sultan's unruly soldiers, and the girls' elbows and ankles, as well as their faces, must be hidden from sight.

The landscape is starker now. Yesterday's forests have thinned out into a ravaged plain covered with cracked stones and ancient rubble, the ruins of a sprawling fortress laid waste by Alexander the Great on his march deeper into Asia. Alexander's thirty thousand men camped here, encircling the enemy with a noxious desert, hacking down trees, shoveling earth and ash into the river, poisoning the waters with oil and manure. Warrior women from across the river joined forces with Alexander, tall and severe in their high feathered headdresses, the severed hands of the enemy strung in garlands to their saddles, their fire spears torching the enemy's granaries. The women blocked the river in front of the fortress, building dams with the bodies of the soldiers they had killed, and then released the waters in a great wave of mud and corpses. The banks of the river are still shattered; the former riverbed, dry and full of stones, coils away from the new river into another valley. The new river's waters are slower and deeper.

The side of the path has fallen away in a landslide, and the horses and mules of the caravan have to climb a steep, narrow trail winding upward over a hill and down again on the other side where the path continues into the valley. Maria is crying silently, her kerchief tied loosely across her face, her parasol tilted toward the priest so he cannot see her. She realized immediately after the morning's service, when all the commotion began, that Lita had run away and was heading back to the barracks, that she had not been seized by bandits or forest spirits as the Drungi villagers seemed to think. Lita's suggestion the day before that they make their way back to the barracks together had not been a sudden whim: she must have been planning her escape throughout the day, Maria thinks, remembering Lita sitting silently on the horse behind her. Maria realizes that she was so immersed in her own thoughts and fears yesterday that Lita's unusual silence didn't strike her as strange. Lita, who had always been so carefree, who hadn't seemed to think twice about leaving her mother and brothers behind in the barracks, a girl who was wandering in air, as people back in the village would have said, clearly had a side to her that Maria had not understood. Maria's first thought this morning was that she had betrayed Lita by letting her run away alone, by not going with her; but by the time the caravan left the Drungi village and it became clear that she would never see Lita again, her feelings of guilt gave way to a much stronger conviction, in which anger mingled with despair, that it was Lita who had betrayed her. Lita had known that as a promised bride, Maria could not have returned to the barracks; once a bride was sent out she could not return, unless it was her husband who sent her back; it was unthinkable for a bride to run away from her own bridal caravan. In her anger Maria thinks that Lita was not as clever as she seemed. She was an unbridled tongue, as Black Melpo would have said, a girl of quick words and flighty action, and what she did would have terrible consequences. Why did she not stay until Father Andreas found her the husband he intended? What prospects would Lita now have? Who would marry her? Maria unties the kerchief from across her face; it is wet with tears, and she dries her eyes on her sleeve. She looks at Father Andreas and sees him reach for his honeypot, trying to uncork it without dropping his horse's reins. She feels queasy and hungry, but does not want to ask the priest if he has some bread in his saddlebag. She turns her head and looks back; one of the guards is now riding Lita's horse, his rifle resting across the saddle as he gazes down the slope at the riverbank. There is a crossing, a floating bridge of chained wooden boats, but the waters have been rising with the melting mountain snows, and the boats are being unchained and moored along the opposite bank.

"The Drungi are obsessed with their saints!" Father Andreas suddenly says loudly. Maria raises her parasol slightly and peeks at him, but sees that he is not looking at her but at the river. The Turk looks back, thinking that the priest is speaking to him, but then looks ahead again. "Before they pray to the Virgin or Christ," Father Andreas continues, "they pray to the Wise Nun Pelagia or Penelope the Holy Princess. If the Archbishop only knew!" He shakes his head.

"Who are the Wise Nun Pelagia and Penelope the Holy Princess?" Maria asks, and Father Andreas turns and looks at her in surprise, as if he has forgotten she is there. He is amazed that a young girl would have the boldness to ask him a direct question. Even a boy older than she would not dare do such a surprising and audacious thing. He knows that in the lands across the border, among the mountain folk where she is from, women are not permitted to even speak in the presence of men. He looks at Maria, narrowing his eyes, but despite her forwardness he is not angry.

"The Wise Nun Pelagia was . . . She danced with a group of girls at banquets. The wise nun was not lewd," he adds quickly, "it's just that her dancing was what one might call . . . Well, she sometimes didn't wear very much." He pulls the pot of honey out of his saddlebag again. "This is medicine I have to take," he explains to Maria, and is surprised that he feels the need to explain himself to her. There is a cleverness in the girl that runs deep and somehow unsettles him, he realizes, though not in a bad way. He knows she can read and write: he had seen her reading one of the Greek Trebizond newspapers he had left outside his shack with a pile of kindling. He had gone up to her, amazed at the sight of a village girl reading a newspaper as if she were a lady from the city, and asked her to read the article to him. This she did, speaking the words with a fluency as if they were her own. He also knows that she has worked for a medicine mixer and probably knows the good and evil in plants as well as any apothecary in the town. He remembers the words from the Tatar epic she recited so unexpectedly when the Turk was first viewing the girls. *From my diamond palace by the emerald lake.* If she were a boy, he thinks, she could have been sent to study at the Greek lyceum in Trebizond, or the seminary. He dips his finger into the sticky poison and raises it to his lips, but then thinks better of it; the honey is confusing him, and he needs to keep his wits. He carefully dabs the glob of honey on the rim of the pot, and quickly pushes the cork back in.

"What about Penelope the Holy Princess?" Maria asks.

"That's Saint Irene," he replies, looking at her again surprised, but relieved that she doesn't seem interested in the dancing nun. "She was Princess Penelope. The Church calls her Saint Irene, but the villagers here still call her Holy Penelope. When she became a Christian she ran through her father's palace breaking all his statues and throwing his jewels to the crowd of peasants who had gathered in front of the palace." He looks toward the pass that is now visible in the mountains before them, feeling a rising anxiety.

"What will happen to Lita, Father Andreas?" Maria suddenly asks, amazed, after the question has slipped from her tongue, at her audacity.

He looks at her, and she lowers her parasol again so he can't see her face. "We'll be able to see the Black Sea from there," he says glumly, pointing at the pass.

There is a sudden clatter of hooves, and a band of soldiers comes galloping toward them around a bend in the path. The Turk's guards quickly lower their rifles and bow their heads. The soldiers are escorting a prisoner, a pale man with white-blond hair who is sitting hunched forward on a black horse. He is wearing tattered trousers and a stained shirt whose collar has remained absurdly stiff. Heavy chains with links thicker than fingers are wound around his torso in what seems an unnecessary precaution, since his hands are bound so tightly to the pommel of his saddle that he is unable to sit upright. As the riders draw nearer, the prisoner shouts a foreign word in a pitiful, high-pitched voice. The Turk waves at the soldiers, but they gruffly motion him out of the way and ride past, veering off the narrow path to avoid the caravan, their horses galloping through the weeds at the edge of the meadow. The blond man shouts the same word again, this time at the priest. As they ride past Maria, the soldier behind the blond man turns his head to look at her, and she catches her breath in fear. But they ride on, and she wonders where the soldiers are taking him, as the only settlement up the path is the Drungi village. She looks at the Turk, who is clearly angry at having been snubbed by the soldiers.

"That was not an Armenian rebel!" the Turk says, leaning back in his saddle to turn and throw a meaningful glance at the priest.

"No, definitely not," Father Andreas replies, shaken that the desperate man singled him out to save him: clearly a Christian man shouting to a Christian priest for help. But what could a priest do? The law is the law, and it is not for a man of the cloth to interfere. "I would say he was too blond to be an Englishman," the priest continues. "Perhaps German?"

"What he was shouting didn't sound like German to me. Not Russian either, though he could have been one of those Russian officers from across the border."

"I think he will need the Last Rites before the day is out," the priest says darkly. The clatter of hooves has subsided in the distance, and the air is filled once again with the sounds of birds and the flowing water of the river.

"Those people have three faces," the Turk says.

"What people?" the priest asks.

"Those Drungi of yours. To me they show their Muslim face, and to you their Christian one, but in truth they are infidel pagans."

"No, no, they *are* Christians!" Father Andreas says, relieved that the Turk is not drawing him into a subversive discussion about the Sultan's soldiers and perhaps tricking him into saying something that he, as a Greek and a loyal citizen of the Ottoman Empire, should not say. "They are Christians, but they have strange ways."

"That elder has more wives than any Turkish village chief!" the Turk says. He leans back in his saddle to look at the priest. "How many? Five, six? They told me he has four wives and two concubines, but that he is legally married to them all." The Turk laughs. "Legally. Probably in that burned-out church of theirs. And do you know why his best mules had their tails cut off?"

Father Andreas looks at the Turk blankly; he had not noticed any mules with missing tails.

"Those mules had belonged to the elder's dead brother," the Turk continues. "He told me so himself. Their tails were cut off to show that the animals were in mourning. I'm surprised that your Church allows that sort of thing."

"Some animals are upset when their masters die," the priest says, realizing that this is a foolish non sequitur.

"The elder's brother was buried in a sitting position," the Turk goes on, and then adds, "together with his favorite horse! What do you say to that?"

Father Andreas shakes his head, shocked that the Turk has found out about these unchristian rites after spending just one night in the village, whereas he, who has been there a number of times over the years to sing Mass and explain the Gospels, knows nothing about them. The Drungi must be forgiven for their strange ways, he thinks; their ancestors were rough warriors, wild early Christians, who in the years of the first Christian Emperors of Byzantium slaughtered the pagan men of these lands and took their womenfolk in holy matrimony. They have lived here in ignorance and isolation for a thousand years, their Christian rites dissolving with the passing generations, until churchmen from Trebizond, with whips and muskets, forced them into the river to be rebaptized, slaughtering all of those who would not bow their heads to Christ. The Turk turns to Father Andreas, expecting him to say something, but the priest smiles at him and looks away.

25

AT THE SIDE OF THE path is a stone chapel, the size of a horse shed, and Father Andreas and the children cross themselves three times as they ride past it. It is the chapel of Saint Judas, and the priest notices that the cross on its roof is missing and that some of the rough columns of its basilica have been smashed. Next to the chapel is a small tomb made of rough slabs of marble in which lie old Bibles, too faded to read but too holy to discard. He asks the Turk if they can stop for a moment, then dismounts, walks back toward the chapel, and pulls the door open by its rusty latch. The chapel is empty: its icons and the casket with its relics have been stolen; the only thing left is a broken candle holder lying on the floor by the door.

Narrow trails descend the steep slopes from hidden villages and join the main path, which broadens into a dirt road. A village woman wearing a man's tunic and a brown, square-patterned dress is coming down the slope, balancing a large basket on her head. Behind her limps a small donkey on which a man seems to be dozing in the saddle. The donkey's harness is made from bits of string and oily tufts of fur knotted together in a tangle, and the reins look as if they might slip out of the man's hand at any moment. When they are within earshot of the caravan the man sits up with a jolt and quickly motions the woman out of the way. "Seen any Armenians?" he shouts to the Turk.

The Turk shakes his head with the air of a man who does not converse with peasants.

"Woman, the beast needs water!" the villager barks at his wife in a show of authority that seems calculated to impress the Turk, and the woman leads the donkey off the path and down toward the riverbank, her husband still bowing in the direction of the caravan.

Maria watches the woman making her way down the slope. Though she is veiled, there is something familiar about her, Maria thinks. It is the dress the woman is wearing, with its drab, quilt-like pattern of brown squares, she realizes. Maria was four or five, wading through knee-deep snow on the mountainside holding on to the hem of her mother's dress, which had the same brown, quilt-like pattern. Like this woman, her mother also wore a man's tunic over her dress, and was staggering through the snow with a large pile of branches and firewood tied on her back, while Maria pulled a bundle of kindling behind her through the snow. These were the shortest and coldest days of the year, as two nights joined into one so that the Virgin Mary could give birth hidden from the rays of the malevolent sun. Maria and her mother trudged past the mosque and the death house, its red stones glittering in the snow, and she remembers Heraclea's cooing, panting voice: "Keep pulling, my treasure, keep pulling! We'll soon be there, my golden girl." Maria had forgotten that her mother once called her "my treasure" and "my golden girl." Heraclea was younger then; in her later, bitter middle years, her endearments were only for her sons. "Look at all the snowflakes," Heraclea had said. "If we had a kopeck for every hundred snowflakes that touch the ground, we would soon have a ruble." Maria looked up at the sky, snowflakes blowing into her eyes. Her mother's shoulders and the large pile of branches on her back were covered in white. The roof of the shack beyond the meadows of Saint Achilles had caved in under the weight of the snow, and Heraclea and Maria were now taking all the firewood and provisions back to the dry storerooms beneath the house. Work needs strong shoulders, the village proverb said, and it is the womenfolk whose shoulders are the strongest. Maria's father had returned from Batum just as the snow began to fall and was sitting in the coffee house on the village square, talking with the other men over small cups of strong, sweet coffee. He had his sons with him so they could hear him discuss trade and learn the ways of buying and selling. Carrying was not a man's job. Men have men's work and women have women's work, Heraclea had told Maria, but as men now often left the village to work far away, women also had to mend roofs, build walls, stoke charcoal kilns, and shoe the horses and mules.

The veiled woman stops and turns to look up at the path, her husband pointing at Maria, a young lady with a parasol seated on a horse, who is looking at them with evident interest. Maria, startled, realizes that she has been staring at the woman.

"The beast needs water!" the villager calls out again and bows to Maria as he sits unsteadily on his donkey.

More villagers and swarms of children in dirty rags come down the trails, many carrying sacks of market produce on their backs. Most are mountain Turks or Greeks, but there are also some Armenian villagers, who seem unaware of the dangers awaiting them in the town. An old man, his face burned purple by the sun, comes hurrying down the path with two large, finely-polished cedar boxes strapped to his shoulders. Two boys of about ten, with field flowers in their tangled hair, are limping after him, carrying bundles and bags. The boxes on the old man's back are decorated with black cuneiform symbols copied from Hittite tablets, a theatrical hint that there might be something ancient and mysterious hidden inside. The old man is wearing a dirty white cap with a stained piece of leather wrapped around its rim, and wide pantaloons held up by a red sash. He calls out to the Turk, pointing to his boxes. At first the Turk tries to wave him out of the way, but then he turns and glances at the priest, raises his hands in a gesture of resignation, and motions the caravan to stop. The old man quickly puts the boxes down in front of the Turk's horse and begins to tug at the latches. The horse tosses its head, and the Turk pats it gently on the side of the neck. The old man is panting heavily and has to steady himself as he kneels. Sweat trickles down his face. He tugs at the latches one last time, and the lid opens. The two boys behind the old man have taken goatskin tambourines out of their bundles and are looking at him expectantly. They might be mistaken for girls, Maria thinks, were they not bare-chested and wearing dusty red loincloths that seem to be made of velvet. The old man claps his hands together and the boys immediately begin to dance around the box, raising their arms and waving their tambourines, jerking their hips rhythmically from side to side mimicking feminine enticement. Maria watches them shake their thin chests the way voluptuous dancing girls might. They are clearly not the man's children or grandchildren, she thinks, for what father or grandfather would allow his boys to draw the eyes of men? They must be orphans, glad for a bowl of food, or children sold to the old man by desperate parents.

The Turk leans forward over his horse's head to look into the box, and then quickly leans back in disgust. He glares at the old man. "Those are creatures of Allah!" he shouts.

"But look how cheerful they are!" the old man wheezes, pointing into the box. "And I taught them all they know!" He snaps his fingers and the two little boys stop dancing, one of them quickly crouching down to pick up some petals that have fallen out of his hair. The old man peers eagerly past the Turk at the priest, Maria, and the unsold girls sitting in their saddles with their dark umbrellas.

Again he points into the box. "Come look, come look! This box is filled with magic creatures, and I taught them everything!" he shouts, trying to attract the attention of the whole caravan. "I taught them everything—to run, jump, swing on swings, pull golden chariots!"

"Those boxes are full of fleas!" the Turk says contemptuously, turning to the priest. "A flea circus! He's glued them to all kinds of contraptions!" He again leans over the horse's head and peers into the boxes. "You taught them all that?"

"Yes, yes! I taught them all they know!"

The Turk motions for the barracks children to come to the front of the caravan and look into the boxes. Maria slides off her mount, almost dropping her parasol in her haste, and hurries with the others to where the boxes lie. Inside one of them is a miniature arena, inlaid with what look like mother-of-pearl tracks separated from each other by a small rim, along which fleas are dragging tiny gold-paper chariots glued to their backs. The fleas are racing along with great energy, but it is unclear whether they are trying to outrun one another or dashing forward in a desperate attempt to shake off their burdens. The second box presents an even wilder spectacle, with fleas dangling from swings and trapezes, whirling at great

speed on merry-go-rounds, and glued to the gondolas of a miniature Ferris wheel, their tiny wings fluttering as the old man spins
the wheel with his finger. The barracks children clap their hands
in delight. Some of the girls step back, afraid that the fleas might
jump out of their amusement park and hop up their caftans. Maria
notices that some of the fleas are dead. One of the dancing boys
grabs her by the wrist, and she tries to draw her hand back. He
tugs her toward him, stronger than she would have thought, and
says something to her in a language she does not understand, his
words rhyming and his voice high as if he is reciting a riddle. His
fingers are gripping her wrist painfully, and he stares at her, waiting
for an answer. Alarmed, she shakes her head, and the boy darts his
tongue out at her and lets go of her hand. The other dancing boy
laughs and jiggles his hips at her. Maria looks around, but nobody
has noticed. The Turk throws two coins into the dust; the old man
rushes to pick them up, and the caravan moves on, Maria hurrying
to climb back into her saddle. The old man leaves his boxes at the
side of the path, closing them carefully, and tries to catch up with
the Turk, holding up three rusty nails, glancing over his shoulder
to make sure his dancing boys are guarding his boxes. "Nails, nails,
they're cheap, almost free, for you almost free!" he pants, but the
Turk waves him away. "You never know when they might come in
handy! You can hammer them in anywhere!" he says plaintively.
"Three nails!" He holds them out to the priest, who ignores him.

•

It begins to rain, slowly at first, then in showers. The Turk seems
unperturbed, but the priest cowers in his saddle, his soaked cassock
clinging to his thighs. Maria offers him her parasol, but he refuses

it. A donkey cart comes rolling toward them, its large wooden wheels creaking loudly. It slowly lumbers to a halt to let them pass. In it sits a thin man, his legs shockingly swollen, behind him a heap of skinned and bleeding animal carcasses, mainly rodents. Some of the red glistening bodies still have strips of matted fur on their haunches. There is a wet stench, though the animals look freshly killed. The man is wearing a wide, blood-speckled caftan, as his legs are too bloated to fit into trousers, and he has raised the caftan immodestly above his knees in order to cool his legs in the rain. Maria and the other girls look away. He lifts his hand, and in a pleasant, singsong voice calls out, "Armenians, Armenians." The Turk nods sympathetically, though it is unclear whether the man is asking whether they are Armenians, or warning them against Armenians, or inquiring whether they have seen any along the way.

"There's war in the town!" the man shouts, pointing back down the path. "War! War!"

Maria looks back at the cart as the caravan rides by and sees the man staring after them, craning his neck over the heap of flayed carcasses. She notices a string of flatbreads hanging from the side of the cart, their crusts spattered with blood. Further up the path, just before the roadblock by the pass, a dead mule lies in the rain. It has been dragged into the meadow, and men and women in wet rags have put down their sacks and bales and are carving pieces of meat from the animal's flanks.

More people are now coming toward the caravan, villagers who have been turned back at the pass. "They aren't letting anyone through!" they call out. "Turn back, turn back!"

At the roadblock there are over forty soldiers in torn and muddied uniforms, but only two are guarding the pass and checking travel permits. The Turk unloads his pistol and raises it in the air for the soldiers to see. Army carts with mounted guns line the road, and unharnessed horses are grazing in the meadow. A small, odd-looking cannon has been set up but then left unmanned on this side of the pass; a row of cannonballs the size of billiards, glistening in the rain, are stacked neatly beside it. Most of the local villagers who have been trying to take their animals and produce to the port are being sent back up the path. A palsied boy of about fifteen is lying on a muddy blanket watching the approaching caravan, his thin arms stretching out and moving aimlessly, the rain dripping into his eyes. He is shirtless, his chest thin and crooked, his torn trousers soiled. There are red marks across his chest as if he has been whipped, and there is a bleeding cut on his shoulder. A group of ragged, mud-caked men in shackles are sitting next to him by the roadside, waiting for an armed patrol to escort them to the prison in town. Maria watches the boy. He looks as if he is trying to say something, his arms reaching out. Someone must have brought him here and left him. It will be terrible if his people don't come back for him, she thinks. How will he live? He will die a terrible death, unable to ask for food or water. She notices that the soldiers and their captives are playing cards and rolling dice as if they were old friends. One of the captives nudges the boy and says something. The men slam the wet cards down onto the drenched ground, shouting obscenities and guffawing. They stare sheepishly at the incongruous caravan of girls, whose faces are hidden by kerchiefs, and who are guarded by muleteers and headed by a Turkish gentleman in an elegant fez and a Greek priest wearing a cassock. The Turk, without dismounting, greets the two soldiers standing guard and hands them the permits and passes for the caravan. The palsied boy moans, and the Turk turns and looks at him. One of the soldiers deferentially holds a newspaper over the Turk's hand so that the documents will not get wet in the rain, and it is clear from his demeanor that he has recognized in the Turk's face his resemblance to General Djemal.

"Has the cripple been fed?" the Turk asks, pointing to the palsied boy.

"Not yet, effendi," the soldier says, bowing. Maria sees the Turk's hand brush over that of the soldier with a flash of shimmering coins. The second soldier on guard walks up to the priest, two quails hanging from his belt, their blood dripping down the side of his trousers, and the priest looks at the dead birds with disgust.

"You a Greek man? Greek? You no Armenian man?" the soldier asks.

"Of course I am Greek, but what does my being Greek have to do with you?" the priest replies, angered at the soldier's insult of speaking broken Turkish to him as if he were an illiterate peasant from some remote province. "And why is that cripple lying by the roadside with the convicts? Have you arrested him too? Have you?"

The soldier, only momentarily taken aback by his sharp tone and elegant Turkish, pinches the hem of the priest's cassock, checking to see whether coins or gems are sewn into secret pouches. He raises his fist and shouts, "Turkey is the Turks!"

"Turkey is *for* the Turks!" the priest corrects him angrily. "Learn some Turkish first, and then we'll talk about who Turkey belongs to!" The soldier grins and walks back toward the army carts by the roadblock. "And for your information," Father Andreas shouts, Turkey is for *all* the people of the Empire!" He sees that the Turk is still conversing with the bowing guard and has not noticed the insults to which he was being submitted. He is about to call out to him but thinks better of it. He sees him point at the pack mule next to him, and one of the muleteers unknots a saddle sack and pulls out a round loaf of bread, handing it to the Turk. The Turk gives the bread to the guard, who again bows and with a grimace quickly tears off a piece and pushes it into his mouth. The Turk nods to the muleteer and then at the guard, and the muleteer gives the man a second loaf. "Feed the cripple," the Turk says.

26

AS THE CARAVAN REACHES THE first shacks on the fringe of the town, the rain suddenly becomes heavier, pelting the fields, and Maria holds her parasol close over her head. The road leads through a wide cemetery with broken and crumbling headstones and grave pillars on either side as far as she can see and there is a stench rising from the shallow graves. A pack of dogs comes running toward the caravan, tattered and mangy creatures. One of the muleteers fires a shot in the dogs' direction, and they run back toward the cemetery wall, where they stand barking and snarling. The stench worsens as the caravan rides on, and Maria raises her scarf to her nose. A flock of carrion crows is circling in the sky. She sees skulls by the roadside, and bones that have been dug up by the dogs. The cemetery seems abandoned but is not; many of the graves are freshly dug and are beginning to flood. A festering body in pantaloons and a torn pink headdress is lying in the watery mud and weeds, dug up by the dogs. Beyond the last graves are the first grimy houses, church domes, and minarets of the town, and behind them Maria sees the gray expanse of the Black Sea. It looks like a desert of steel, hard and cold, not like water at all. Father Andreas has told her that her first view of the sea would be like a revelation, that everyone who saw the sea for the first time was struck with admiration and even fear, its waters unimaginably deep; a ship could sail many days toward the horizon without coming upon land. But Maria is disappointed.

Her red caftan hangs from her shoulders in wet folds, and she holds the reins against her chest. The rain streams down her legs and over her stockings and slippers. The caravan comes to another roadblock, where drenched soldiers are sitting on sacks of sand. A row of glistening machine guns points aimlessly into the fields. A young soldier comes forward, holding a rifle from whose barrel hang rabbit feet for good luck and blue-eyed beads to ward off the evil eye. Two cartridge belts are crossed over his chest, and slung over his shoulder is a third that he must have just taken from a traveler. He speaks to the Turk, looking up at him with admiration, shielding his eyes from the rain. He, too, has noticed his resemblance to General Djemal, and is showing the deference he would have shown the general if he had appeared unannounced on the outskirts of the port. As the Turk knows, these illiterate soldiers might in fact think that he is the great Ahmed Djemal traveling on some secret mission, and is amused that word will soon make its way through the ranks that General Djemal is visiting the town; as if the general would come to this godforsaken end of the Empire. He looks at the soldier standing barefoot in the mud before him. He has heard that in the rioting province of Yemen the Sultan's soldiers are so starved that those who have boots gnaw at them to still their hunger; they are hacked down with machetes, too weak to stand up to the warriors of the desert, and the Imam of Yemen is proclaiming a new holy Caliphate, with himself as Commander of the Faithful. It is clear that the Empire is at its end. The Turk drops some coins into the soldier's open palm and raises his hand in a military greeting, the way the General might. The young soldier bows low and hurries along the caravan through the rain, shouting to every muleteer and barracks boy: "Armenian? You Armenian?" The Turk watches him coldly.

Lightning strikes close by with a loud crack, and the rain begins to fall even harder, the sharp volley of drops turning into cascades. The caravan rides on, and the Turk spreads his arms wide, his soaked shirt clinging to his body. The priest looks at him, repelled by his obvious delight. Lightning strikes again, and the priest almost loses his balance on his horse.

The Turk grins. "Great weather, don't you agree?" he calls out. "'Seest thou not that Allah sends down rain from the sky to clothe the earth with green?'" He winks at the priest.

"'Seest thou not that Allah stops the sky from falling on thine head, except by His will?'" the priest shouts back, pleased at the opportunity of displaying some wit despite his discomfort.

The Turk laughs and claps his hands, dropping the reins for an instant, but snatching them up again before they can slide down the horse's neck.

The town stretches along the shore in a tangle of wooden shacks and gray stone houses, some of which were wealthy mansions when the port, a few decades ago, was the gateway to the Empire's eastern lands. Every village in the borderland mountains has its own name for the town, but its inhabitants call it *Nusret*, the name of a great wooden warship that ran aground in the nearby shallows two hundred years ago. The ship's skeleton still lies on the beach. But it is an ancient Greek town, the priest has told Maria. A golden fleece was hidden upriver, an ancient magic fleece that had belonged to a sacred ram with wings. Princess Medea seized the fleece and sailed her ships for Greece, the warrior women of her guard using slingshots to hurl nests of scorpions onto their pursuers' ships. The leader of the pursuers, her brother Absyrtus, boarded her ship, expecting to find his sister cowering beneath deck, but Medea hacked him to pieces and scattered his body over the beaches outside the town. Her pursuers had to withdraw from the battle and gather the body parts, honor-bound as they were to put them in order and bury them. Father Andreas said he would show Maria the tomb, but he seems to have forgotten his promise, and Maria looks uneasily at the town stretching out before them with its crumbling minarets, stunted trees, and desolate houses. A thousand people living here, she thinks; you could walk all day through the streets of such a place without meeting anyone you knew. In the villages in the Caucasus, one never met strangers—even the peddlers and merchants from far away were known to everyone.

Father Andreas looks ill. The rain is not cold, but he rocks back and forth in his wet cassock as if to ward off a chill. Stray dogs with festering wounds limp out from behind roadside bushes and stand cowering in the rain, the caravan guards jabbing their rifles at them. Maria looks at the Turk sitting upright in his saddle, unperturbed by the rain. She thinks Lita must be back at the barracks by now, dry and safe, having walked much of the night and all day. She wonders how Lita was welcomed, and through her mind flit images of the men and women of the barracks rejoicing or cursing and raising sticks to hit her. She concludes that they will not be happy to see Lita again. They will be angry at her selfishness, her turning her back on the priest's effort to find her a wealthy master who would provide her family with riches and the priest with a commission that would help save the other refugees. No cat will leave a feast of plenty, yet Lita has cast aside a prosperous future. Lita will not be chased away from the barracks, Maria thinks, but she will be an outcast. Homeros will surely protect her. Perhaps he will even marry her; and yet, if she herself had remained in the barracks, Homeros might have wanted to marry her instead. But Kostis would not have given Maria to Homeros, for he knew, as she did, that a marriage to him would be one of hunger and poverty. Father Andreas has told Maria that if she does not disappoint her master, who will save her parents and secure her brothers' future, she will become happier and wealthier than anyone she has ever known. You cannot spin your own fate, Black Melpo always said, but you can sometimes choose the threads. Black Melpo could see the threads of fate in the animal entrails she cast, their tangle of membranes and veins revealing future secrets. The dead veins sucking in the sunlight are the paths of life, Maria knows, and the dark and dry blood clots are the people along those paths. Rings and loops at the ends of veins are nooses that mean death. What future would Black Melpo have foretold for Lita and Homeros? Would they ever make it to Greece? Lita's father and uncles now lived in Athens, but would they help her, Maria wonders, if she arrived there with a penniless husband they had not chosen for her?

The last time Maria saw Black Melpo was the day before the marauders ransacked the plantation and the village. On the morning of the raid, Black Melpo was nowhere to be found. Maria had gone to her hut before dawn as she did every day, but found it empty: Black Melpo, her cart, her mules, and her chickens were gone. There was an orange tree in the garden, and in the early morning light Maria saw that all its fruit had been plucked; all the artichokes had also been picked, a task Maria was supposed to do that week. Black Melpo must have loaded her cart with everything she

owned and left in the night, a strange thing to do in such dangerous times, when the whole Caucasus was in turmoil; and what is
even stranger, Maria thinks now, is that Black Melpo had managed
to leave without anyone noticing. Her hut was at the top of the village, shielded from the other houses by the ancient mosque, and
she must have left late in the night, rolling her cart carefully along
the dark path that coiled away from the village past the leper shacks
and the chapel of Saint Achilles, far from the barking dogs. It has
been clear to Maria, ever since they fled the fire and the killing, that
Black Melpo had foreseen what was to come and had abandoned
her to her fate. This was a terrible thing, Maria had thought, a terrible betrayal, for Black Melpo had been like a mother to her, in many
ways more than a mother. Almost everything she knew, besides the
household chores Heraclea had taught her, she had learned from
Black Melpo. That Black Melpo had not warned her of the impending danger was something she would never be able to forgive, Maria
has thought all these weeks; but now she wonders if Black Melpo's
silence was not an act of kindness. On the day before the raid Black
Melpo slaughtered a cockerel; Maria remembers that his name was
Kanelli—cinnamon—because his white feathers were sprinkled
with brown speckles. Black Melpo threw his entrails onto a large
stone slab in her yard, and Maria saw the many reds and yellows in
the membranes around the animal's intestines. A cockerel's entrails
were a better oracle than the entrails of a sheep, Black Melpo said,
because the cockerel had been favored by Jesus, who had given it
a gift of a thousand years in Paradise for revealing to him the ways
in which Judas was planning his betrayal. The old woman peered at
the raw tangle, leaning closer and closer, and then, crouched over
the entrails as she was, looked up at Maria in horror. But, as Maria
thinks back on it now, there was also amazement in that look. The

cockerel had belonged to Black Melpo and could only reveal its owner's fate; but Black Melpo must have seen something that had to do with Maria as well.

•

The caravan trudges slowly down one of the main streets toward the harbor. The rain has already flooded the open sewers that run from the houses across the beach and into the sea, and human waste and animal dung are seeping into the mud and water covering the streets. The townsfolk hurry through the ankle-deep water carrying bundles and baskets, salvaging belongings from their flooding houses. A dog stands barking on a raised slab of pavement, and a child of about six is sitting in the water nearby, looking for something in the mud and filth.

There is another roadblock, but the soldiers are dismantling it and the caravan stops only to let two stretchers pass, carrying corpses covered with bloody sackcloth. The priest crosses himself three times. A group of some fifty men gallops past in tight formation, the big badges of the Kurdish militia pinned to their tall caps for all to see. The men in front are carrying their carbines pointed forward, the others behind holding lances and broad-bladed daggers. Maria sees that one of the riders is missing a hand; he has the reins wrapped strangely around the stump. His rifle is slung behind his back, and she wonders how he can aim and fire it.

"The town isn't safe," Father Andreas says to the Turk, who nods, glancing at Maria.

"They've brought in the Kurds," the Turk says, his eyes following the cavalrymen, who suddenly turn their horses and race up one of the streets leading away from the port. He shakes his head.

"If they've brought in the Kurds, there's trouble brewing." He looks at Father Andreas.

The caravan makes its way through a throng of vendors and carters who are arguing and haggling along the waterfront in spite of the rain and the fighting in the streets. There is a battleship in the harbor, its guns aimed at the docks, ready to fire at the first sign of an Armenian insurrection. But the only Armenians in the port are small groups of frightened women sitting on wooden crates in front of wet squares of cloth heaped with useless knickknacks. One of the women is arguing with a thin, sickly man who is trying to buy a tin bowl from her. She suddenly begins to shriek and runs at him, hitting him with quick hard slaps as he hurries away.

The caravan passes a shabby mosque with a minaret whose brick walls are badly battered, as if the mosque has been under siege. There are beggars sitting in a line before tin bowls, while an old woman stands next to them singing in a shrill, childlike voice. The words sound to Maria like Tatar Turkish: "You are the sun, you are the moon, you are the light of light, you are the soul of life, you are the lanterns burning in my breast, O my beloved one, O my Mohammed!" The old woman rocks back and forth in a trance. Maria thinks with horror that she might be possessed. At every verse, the old woman raises her hands to her eyes and covers them tightly as she sings, shutting out the rain and the commotion, then lowers her hands again and covers her face with her veil while the beggars drum long refrains. Maria listens to the beautiful words. It is much easier to understand the simple Turkish of these eastern streets, so similar to Caucasian Tatar, than it is to follow the formal language that the Turk and the priest speak.

The Turk gives a handful of coins to one of the caravan guards, who hurries across the street and runs crouching along the row of beggars, placing a coin in each bowl. The beggars nod rhythmically in gratitude, while the woman continues her shrieking song: "A moon has risen over me, eclipsing every other moon! Beauty like yours I have never seen! Never, O face of radiant delight!"

27

MARIA IS SOLD THE FOLLOWING day. The transaction is completed in a large office facing the customs sheds and jetties of the port. A magistrate with an olive complexion is sitting behind a long mahogany table covered with neat piles of paper and rows of inkpots with different colored inks, two pens lying beside each pot, Maria notices, their iron tips pointing toward the magistrate in perfect symmetry. A wooden tray, its sides lined with chiseled Doric columns, is filled with a stack of folded newspapers so smooth that they look as if they have been carefully ironed to remove all the creases. The magistrate's crimson fez sits at a peculiar angle, and a few strands of glistening black hair have been carefully combed forward and pasted across his forehead.

Maria is standing heavily veiled at the back of the room; she knows that the meeting has to do with her, but can't follow the elegant repartee of the men. The Turk and the priest sit facing the magistrate, sipping sweet coffee, and, as a polite preamble to the completion of her sale, are discussing the political situation in the Empire, careful not to express any opinions that might be thought too controversial. They talk about the unrest in

Constantinople, and the magistrate says he has heard that battles are being fought in the streets and that there are regiments marching on the Sultan's palace. What is one to think? "We received a wire from Constantinople last night," the magistrate says gravely. "Apparently there have been more skirmishes between regiments loyal to the Sultan, commanded by the Grand Vizier's son, and the revolutionaries camped in front of the parliament buildings. The Grand Vizier's son, can you believe that? And then today's newspapers say that the Vizier's son has been hiding in Athens for the past two weeks." He clicks his tongue and shakes his head. "It's all nonsense, nonsense, nonsense. Who is one to believe? Traveling to Constantinople these days might be difficult; it might soon be impossible," he says, glancing at the Turk.

"Everything has been arranged," the Turk replies coolly, "we have no cause for concern."

The magistrate picks up the telegram he has received from the capital, looks at the Turk, and reads: "The Ministers of War and Justice were in their carriage on their way to the Sultan's palace when they were stopped on the Galata Bridge, which the rebels had seized. Nazim Pasha was ordered by a soldier to hand over his revolver. But the pasha refused, whereupon the soldier shot him dead and wounded the Minister of War." The magistrate looks up and sees the shocked face of Father Andreas, who is as much taken aback by the news as he is by the telegram's expensive wordiness. It must have cost at least ninety piastres. "Other victims," the magistrate continues, "included Emir Mehmet Arslan, the Deputy for Lattakia, whom the soldiers bayoneted outside the parliament building, mistaking him for Hussein Cahid Bey, the editor of the Tanin newspaper."

"There must be many dead," the Turk says, apparently unconcerned.

"A hundred and three," the magistrate eagerly replies, pointing to the telegram. "And that is only the official count. Unofficially—who knows?" He leans forward to his tray of newspapers, takes one, and carefully unfolds it, the rubies on his rings catching the light. "And listen to this," he says, shaking his head, and in the tone of a mullah delivering a sermon, reads: "There has been an attempt on the life of the Sultan's brother, His Imperial Highness Prince Reshad. The perpetrator, a traitorous guardsman, was shot sometime after midnight on Thursday in the Prince's bedchamber. An investigation is underway to ascertain whether the would-be assassin was acting on his own." He puts the paper down, looks at the Turk and the priest, and then picks up another newspaper, holding it out to them as if they could read the small print from where they are sitting. Both men lean forward in a show of interest. "What I just read to you, gentlemen, was from yesterday morning's edition, and here in today's edition we read"—again he assumes the tone of a preaching mullah—"His Imperial Highness Prince Mehmet Reshad has stated that the attempt on his life is a pure invention by enemy factions in the government. The trusted guardsman, who was accused of breaking into the Prince's apartments, had been in Edirne with his two sons at the time, but has now returned to the capital."

The Turk and the priest shake their heads, demonstrating polite disbelief at the state of affairs in the distant capital. The Turk turns and glances at Maria who is still standing motionless at the back of the room. Neither the three men, nor any of the newspapers, are prepared to address the toppling of the Sultan that will inevitably take place any day, if it has not already; nor do they touch on his heirs, who are wrangling for the throne. Adding to the Empire's misery, the men agree, are the rebels here in the borderlands, and they exchange ideas on what measures should be taken.

The priest points out that the Greeks are among the Sultan's most loyal subjects, while the Armenians seem intent on causing trouble, their rebels ready to attack other Armenians who sympathize with the Empire. The magistrate agrees and says that he was once forced to hide in a Greek Church on a visit to Constantinople when Armenian rebels were marching through the streets. "As the saying goes," he adds, "two Greeks make one Armenian, one Armenian two devils."

The priest looks at the magistrate aghast, but realizes that he has not intended the offensive proverb as an insult to him.

"May I offer you a cigarette?" the magistrate says, opening a drawer in his desk and taking out a silver box studded with blue and purple gems. He snaps the lid open and there is a burst of tinkling music. He holds the box out in the general direction of the Turk and the priest, uncertain which of the two men outranks the other. The sudden music has startled them, which pleases the magistrate. "These are Ramses IIs, an excellent brand, the cigarette the Pharaohs would have smoked if cigarettes had existed in those days," he says, and then nods at the box. "And perhaps they did exist in those days, who knows? The Egyptians invented everything. After all, they invented matchsticks, so why not cigarettes?" He leans forward. "These are an American brand, not the rubbish we get here, though of course they are made with our tobacco." He smiles encouragingly.

The Turk holds out both his hands toward the box and bows to the priest in the manner of an elegant man favoring one he outranks. The priest takes a cigarette and thanks both the magistrate and the Turk.

"And now to the matter at hand," the magistrate says, twisting the rings on his fingers.

Maria has been watching the lengthy preambles to her sale through the narrow slit of her veil. The Turk insisted that she be heavily veiled: after he and the priest have stamped the sale papers, she is to be officially in his charge, and he cannot appear in public with a woman who is not fully veiled. The veil provides a welcome screen for Maria to hide behind, though the heavy brown-black cloth covering her mouth is hot from her breath. She does not feel as shy or uneasy as she would have standing before these men with just her kerchief, but she is thirsty and wishes she could go out into the yard where there must be a well. Though the men are sipping coffee, and there are little glasses of water on a tray next to their cups, she has not been offered anything to drink. She no longer tries to follow what the men are saying, though she knows they have been talking about deaths and killings in the big city to which she is to travel. She stares at the strands of the magistrate's hair; he has a prominent beak-like nose, and she imagines him perched on the edge of the table pecking at bowls of sunflower seeds. The door is only a few paces away. Perhaps she should have gone back with Lita when she had the chance, Maria thinks. Now it is too late. She will never see her mother and her father again, but that is the fate of all brides who are sent to their bridegrooms' distant villages, or who are lucky enough to be married to a man in a town. She looks at the door. If her father would only walk in and take her away, pulling off her veil, angry at her masquerading as a Muslim girl, his hand gripping her wrist: my daughter is not to be married into the big city, she will come with me, I will take her to Athens. He would hug and cuddle her the way he had before her womanhood got in the way of his affections. She misses her mother too, but in a different way. She misses her presence in a way she cannot explain. There is something comforting about being in the same house with her mother, even if not in the same room, even if they do not speak, which they often did not for an entire day. She feels sadness trickling through her body like a poison.

Behind the magistrate there is a large window through which she can see the battleship in the harbor pointing its guns at the back of his head. It has stopped raining, and the ship is gleaming in the sun. Maria sees small, apparently helmeted figures marching on the decks. It is as if the towers of a castle have toppled into the sea and by a miracle managed to stay afloat, with warriors swarming over the capsized ramparts, wielding the swords of Tatar epics— "Golden men with golden swords, gleaming in the golden sun." Black Melpo said that there were bards in the mountains who could sing the epics so well that the warriors of the ancient songs appeared in the sky with their armor and horses, listeners fleeing as the horde came galloping from the clouds, and the bard had to be seized and shaken out of his trance. Maria hears the magistrate say *altin*, the Tatar word for gold, and looks up; the word must be the same in Turkish, she thinks. The priest and the Turk turn and look at her, and she lowers her eyes.

The document of Maria's sale is written in cursive Ottoman script. The priest and the Turk agree with the wording, and the magistrate sends for his clerk to have two handwritten copies made. The three men continue discussing the dire state of the Empire and the Armenian problem, and the priest tells the story of how the legendary Armenian Prince Hamam's arms and legs were cut off, but that he still managed to swim to safety across the river that flowed past his burning palace, an amazing feat of prowess. The magistrate and the Turk look at him blankly.

The clerk returns with two copies of the sales contract, and the priest and the Turk stamp them with their seals.

•

The unsold girls and boys are waiting in an empty office on the second floor of the building. The priest tells them that if they are as well behaved as Maria, they will all be traveling in ships that are even grander than the battleship in the harbor, and the children turn and stare out the grimy window at the sea. Maria starts unpinning her veil, but the priest hastily motions her not to. A few minutes later the Turk enters the room, accompanied by a very old man in a long, dark blue caftan that, except for its color, resembles the priest's cassock. All the girls are motioned away from the window, and the boys are lined up for inspection. They are told to remove their shirts.

Maria watches the old man shuffle past the first boy without looking at him and stop in front of the second—a handsome, black-haired boy of about twelve.

"Teeth?" the old man says in a breathless voice, as if worried the boy might be toothless.

The boy looks at Father Andreas, who bares his teeth, motioning him to do the same. The boy opens his mouth, and the old man pokes his finger inside and begins prodding each tooth.

"I too used to have teeth," the old man says, turning to the priest. "But . . . Allah gives teeth and Allah takes teeth away, and we all know that a man's appetite sits behind his teeth. If you can't chew, you can't eat, and if you can't eat . . . " He points at his thin midriff and shrugs his shoulders. "It is Allah's will that I grow thinner every month, so I grow thinner."

Father Andreas nods sympathetically.

"You're Greek, aren't you?" the old man says to Father Andreas, more as a statement than a question, still prodding the boy's teeth, and Father Andreas nods again. "I can always tell," the old man says.

"I mean I can always tell who's Greek and who isn't. I can see from across the street who's Greek, who's Turk, and who's Kurd. It's a useful knack to have nowadays. You never know who'll be pointing a gun at you." He smiles at the boy and clucks his tongue. "You have good teeth. You're a good little boy with good little teeth. Blow at me, do foo-foo!"

Maria watches the old man and the boy—the boy is confused, she sees, and for a moment doesn't seem to know what the old man wants; but then the boy suddenly grins and blows into his face. The old man nods, reaches out his hand unsteadily and prods the boy's bared stomach, then pats the boy's bottom with an alarming grimace, which he evidently means as a pleasant smile. "What has four legs and a tail, but no hands?" he asks the boy. "Boys like riddles," he says, turning to the priest, "and riddles lighten the mood. If a boy can think of the answer, he is happy, and if he is told the answer, he laughs. Riddles are always good."

"The boy does not yet speak Turkish, effendi," the priest says politely.

"What has four legs and a tail, but no hands?" The old man hesitates and looks at the other boys. "The answer is a ... a ... " He claps his hands together. "A horse, it is a horse that has four legs." The old man grins and then chuckles. "A horse, a horse, you'd never have guessed, would you? No one ever guesses my riddles."

He nods and smiles to himself.

"This one is a 'yes,'" he quickly announces, pointing at the boy. "Too many stairs!" he says to the priest, who, Maria notices, doesn't seem to know for a moment what the old man means. "Too many stairs! A building should never have more than two floors, especially buildings of business; look at me, I can't even breathe— more than two floors is disrespect to elders!"

210

"Yes," the priest agrees. "Stairs are the invention of Satan."

"One of the punishments Allah sent down upon Cain for his sins was that he had to live for eight hundred and eighty-eight years. He grew older and older but couldn't die. He had to live on and on, even when he didn't want to anymore."

The priest nods sympathetically.

"A great penance. Allah knows how to punish. I have already lived through my first eighty-eight years." He looks at the priest. "You're surprised? Yes, I'm eighty-eight, almost eighty-nine." He shakes his head. "I wonder how many more years Allah will punish me with. There are only two men in this town older than I," he quickly adds and smiles. "Only two."

The old man buys all the boys except the first, whom he did not even glance at. He is a particularly handsome boy with unusual copper-brown hair, and Father Andreas cannot understand what fault the buyer of boys might have seen in him. The boy is told he will be sent back to the barracks with the priest.

28

SELLING THE OTHER GIRLS PROVES harder than the priest or the Turk anticipated. A few hours after the old man purchased the boys, a group of rebels guns down three officials from the capital who were walking in the streets of the port without guards, despite the mounting unrest. Throughout the afternoon, soldiers in ragged uniforms run through the town, shooting at anyone who might be an insurgent. Most of the visiting traders leave on the evening boat to Trebizond. The Turk would also have taken Maria and left, but he knows from experience that, if there is unrest in this town, Trebizond will be just as bad. There is also still the possibility of getting a further commission if he can find a buyer for the four unsold girls once the town calms down in the morning. While the Sultan in Constantinople, now without food or water, is besieged in his palace by mutinous troops, here in the outpost of the Empire the Armenians, the Greeks, and the Laz are each claiming Trebizond and its hinterlands as the jewel in the crown of a greater Greece, or a Kingdom of Lazistan, or a Republic of Armenia. The Syrians want a Syristan, the Dimlis a Dimlistan, the Soranis a Soranistan, the Yazidis a Yazidistan, and the Kurds a

Kurdistan. If the Sultan is to give independence to all the groups who are demanding it, the Empire that once stretched from the outskirts of Vienna to the Persian Gulf and beyond will quickly shrink to a few acres in darkest Anatolia. Even Constantinople, the capital of the Empire, is being claimed by the Greeks, who declare themselves the rightful heirs of Constantinople and Byzantium. The Empire is crumbling.

As the afternoon progresses more shots are heard in the streets. Father Andreas becomes increasingly alarmed. He is torn between the conviction that he might sell the girls at a good price if he stays in the town and the instinct to flee back to the mountains, to the relative safety of the barracks. The sale of Maria and the boys has already brought him a good commission, enough to ensure that he and the refugees back in the barracks can escape by sea, at least as far as Trebizond, once the revolt dies down. But if the sale of the remaining girls went half as well as Maria's, there would be enough to relocate all the refugees and give each family a small sum.

The Turk has taken rooms at an inn some distance from the port, away from the street fighting and the shooting. The rooms are on the second floor, the only clean, private rooms in the inn; most of the visiting merchants and peddlers sleep on the benches and the floor of the large taproom below, using their saddles and saddle blankets for pillows. His guards and muleteers stand with loaded rifles at the doors. As the rioting increased, the inn emptied out, and now the innkeeper is sitting alone in the courtyard, sullenly drinking plum liquor. The ground is black with mud and manure, and his boots are immersed to the ankles in the stinking slime. Beyond the stables of the inn stand the ruins of a doll factory that burned down a few days before: in the early hours of dawn a night watchman had dropped his kerosene lamp, the flame and liquid pouring out onto the bales of linen and cotton that were to become the dolls' crinolines. Despite the heavy rain, the odor of smoke still hangs in the air. The wooden facade of the factory burned away, leaving the large blackened shell of the building intact. From the window of her room, Maria can look into the factory's courtyard, where two men, a father and his son, she thinks, are sorting through hundreds of life-sized charred baby dolls whose rouged wooden faces are still smiling. From where she stands the dolls look like babies being hurled onto a growing pile of small corpses. Whenever shots ring out in the street, the men run for cover into the burned-out building.

A seamstress—the wife of the innkeeper—comes with two women to sew the undergarments and dresses that Maria will need for her journey to Constantinople. Squares and triangles of cloth are strewn over the dusty cushions and carpets of the room. The seamstress is a jovial matron in a bright dressing gown and pantaloons who appears completely unconcerned by the growing unrest. She is clearly from the Caucasus and, without making any attempt to give her speech a Turkish veneer, speaks in a stream of village Tatar. She keeps exclaiming how pretty Maria is and how happy her future master will be when he sets eyes on her. "*Ftou, ftou, ftou!*" she says before every compliment, spitting lightly over her shoulder to chase away the evil eye. "Mark my words, your master will prefer you, he'll prefer you above all the rest. That's what fate has in store for you. I don't need to look at any coffee grounds to tell you your fortune. And he'll like these clothes. I know the fashions of the capital. Your master *will* be pleased. Men like drawstrings and frills; nothing vexes a man more than when everything comes down with a single tug. A man likes to work for his pleasure."

Maria has no idea what the woman is talking about, but she

likes her rough, motherly ways. She reminds her somehow of Black Melpo, though she neither looks like her nor speaks the way she did. Her hair is the color of carrots and beets, with the unreal orange and red hues of herbs and henna, and she has the slim arms of a young girl but the fat legs of an older woman. Maria has never seen anyone like her. She can't tell her age, but thinks that her hair must be gray or even white beneath the reddish colors. The matron picks up a shapeless undergarment and holds it up to her face like a veil. "Come to me tonight, tonight," she sings in a high, quavering voice, her big hips swaying in mock enticement as she dances toward Maria. Maria laughs and holds up her hand to ward her off. "Come to me tonight! Yes, he *will* prefer you. He'd be a fool if he didn't. I mean, look at you—such a beauty!" The seamstress turns around to the women. "Have you ever seen such a beauty? Be honest, have you?" The two women quickly shake their heads. "See?" She holds up her hands. "What did I say?"

Maria steps back, suddenly realizing that she is expected to wear the strange garment.

"It's silk," the matron explains. "I like silk, but I never wear it. My lord and master—" she says the words sourly, pointing toward the window "—my lord and master can't tell the difference. I could wear bloomers of velvet and fur and he'd look right past them!"

The two other women, Maria notices, seem frightened of the matron, leaning away from her whenever she draws near, as if she might suddenly slap them. Maria takes the bloomers, not sure which end is the top.

"Your master will be delighted," the matron says. She snatches a pair of scissors from one of the women. "The softer the bloomer, the more a man pants. Men like rubbing up against bloomers like these, smooth and soft as they are." One of the women snorts, suppressing a laugh, and sits there, stitching rapidly, her head lowered and her lips pressed together. "We don't wear these things for our own pleasure, you know," the matron adds. There is a large opening at one end of the bloomer from which silk drawstrings hang; another opening laced with frills on either side; and a much smaller opening at what Maria thinks must be the bottom of the bloomers. Here, too, there are delicately looped drawstrings and rows of frills.

"This is the top," the matron says, crinkling her nose and tapping the bloomers with her scissors. "One pretty leg goes in here, the other in there—and this little opening . . ." she pauses and smiles with feigned bashfulness, swaying her head from side to side, ". . . this little opening your master might want to unlace if he's in a hurry."

The matron strides over to the window, opens it, and, draping the lace curtain over her head and mouth to veil her face, barks an incomprehensible order down to the innkeeper who is still sitting in the courtyard drinking. She shuts the window, but reopens it quickly and yells, "Fine! You can have one more jug, but that will be that! Any more and I'll come down myself!" She slams the window and pulls the curtain off her head. She smiles at Maria and takes a few gulps from an invisible glass, tossing her head back each time. "Drink, drink, drink, that's all he does, and work, work, work, that's all I do! May Allah not torture you with such a master!"

"You are his wife?" Maria asks in Tatar. "I thought you came from the port—"

"From the port?" the matron shouts, and begins to laugh. "In a dressing gown and pantaloons? What do you think I am? Do you think I'm some . . . some . . ." she falls silent as if she can't think of the word, and looks at the other two women, throwing up her hands at Maria's simplicity. The women grin. "Yes, he's my master, the one down there in the courtyard." She smiles at Maria wistfully. "That man is the one Allah has sent to torment me. Everything he touches turns bad, under every hair he finds a devil. If I didn't work," she says, waving her needle, "we'd be out on the street by now, holding out beggars' cups. Go to the window and take a peek at him, but don't let those brutes from over there in the factory see you: use the curtain to hide your face and your hair. They are lewd, those men, they have only one thing on their minds."

Maria drapes the curtain over her head and face and peers out of the window. The drunken innkeeper looks up at her in surprise.

"What do you think of my curtains?" the seamstress asks Maria. "They're lace—they came by ship from England. I'm the only one who has them. People from all over town come visiting and ask to see my curtains."

Maria touches the material and looks at the stitching.

"They're made by machines, big machines, not by hand; they spin them out in minutes!"

Maria nods admiringly.

"And I have glass in all my windows," the seamstress says, walking over to a window and tapping the pane. "I'm the only one here who does. My house is as good as those in the capital."

"How long have you lived here?" Maria asks the matron in Tatar.

"Years and years," the matron says. "How old do you think I am?" she suddenly adds, looking at Maria expectantly.

"Thirty?" Maria replies.

"I used to be thirty," the matron says quickly, running her hand through her hair. "So you're Greek?"

"You can tell?"

"No, you sound just like a Tatar girl, though you don't look it. The priest told me. One look at him, and I knew he was Greek. I know a Greek priest when I see one. But don't let them catch you speaking Tatar in that fancy house you're going to. They'll send you right back to where you came from. They don't like Tatar over there."

"I know."

"I too could have been sent to a nice house like where they're sending you if I'd looked like you." She spits lightly over her shoulder three times to ward off the evil eye and cracks her knuckles. "Then I wouldn't be here. But Allah chose me as a martyr, and so I suffer. But I don't complain. It's not my way."

"This is a nice house and a nice room," Maria says uncertainly, looking at the other two women, who continue sewing without looking up.

"You didn't see downstairs, with all the drunks and robbers we get. No, Allah has chosen me as a martyr. Of course, if I had your looks, you'd never find me here. The only thing Allah gave me is beautiful hair," she says pointing at her head, again looking at Maria expectantly. "It's a gift from Allah. Have you ever seen hair this red?"

Maria shakes her head.

"Well, much good it did me. If I'd been prettier I could have ended up in a good house like you, a big house. But we never know what's in store for us, what to expect."

"I didn't expect to be here and on my way to Constantinople," Maria says.

The matron leans forward as if she hadn't heard right.

There is a knock at the door, and the matron and her women quickly pin their veils over their faces. Maria feels a pang of anxiety. There is another knock, and the matron tiptoes toward the door.

"Who may I ask who it is what is present?" she asks in an unsuccessful attempt at formal Turkish.

"This is Father Andreas," the priest answers. "Is permission for entry granted?"

"If you are pleased to linger for some instants," the matron calls out, and hurries over to Maria with a wide scarf, frantically motioning for her to drape it over her hair and pin it over her face. Maria shakes her head, but the matron raises a finger at her sternly, and she takes the scarf. The women gather up the undergarments and quickly go to the far end of the room.

The priest enters, and a white Persian cat, its tail and legs pink with henna, comes darting into the room before the door closes. The matron calls out, "Shoo, shoo, you naughty thing!" flicking her hands, and the cat jumps onto the windowsill and disappears, scurrying over the courtyard wall. The matron shakes her head and shrugs her shoulders helplessly, smiling at the priest.

"Please pardon the beast," she says. "It has no manners."

Father Andreas smiles and nods. "What beautiful clothes," he says to the matron. "Very good, very good, indeed."

The matron titters with pleasure behind her veil and bows her head. "Thank you, thank you, effendi."

"By your leave," the priest says to the matron, "I have come to say farewell to the young lady."

The matron bows again, utters a string of conventional expressions of sorrow at his departure, and goes to join the women at the other end of the room. The priest does not look at Maria, but keeps glancing out the window at the charred remains of the factory. He turns and pats her on the shoulder. The matron, shocked that he would touch the girl, looks at him in alarm. He wants to tell Maria "Health to you, till we meet again," but he knows this is the last time he will see her. His silence unnerves her, and she feels fear rising inside her and her blood beating. He gives her a consoling smile. She opens her mouth to say something, but he turns around in silence and goes out of the room, closing the door carefully behind him.

29

A ROW OF WOODEN SHACKS at the eastern edge of the town has been set on fire, and acrid smoke is creeping over the inn. From her window Maria sees the priest and the unsold children running through the courtyard and out past the stables. He is ducking as he runs, as if he is dodging bullets, clutching a saddle-bag in one hand, holding onto his priest's hat with the other. The matron and her two women are throwing bundles onto a wagon to which the innkeeper is frantically harnessing the horses. Maria is gripped by fear. There is a loud rap at the door, and the Turk enters the room. He tells her to pack, mimicking with his hands the folding of clothes.

"We are leaving," he says and, pointing to the sea so she will understand, adds, "Constantinople."

His cool demeanor reassures her. He picks up one of the long jackets the matron and her women have sewn and points at a large cloth bag. His movements are calm and measured.

·

Maria hurries down from her room, fully veiled and carrying the bag filled with her new clothes. The inn and the courtyard have emptied out; the innkeeper and the matron have already fled; and the stables are empty. The thickening smoke stings Maria's eyes. The Turk is loading trunks and sacks onto a cart and takes Maria's bag and carefully places it among his belongings. He is elegantly dressed, wearing a European suit and his new fez—a signal to the soldiers that he is a Turkish gentleman from the capital.

"The innkeeper and his wife left without even locking the doors!" he says and, not expecting Maria to understand, mimics the turning of a large key in a lock. Beyond the courtyard wall she sees that the sky behind the doll factory is black with smoke, like it was when she and her parents fled their village. The Turk coughs and waves his hand in front of his face as if to dispel the smoke. "Every year these rebels make trouble, and every year the townsfolk run away! Big trouble! Not that it's any better in Constantinople. Bang—big bang!" He throws his hands up in the air, his fingers mimicking falling debris.

Maria wonders where the guards are and what has happened to the caravan and the horse she has been riding. She feels a wave of panic. Her parents, Father Andreas, Lita, everyone is gone, and she is alone with a man she does not know in a town that is burning. He seizes her hand, and she pulls it back. "No . . . no!" she says. He looks angry. He seizes her hand again, grabbing her wrist hard, not letting go this time though she is struggling to break free, and he pushes her roughly up onto the cart. She begins to cry; he motions her to stay calm. Her veil slips, and wiping her eyes with her sleeve, she pins it back into place. He whips the horses, and the cart tears out of the courtyard into the street, the wheels thudding against the cobblestones that have cracked and sunk in the mud. Maria is thrown against the Turk and holds onto him. It looks like they are heading toward the mountains: the Turk must have taken a wrong turn—this is the way back to the barracks—but then the street veers around a mosque, its courtyard filled with shouting men, and suddenly Maria sees the sea in the distance, now wide and gray and terrifying. There are a thousand houses between them and the port, how can they find their way? Maria sees a man pouring kerosene through a smashed window. He is hunched forward, looking nervously up and down the street, ready to drop his can and run if he has to. People carrying bundles are hurrying in all directions through a haze of smoke. Some are heading toward the sea, others running toward the fields and the mountains. Torn sacks and bales lie covered in mud, dropped luggage cracking and splintering under the wheels, Maria steadying herself as she is jolted forward. There is a roadblock next to a burning building, but the soldiers are not stopping anyone, and people are jostling one another as they pass the barrier, wading through the reeking slime. The Turk slows the cart, but the soldiers wave him on. Shots ring out, and the Turk instinctively ducks, whipping the horses on. They drive past a row of dilapidated mansions, monuments to the town's former wealth, their decaying facades blackened by fire. The intricate lattices of the windows are smashed, and there is a foul odor of rot and smoke.

"I wonder if they'll bother to rebuild the town!" the Turk shouts to Maria. "We should leave the place to the Russians—then good luck to the rebels!" For the first time since fleeing the Caucasus, Maria is frightened for her life. She doesn't understand everything he is saying, but she knows that he is only speaking in order to say something.

In the distance, small boats filled with fleeing families are setting out to sea. More shots ring out, and a barefoot young man darts across the street right in front of the horses. The Turk shouts at him and pulls back the reins just in time. Two soldiers come running and shoot the man in the stomach. He falls in the street and begins screaming, his legs kicking. The horses bolt. The cart tears around a sharp corner by a barricade; one of the wheels hits a stoop in front of an empty shed, and Maria flies backward and to the side, falling off the cart into the mud. She hits her head and there is a thudding pain that is both dull and sharp and she sees darting yellow and white lights that blind her for a moment. She hears the wounded man's shrieks and looks back. He is trying to get up, skidding and sliding in his blood. More shots ring out and she scrambles toward a nearby door, her tunic and veil covered with mud, but then swings back around, realizing she is heading toward danger. She has to get back to the cart, but the cart is gone. Before her on the front step of a wooden shack lie three dead men side by side, their beards ripped out, their faces bloody and twisted. She hears a shot and a bullet whistles past her: a soldier across the street is aiming a rifle at her, and she jumps up, grabbing the hem of her skirt, and runs back down the street past the unmanned checkpoints, holding her veil over her face, gasping for air; there is another shot, the bullet pierces one of the folds of her skirt; she runs around a corner, tripping over a bundle of kindling lying abandoned by the side of the street, falling down, bruising her hands. She scrambles up before the soldier can cross the street and shoot her point blank, and she runs blindly past stores and warehouses, past smaller streets leading to lanes and alleys that burrow deeper into the town. She hears more shots, but they seem farther away. She cannot understand why the soldier took aim at her. Perhaps he mistook her for somebody else. Perhaps in all the confusion and violence he was shooting in all directions. She runs panting until she can't run anymore and stumbles on, slipping in the mud and steadying herself on the battered wooden walls of the buildings. She stops under the awning of an abandoned street stall, pulling off her veil, leaning against the frame. It is perhaps a mistake to unveil herself, she suddenly thinks, but there are no soldiers in sight, just townsfolk running in all directions, and she notices that some of the women, probably Greek, are unveiled. She feels the blood pulsing painfully in her head. On either side of the street are abandoned stores, some of whose shutters have been left open. Across the street she sees a man, whom she mistakes at first for a Muslim cleric as he is wearing a white turban; but then she sees that he has a revolver in his hand. He is looking the other way. He raises the revolver and points it at a man hurrying toward him, but the man stops and darts across the street, hunched forward and holding his head as if to protect it from bullets. Maria catches her breath and edges backward toward the open store behind the stall. There is a tangle of halters and stirrups hanging from the ceiling, and piles of ripped saddle flaps and blankets strewn across the floor. Looters have clearly been here, and Maria is surprised they didn't take at least the stirrups, which seem in good condition. There is blood on the floor and on the bench where the storekeeper would have sat; it is a lot of blood, that of a fatal wound, and it is fresh: she can smell its strange metallic odor.

She presses herself behind one of the wooden columns propping up the roof, and the man with the revolver turns and looks in her direction. Their eyes meet; he stares. She looks away and holds her breath, leaning as far back behind the column as she can, and begins to count; if he is not here by the count of fifty, she will look again. She closes her eyes and counts slowly, to give him time. She thinks of children who close their eyes and believe they can't be seen, without a doubt the worst thing one can do in the face of real danger such as this; she must keep her eyes open and look for a way to escape. But she keeps her eyes shut. She can hear the sound of boots coming nearer but isn't sure if they are his, as she can also hear the footsteps of people hurrying past. There is a click, perhaps a pistol being cocked. There are voices, a woman whimpering, "Allah-Allah!" Maria stands behind the column and waits. "My death has come," she thinks, "it will be now." The store is shaped like a horseshoe, the only way in or out is from the front. She knows she is trapped; and yet, if the man with the gun was coming, he'd have come by now. She leans forward, and sees that he is still there, across the street, but now a little farther away, talking to two men, patting one of them on the shoulder and then hugging him and kissing his cheeks. He seems to have put his revolver away. He is perhaps a kind man after all, a good man, for what evil man will kiss another? Maria steps back behind the wooden column so he will not see her if he turns around.

People are hurrying past in both directions—if she joins the crowd she will be safe from the man with the revolver, and perhaps from the soldiers too. Nobody will notice her or wonder why she is there, or why her clothes are wet and covered in mud. She will be safe unless they begin shooting into the crowd. She hesitates. To the left, past the turbaned man, the street leads toward the edge of the town and through the fields back up into the mountains, to the barracks. To the right, the street goes down to the port where the ship is waiting, and perhaps the Turk too. There are so many houses, so many streets. The town is many times bigger than her village was. She wonders if being separated from the Turk is a sign that she should try to return to the barracks. If she goes back now, she thinks, she cannot be blamed; it will not be her fault, it is not as if she has run away from her future husband. She imagines her father and her mother outside the barracks; Homeros and Lita would be there too. But even if she gets out of the town unharmed, there are soldiers and rebels along the way, and men coming down the mountain paths. If she isn't murdered in the town, those men will murder her. She remembers the last thing she saw in her burning village, Widow Manthena in a ditch, two murderers hugging her, rolling with her in the mud, a third murderer jumping into the ditch, and a fourth. That will be her fate too, she thinks, and if the men at the checkpoints do not murder her, death will be lurking at every bend in the path.

She raises her hand to where she hit her head when she fell from the cart and looks to see if there's any blood. There isn't. The floorboard creaks and her breath catches in her throat. She hears her pulse beating in dull soft thuds, as if her head was under water. A shadow crosses the wall and she wheels around, a man's hand just missing her face and swiping her shoulder. She staggers back, falling against the hanging saddle straps, clawing at them to steady herself, and in a blind panic violently hurls the straps against the man, hitting him in the face. He is taken aback by her strength and violence, and almost loses his balance, tripping over a battered wooden saddle and a coil of whipcord. It is the man with the revolver, and he is holding it in his hand, though he is not pointing it at her. "Get away from me, get away from me!" she shouts in Tatar, and snatches up some horseshoe nails on the floor and flings them at him, hitting him in the face. She tears past him and runs out into the street, certain she will feel a bullet in her back, any moment now, a fatal sting, like the sting of ten bees. He catches up with her across the street, grabbing her by the wrist and dragging her back toward the store, as she kicks and tries to hit him with her fist, shouting out to passersby for help in Tatar. But the people hurrying to the port make way for the man as he drags her through the muddy street past the stalls and back into the store; to them he is a man with a wayward daughter, perhaps a wayward wife, and it is for him, and only him, to see to his womenfolk. Inside the store, he seizes her by the shoulders and pushes her down; her head hits the floor. She lies there, stunned, but only for an instant as he falls on her, his chin banging against her shoulder, his hips rolling and pushing, his lips on her mouth. She frees one arm from under his weight, overcome by his odor of acrid tobacco and unwashed clothes, and tears off his turban and claws at his hair. She gasps for air, feels she will vomit, and he pulls up her dress and tugs frantically at his trousers, the buttons tearing, and as he rolls and pushes, his trousers slide down to his thighs. He reaches down to force her legs open, and she frees her other arm, digging her nails deep into his cheek. He leans back, raising his hand to strike her, and she pushes his shoulder with full force, tipping him off her, jumping up and running to the front of the store. In the blindness of her fear, she grabs the wooden saddle and the whip coils and throws them back at him as he stumbles toward her, tripping, his face bleeding, his trousers around his ankles, covering himself with his hands so that passersby will not see his nakedness. She runs out into the street, panting, covering her face with her ripped and soiled veil, and joins a crowd of people hurrying with their bundles toward the port.

30

Grandfather's Decision, Summer 1909, Constantinople

FROM THE ROOM IN THE harem where she continues to be sequestered after Grandfather has viewed her and the other girls, Maria can look out into a large courtyard with a palm tree in the center, surrounded by a bright strip of marble mosaic. Though he has paid the Turk and her father a great sum of money, it is now unclear to her whether he will keep her in his house or send her away. She feels a simmering fear of uncertainty. He is older than she expected; there is silver in his hair. His monocle with its gold rim and gold chain is worth a house back in her village, and she is amazed that the round piece of glass can remain in place in his eye. He is clearly a good man, a kind man, she thought as he viewed her and the other purchased girls, even if his eyes were difficult to read. He smiled at her, which probably meant that he was pleased. He had saved her by sending her father so much money before he even set eyes on her, a great act of kindness. His eyes were a bright hazel color, and were the first thing one noticed about him. They were unusual eyes.

The door of the room is locked for her protection, she has been told, though this is surely a safe and secure home. From her window she watches a piebald mare that walks around the palm tree all day, its hooves never straying off the mosaic, and she spends much of the time watching the women and girls in German riding dress taking turns riding sidesaddle on it, reins in the left hand, white parasol in the right. A eunuch wearing the red coat and white breeches of a British master of hounds calls out instructions, and from time to time looks up to Maria's window and waves to her. She waves back. She soon realizes that the young women have a fixed time every day for riding. They have been dressed by their dress girls and make their way down to the courtyard, where they ride hour after hour around the mosaic in the same tight, never-ending circle. The horse stops only long enough for one girl to glide off the saddle and the next to mount. She takes the whip and reins in one hand, the eunuch bends forward, she places her foot in his palms, and in a second she is up on the horse, gathering her skirts, raising her leg over the pommel so that she is sitting sidesaddle. As the horse trots, the yard maid waits by the wall, ready to dart into the circle to scoop up its droppings and spray patchouli into the air.

Two weeks have passed since Maria arrived in this house in Constantinople. She had found the Turk waiting for her in the port by the moorings of the last ship that was to leave the burning town. He had sent out his guards to look for her in the streets and had been surprised to see her walking calmly, almost coldly, toward him, her veil covering her hair but not her face, her dress muddy and torn on the side. A shrill throng of people was trying to board the ship, but only those with tickets and traveling passes were allowed through. Maria and the Turk made their way across the deck, three porters carrying his trunks and bags. The engines were rumbling loudly, and the ship's gray walls and the planks underfoot were quivering. The deck was filled with steerage passengers carrying bundles and dragging boxes and luggage down to the lower levels, men with dark beards in turbans and fezzes, veiled and unveiled women, frightened and angry people calling out to one another, yellow feverish faces. Officials and police officers were making their way through the crowd, checking papers. Some people were being dragged off the ship, and a woman began to shriek. The other passengers were herded to the side, the men separated from the women. The Turk showed his travel papers and first-class tickets to the officials, who bowed as he and Maria passed. Black smoke was pouring from the big funnel, and she quickly stepped back, turning to look at the Turk, but he grabbed her wrist, his grip hurting her. She wanted to tell him that she had changed her mind, that she had decided he should take her back to the barracks, but she suddenly remembered that it hadn't been her decision to come, that her mind wasn't hers to change. As Black Melpo had said, she had to tread the path that had been chosen for her. Perhaps her path had come to an end, should come to an end, and she should topple over the railings, the waves reaching out for her, her bloodied face dragged over the sharp rocks of the seabed, fish darting through her hair, Saint Nicholas of the Waves holding her down till her body filled with water. The Turk said something, but his voice was drowned out by the engines. She saw the piers moving back, the black water churning and spraying white as the ship turned away from the burning town and set out to sea in the direction of Constantinople.

•

From her window in the harem she sees that the house, which she imagines will be her new home, is in fact a group of buildings, a labyrinth of rooms and apartments. She can see roofs and parts of other courtyards and gardens stretching over an area almost as large as her village in the Caucasus. Some of the buildings seem new and some very old, connected by walled paths and garden walkways, the house having over the centuries expanded like an oriental puzzle box unfolding in unexpected directions. Everywhere groups of small figures are sweeping, cleaning, and whitewashing. She can see minarets beyond the outer walls, the muezzins' calls to prayer ringing out in melodious discord over the city. From the matron who brings Maria her meals she learns that all the wives and women of the house have been brought from the Caucasus, even Zekiyé, the senior wife who arranged the viewing of the purchased girls. Zekiyé's elegant clothes and elegant speech, the slightly foreign Turkish into which she mixes French and German words, might lead one to think that she is European, but she is in fact from Batum, the rowdy and dangerous port town across the border in the Caucasus. The matron sits with Maria as she eats her meals, speaking to her in whispered Tatar, the rough borderland language that none of the women of the house are supposed to know, but which for most is their mother tongue. In one of the windows on the other side of the courtyard, Maria can see the back part of a room and a group of veiled women sitting at small tables. A man with a walking stick, clearly a tutor, is strolling past the open window, gesticulating as he speaks. Those are ladies of the household, the matron tells Maria, who are sitting with the master's sons and daughters at their lessons. The ladies are expected to know Persian and French poetry as well as the master's sons and daughters do, and to be able to converse with the master on any topic that might interest him.

"Do you know Persian?" Maria asks the matron.

"Yes. You, too, will learn Persian," the matron says, "if you stay."

"If I stay?"

"If you stay."

Maria's isolation ends with the arrival of an Italian nun called Sister Ernestina, the physician for the women of Grandfather's household. The nun eats the assortment of miniature pastries she is served in the harem's front garden, and then enters Zekiyé's drawing room, where Maria is lying propped up with cushions on a chaise longue. Sister Ernestina plants a sticky kiss on Zekiyé's rouged cheek; Zekiyé leans back as far as delicacy permits.

"You look wonderful!" the nun says to her in a loud, cheerful voice. "A picture of rosy health!" Before Zekiyé can answer, Sister Ernestina abruptly turns and marches over to Maria. "Skirt up, legs apart!"

Zekiyé sits down at her escritoire, takes a piece of parchment-like paper from a drawer, and begins drawing large Arabic letters with calligraphic loops and curls.

"This girl has come with the usual certificate?" the nun asks in her sharp, rough Turkish.

"*Oui*," Zekiyé answers distantly.

"A certificate of virginity!" Sister Ernestina says. "A certificate! As if remaining a virgin till you're ten is an accomplishment!"

"The girl is fifteen," Zekiyé replies.

"Fifteen?" the nun says with feigned surprise.

Maria watches her take a small iron rod out of her bag and place it on a tray. A hissing pan of water is balancing over a large blue flame on a spirit burner. One creak of the floorboard, and the water will spill onto the carpet with its strawberry- and plum-colored patterns. There is a shrill noise as a golden cuckoo in a red waistcoat and sparkling crown darts out of a large clock.

"Open your legs!" Sister Ernestina says to Maria, stretching her arms out wide. "Open, open!"

Zekiyé turns and looks at the nun, who winks at her. "One of those Circassian girls?" the nun says.

"*Non, Grecque.*"

"Aha! *Kalimera!*" the nun says to Maria. "*Kalimera!*"

Maria stares at her.

The nun looks at Maria expectantly. "*Kalimera!*" she repeats in a louder voice. "She doesn't seem to know much Greek," she says to Zekiyé. "Are you sure you weren't duped?"

"*Pardon? Je ne . . .*"

"Duped; you know, hoodwinked. If I'm buying an Ayvalik goat, I want it to be an Ayvalik goat and not some Mugla animal. If this girl doesn't even understand the word for 'good morning' in Greek, then Heaven above knows where she's from."

"I am pleased with this girl," Zekiyé says firmly, speaking to the nun for the first time in Turkish, prepared to cross swords with her if she continues her militant tone. "I would like her for my household. Even if it turns out that she is from Zanzibar I would not consider myself duped or 'hoodwinked,' as you put it. I marvel at your Turkish, my dear Sister Ernestina! You speak our language in a manner that is quite *extraordinaire*. If she is intact, we will keep her."

"What's *extraordinaire* is the girl's beauty," the nun continues, surprised by Zekiyé's uncharacteristic directness and her sudden switch to Turkish. She looks at Maria and clicks her tongue. "Well, well, well, a fifteen-year-old Greek virgin with a certificate! I am a fifty-two-year-old Italian virgin—perhaps I should have a certificate, too?" She laughs, hoping that Zekiyé will interpret her words as a pleasant witticism.

"Is Doctor Haufbach keeping well?" Zekiyé quickly asks. The

German doctor is Grandfather's physician and the director of the hospital that Sister Ernestina runs with her fellow nuns. The nuns go on house calls to wealthy Constantinople ladies who live in the seclusion of their husbands' harems and cannot appear unveiled, let alone undressed, before a male physician.

"The Doctor is keeping very well," the nun says. "We hardly ever see him. He rushes from villa to villa and from one palace to the next. Doctor Haufbach has only the best clients, as you know, and all the new Sultan's entourage is suffering from stomach ailments."

"*Ah, oui?*"

"*Oui*, indeed! Either the palace cooks are plotting to poison all the ministers, or the new Sultan's politics are already corroding their stomachs!"

Zekiyé abruptly puts down her calligraphic pen, its wooden holder slamming on the tabletop. To her surprise, the ink spatters across the parchment. She looks directly at the nun, who quickly averts her eyes and dips the rod into the boiling water. A burst of birdsong comes from the garden, and Maria and the two women look toward the French doors leading out onto the terrace.

"You should see how virginity tests are done in the Caucasus," the nun continues in Turkish, changing from politics to a subject that Zekiyé will find equally disturbing. "Twenty girls in a row on the floor, and an old crone goes from one to the next slipping her finger in. Does she wash her hands? No. And I don't mean, does she wash her hands before she comes in from the fields! I mean, does she wash the probing finger between prods? She doesn't. And then everyone wonders why the poor girls arrive here in Constantinople sallow and full of infections."

Maria winces, and her lips begin to tremble.

"Ha ha!" the nun says. "The pretty girl might have forgotten her Greek, but I see she understands Turkish well enough. Don't worry, my dear," she continues in a kinder tone. "I boil all my utensils, and here in the capital we use preparations that destroy all bacilli. *Ba-ci-lli*," she repeats slowly, stressing each syllable as if she is teaching Maria the word. "I promise, you won't feel a thing, just a tickle. I will slip the little rod inside for a second or two so I can check that you are as much of a virgin as your certificate says, and then you can go out into the garden and play with the other little girls."

She fishes the rod out of the boiling water and waves it in the air to cool. Beads of sweat trickle down Maria's face.

"Some of the girls in the Caucasus have their virginity refixed, did you know that?" the nun says, looking over her shoulder to Zekiyé, who is now standing by her escritoire, looking at her coldly.

"Refixed?" Zekiyé asks.

"Yes."

"How refixed?"

"A little needle, a very light thread: and, one two three, the former virgin is a virgin once more."

"Might we have been . . . affected?" Zekiyé asks carefully in French, looking at Maria.

"Affected?"

"This girl here, and the girls that we . . . that we have introduced into our house in the past."

"As far as I know, I am your only physician, and I don't remember sewing up any of your deflowered girls," the nun says brusquely.

Zekiyé smiles. She wonders how she should handle the nun's hostility; she is invaluable to the harem as a physician, and is in a sense almost Dr. Haufbach's equal, so instant dismissal is out of the question. Zekiyé decides to treat the brusque remark as a pleasantry.

"I did not mean to suggest that you are a de-deflowerer, *chère soeur!*" Zekiyé says lightly. "What I want to know is, might we have introduced any sewn-up girls into our household? Girls that we thought were virgins but were not."

Sister Ernestina grins, again caught unawares by Zekiyé's sudden change in tone. "Me a de-deflowerer, what a thought!" she says, moving toward the French doors, chuckling. She turns back to say something to Zekiyé, but falls silent as their eyes meet.

"The question is," Zekiyé says firmly, "did we acquire any deflowered girls without our knowledge?"

"No, your household would not have been affected," Sister Ernestina replies. "It's a relatively new procedure—and anyway, I would have noticed. A discerning man would notice, too—there are bumps on the hymen that should not be there." She looks at Zekiyé coldly. "But from what I am told, most men, when they set about to deflower maidens, are too breathless to notice anything."

Sister Ernestina turns to Maria, motions her to open her legs wider and unbutton her pantaloons, and slowly inserts the warm rod. Maria winces and presses her knees shut over the nun's hand. The nun wriggles her hand free and pulls the rod out. "This one's a virgin," she says, looking over her shoulder at Zekiyé, who has come closer. "A genuine virgin."

Acknowledgments

Thank you, Dad, for reading the first drafts of *The Purchased Bride* and enthusiastically supporting my version of how your mother met your father.

Thank you, Jennifer Lyons, my friend and agent, for your relentless encouragement and wise editorial advice. Thank you for inspiring me to persevere and continue writing this novel from start to finish over countless drafts, while also encouraging me to work on all the other fascinating translation projects. Working with you has been such an exciting literary journey.

Thank you, Judy Sternlight, my friend and my editor for so many years at Random House, for energetically encouraging me to embark on this first fiction project, and for all the editing and advice. Thank you for sharing your insights on building the characters and developing the narrative and action of this novel. Our work together on Machiavelli, Tolstoy, and Gogol projects at Modern Library taught me so much.

Thank you, Motti Lerer, for being my first reader and for your very encouraging response that made me see this book as a possible novel.

Thank you, Rene Steinke and the wonderful MFA Program at Fairleigh Dickinson! Thank you for seeing a potential in this novel.

Thank you, David Grand, for being a great novelist and teacher, and for your help and detailed advice in consolidating the point of view and plot.

Thank you, Jake Syersak, for reading my drafts and for your generous edits.

Thank you, Henry Gifford, for your many hours of careful editing and your amazing eye for tone and style.

A special thanks to Dimitri Gondicas and Princeton University's Program in Hellenic Studies for offering me a writing residency and for making available Princeton's remarkable and vast resources on Greek and Ottoman history.

Thank you all
for your support.
We do this for you,
and could not do
it without you.

PARTNERS

pixel ||| texel

EMBREY FAMILY
FOUNDATION

ADDITIONAL DONORS, CONT'D

Mark Haber
Mary Cline
Maynard Thomson
Michael Reklis
Mike Soto
Mokhtar Ramadan
Nikki & Dennis Gibson
Patrick Kukucka
Patrick Kutcher
Rev. Elizabeth & Neil Moseley
Richard Meyer

Scott & Katy Nimmons
Sherry Perry
Sydneyann Binion
Stephen Harding
Stephen Williamson
Susan Carp
Susan Ernst
Theater Jones
Tim Perttula
Tony Thomson

SUBSCRIBERS

Alan Glazer
Amber Williams
Angela Schlegel
Austin Dearborn
Carole Hailey
Caroline West
Courtney Sheedy
Damon Copeland
Dauphin Ewart
Donald Morrison
Elizabeth Simpson
Emily Beck
Erin Kubatzky
Hannah Good
Heath Dollar

Heustis Whiteside
Hillary Richards
Jane Gerhard
Jarratt Willis
Jennifer Owen
Jessica Sirs
John Andrew Margrave
John Mitchell
John Tenny
Joseph Rebella
Josh Rubenoff
Katarzyna Bartoszynska
Kenneth McClain
Kyle Trimmer
Matt Ammon

Matt Bucher
Matthew LaBarbera
Melanie Nicholls
Michael Binkley
Michael Lighty
Nancy Allen
Nancy Keaton
Nicole Yurcaba
Petra Hendrickson
Ryan Todd
Samuel Herrera
Scott Chiddister
Sian Valvis
Sonam Vashi
Tania Rodriguez

AVAILABLE NOW FROM DEEP VELLUM